W9-APH-378

BELLA BALISTICA

AND THE INDIAN SUMMER

India Bachelor
christina

India
Bachelor christina

ADAM GUILLAIN

ILLUSTRATIONS BY RACHEL GOSLIN

Milet Publishing Ltd
6 North End Parade
London W14 OSJ
www.milet.com

First published by Milet Publishing Ltd in 2005
Copyright © Adam Guillain, 2005

ISBN 1 84059 407 1

Adam Guillain has asserted his moral right to be identified as the author of this work, in accordance with the Copyright, Design and Patents Act 1988.

Cover and chapter illustrations by Rachel Goslin.

Milet's distributors are as follows:

UK & Ireland
Turnaround Publisher Services, Unit 3, Olympia Trading Estate, Coburg Road, London N22 6TZ

North America & Latin America
Tuttle Publishing, 364 Innovation Drive, North Clarendon, VT 05759-9436

Australia & New Zealand
Tower Books, Unit 2/17 Rodborough Road, Frenchs Forest NSW 2086
Global Language Books, PO Box 108, Toongabbie NSW 2146

South Africa
Quartet Sales & Marketing, 12 Carmel Avenue, Northcliff, Gauteng, Johannesburg 2195

Printed in Great Britain by Cox & Wyman

For our gorgeous son, George

INDIA

BELLA BALISTICA

AND THE INDIAN SUMMER

"You must be the change you wish to see in this world."

Mahatma Gandhi

CHAPTER ONE

FAMILY TENSIONS

"Bella, slow down!" Annie Balistica craned her head around from loading the dishwasher to cast a critical eye over her adopted daughter. Bella pulled a face before noisily spooning up the last dregs of sweet, creamy milk from her cereal bowl. Annie was apprehensive. What she had to say next wasn't going to go down well.

"Bruce is picking me up from work at one," she said firmly, giving her hands a quick swill under the tap. To Annie, the look of exasperation on Bella's face was as predictable as it was annoying.

"But why does he have to come?" Bella pleaded, banging the end of her spoon onto the table. Bella's tantrums over Bruce were getting out of hand. Annie was sick and tired of always being the one in the middle trying to make the peace.

"Because he wants to be more involved in the things that matter to you," Annie sighed, wiping her hands on a towel and coming to sit by Bella.

"Ugh," Bella grunted, scrunching up her face.

Annie bit her lip. "The day's just started," she told herself.

"Don't have an argument now."

Bruce Anders was in his early thirties – a good ten years younger than Annie. Bella knew her mum was embarrassed about it because she got so defensive whenever people passed comment.

"You hardly know anything about him," Bella had heard Imogen Meeks' mum tell her. "About his family and friends, I mean."

"They're all in Australia," Annie tried to explain. "Bella and I are Bruce's family here."

Bella considered this a little overstated but had tried to keep a lid on her reservations, at least for the first few weeks. Unfortunately, the weeks had turned into months. Four of them. A period of time during which the familiar mum and daughter routines had been severely disrupted. Bella had just about had enough.

"Bella, you know you're still my biggest love, don't you?" said Annie, raising a smile and giving Bella an affectionate finger nudge on the nose. Bella grimaced and pulled away, too mad with her mum to be so easily cajoled into good humour.

"I don't want him to come!" she snapped, slamming down her bowl and storming out.

Bella cursed the day they had first set eyes on Bruce Anders. She and her mum had just got to the end of a demonstration walk in London against cuts in aid for overseas charities. Bruce was hanging off the statue of Sir Winston Churchill outside the Houses of Parliament waving a rather tatty placard when Bella saw him. "What an idiot," she muttered, as she threw down her banner and flopped out on the grass.

Despite the blazing sunshine, Bruce was dressed in black tight-fitting jeans and a T-shirt that accentuated, rather too calculatingly in Bella's opinion, his athletic physique. Even worse, he was wearing a pair of green-tinted skiing glasses, which made him look like a poser even without the long blond ponytail. "He looks like a slippery eel," she thought, taking an immediate dislike to him.

"Hi there, girls," he'd shouted across to them in his laidback Australian accent. Bella imagined that the small silver earring glistening in his left ear could be pulled like one of her old toys, revealing a retreating cord and a never-ending string of inane phrases. Apart from the cord, she wasn't far wrong. Unfortunately for Bella, her mum had blushed bashfully, a signal Bruce Anders was all too familiar with. He jumped with acrobatic zeal off Churchill's plinth and slipped with suspicious ease into her mum's affections and, consequently, Bella's life.

Whether it had anything to do with Bruce or not, Bella had been wondering about her birth father more and more since her Guatemalan adventure last Christmas with the Quetzal bird. She found the whole idea of her mum having a boyfriend disconcerting and deeply objectionable.

As usual when Bella was upset, she quickly made her way to the landing and pulled down the ladder to the attic. Making as much noise as she could, she stomped up and yanked on the light cord. Before the fluorescent lights had even stuttered into full beam, Bella had thrown herself into her hammock and buried her watery eyes into a musty old cushion.

"Don't think I'm going to let you hide away up there all

ɔrning," her mum called from downstairs. Annie Balistica was feeling stressed. It had been a strain right from the start, dealing with Bella's negative attitude towards Bruce, and things were getting worse – particularly since Bruce's recent business trip to India. "I want you downstairs ready for school in ten minutes," Annie ordered. "And don't forget to brush your teeth and comb your hair."

Bella thumped the cushion with her fist.

The attic was Bella's favourite room in 14 Birdcage Crescent, the small semi-detached house in southeast London where she lived with her adoptive mum. She loved the smell of the timbers and the cosiness of the low ceiling and rafters. But most of all, Bella liked the fact that her mum never came up uninvited. It was her space. A place where she could go and be by herself – whatever her mood. She didn't even mind that it was dusty and full of cobwebs.

"I thought you hated spiders," her mum had commented only the other day, seeing Bella pick one up from the living-room floor and carry it all the way up to the attic. "I used to have to come up and rescue you from them twice a week."

Following her adventures in the Guatemalan rainforest and Bruce's unwelcome arrival, Bella now talked to spiders more than she talked to her mum. Even when she did speak to her, it was often to complain. "And why does Bruce have to leave his toothbrush and shaving stuff in the bathroom?" she had protested last night. "He's not even living here."

Bella had the niggling suspicion that Bruce and her mum spent time together in the house when she was at school, but when she thought about it, she got upset.

"Bella, I'm waiting." Annie called from the bottom of the

stairs. Rolling herself out of the hammock, Bella made her way to the far corner of the attic and lifted up the floorboards. Lying on the floor, she reached under and pulled out the beautifully handcrafted jewellery box that had once belonged to her birth mother. "There," she sighed with pleasure, as she rested it carefully on the floor.

Up until last week, Bella had kept the box tucked away beneath all her mum's old travel souvenirs at the bottom of a large Guatemalan chest. Recently, however, she'd become suspicious that Bruce had been up there rummaging through her things. The evidence was clear. Things she usually left lying around on the floor had been stashed away into boxes, while others she hardly ever used were left out. "He's been trying to cover his tracks," Bella thought. In addition to this, there was the lingering aroma of Bruce's revolting aftershave.

"Have you been up in the attic recently?" Bella asked her mum.

"You know I don't go up there unless you ask," said Annie. "That's your space. Although I dread to think what kind of a state you leave it in."

"Then Bruce has been up there," Bella continued, feeling more confident by the day that her mum's boyfriend couldn't be trusted. "I could smell him."

"Now why would he do that?" Annie replied dismissively. Bella didn't answer, but felt sure that it had something to do with the pendant she kept hidden away inside a secret compartment in her jewellery box. Since coming back from his trip to Mumbai and Delhi last month, Bella thought Bruce had been acting shiftily.

"He never takes those stupid sunglasses off," she'd said to

Charlie the other night. "It's like he's pretending to be some kind of undercover agent or something."

"Maybe he's afraid to show his eyes," said Charlie mockingly. "You know the eyes are supposed to be the window to your soul." The two friends stared fiercely into each other's eyes. Bella slowly rolled hers together and stuck out her tongue. Charlie tried to copy her and managed to keep a straight face until Bella blew a raspberry. Bursting into hysterics, they grasped each other's ears and tumbled to the floor.

"I looked into your soul," Charlie laughed, pretending to be spooked.

"And what did you see?" Bella giggled.

"I dunno," said Charlie. "The curtains were drawn."

Opening the secret compartment inside Bella's jewellery box was quite an art. Today, as always, Bella turned both of the bottom drawer handles in unison. She then put one hand on the base and the other on the rim just below the lid and twisted. Even though she'd opened it a thousand times, it still felt exciting when the base swivelled open. "It's like magic," Charlie had told her the first time Bella showed her how to open it. In truth, that was how it felt.

As the base of the box swung open, Bella tipped the pendant out into the palm of her right hand. Raising the silver chain up to the light, she gazed in awe at the resplendent multicoloured gems, carefully crafted into the crest, body and wings of her quetzal twin – her nahual. The pendant had been a wedding gift from Bella's birth father to her Guatemalan mother. Bella knew that it was valuable, because her mum had got it insured, but she really dug her heels in when Annie suggested they should deposit the pendant in the bank.

"My mother didn't pass it on to me so that I would be rich," she told her mum firmly. "It's to remind me at all times of who I am and where I come from. You can't put a price on that."

Annie couldn't object. These had been the very sentiments Bella's mother had expressed the day she handed Annie the jewellery box containing the pendant. As Bella now knew, Annie had been the midwife who had delivered her into the world at the Santa Maria Orphanage in Quezaltenango. She also knew that only a few days after her birth, her mother had died but not before giving Annie her blessing to adopt her spirited baby.

For a few moments Bella let the pendant swing hypnotically before her eyes, imagining that the Quetzal might once again appear at the skylight, ready to whisk her off on another hell-raising adventure. "And where are you when I need you?" she chastised her absent friend. "We were such a team!"

Bella missed the Quetzal more than she would admit. The great bird was Bella's link with her mystical past. Using the pendant to summon her powers, Bella had discovered that she could understand the natural world in quite an amazing way. The fact that she could fly like a bird, understand the whispers of the wind and converse in almost any language in the human and animal world was now something that Bella was entirely at ease with.

"Many moons ago," the Quetzal had informed her, "during the centuries in which our own mythologies were first formed, it was foretold that a girl with exceptional powers would be born. She would live amongst her own kind, but her ability to communicate with the animal world would form a new bond between species. Together, we would fight a great battle, the outcome of which would become destiny itself and the start of all mythologies to come."

Certainly, since discovering the pendant, Bella was aware of how the animals around her could sense her power. She was also becoming increasingly conscious that the pendant had an intuition all of its own. When things were fine, it radiated a warmth that effervesced through her whole body, making her feel safe and good inside. Whenever there was even the slightest hint of trouble or danger, it would warn her by turning cold. But the pendant wasn't the only source of comment in Bella's life. Today, just as she was about to head downstairs, a familiar voice inside her head caused her to turn to the old oil painting that hung from a rusty nail on one of the rafters. "He's alive," the voice whispered.

Bella gazed at the painting of the beautiful Mayan woman in tribal robes standing before the Great Temple of Tikal. No one, not even her mum, had any idea how it had got there. Bella had learned during her last adventure that it was a portrait of Itzamna, the supreme Mayan deity, in female form. Bella's conversations with the portrait – sometimes out loud – had become eerily real over the years. They communicated in ancient K'iche', a language still used by a small tribe of K'iche' Indians living deep within the tropical rainforests of Guatemala. To Bella's amazement, she had discovered that not only was she K'iche', but she was a direct descendant of the Itzamna dynasty.

"What do you mean – 'he's alive'?" Bella mimicked back. "Who's alive? You're always talking in riddles. It's really annoying!"

Venting her frustrations with a loud groan, Bella made her way down the ladder to the landing and made a quick dash to the bathroom to freshen her breath with mouthwash.

"Have you cleaned your teeth?" enquired Bella's mum suspiciously, looking up the stairs as Bella bounded down.

"Yes," Bella lied, with more than a hint of irritation. Her long, jet-black hair dangled in chaos around the hastily unaligned buttoning of her school dress. The summery, blue-and-white chequered uniform was a welcome change from the dowdy colours of the old winter uniform.

"Bella!" gasped her mum. "I'm not letting you leave the house looking like that!" Ignoring the fiery look in Bella's eyes, Annie took her dishevelled daughter by the shoulders and manoeuvred her over to the mirror in the hall. There, she pulled off Bella's colourful, Guatemalan scrunchie and tried in vain to brush the wildness out of her hair. As she reluctantly rebuttoned her dress, Bella looked up into the mirror and compared her mum's immaculate olive skin with her own, more reddened complexion and rounded Mayan features. "It's no wonder people on the streets stare at us," Bella thought to herself. "On first impression, the only thing we have in common is the fact neither of us looks English." The "odd couple" was how her mum often joked about it.

"That will have to do," said Annie dejectedly, laying down the hairbrush and handing Bella her sports bag.

Sports Day normally fell in the week before the end of term, but the unseasonable weather and a full school calendar had forced a hurriedly rescheduled event on the final afternoon of term. Annie opened the front door and stooped down to give her moody eleven-year-old a kiss. But Bella was having none of it. She felt so cross with her mum this morning that it was all she could do not to mumble something horrible about Bruce and run off. She glared into Annie's emerald-green eyes, which sparkled with the same passion for life and adventure as her own.

"Shhh," Annie hushed, laying a finger across Bella's lips. "Put all your energies into winning that trophy this afternoon. I know how much you want it."

However much her mum wound her up sometimes, Bella loved her to bits. Instead of lashing out with her tongue, she ducked away from her mum's conciliatory kiss and sprinted up the garden path. Annie was about to shut the door when she remembered:

"And where's your present?" she bellowed down the street. Bella was almost out of sight and could have carried on running but decided to stop.

"Damn!" she thought, feeling a little guilty. She turned around and began to jog back while her mum nipped into the house to get the bottle of red wine Bella had picked out for Mr. Alder.

"Thank goodness I remembered," she smiled, handing it over to Bella. "How that poor man has put up with you lot for a whole year, I've no idea. Now whatever you do – don't drop it!" Bella shoved the wine into her sports bag, jerked forward and gave her mum a quick peck on the cheek.

"You'd better tuck your necklace away," Annie advised calmly, noticing for the first time that morning that Bella was wearing her mother's dazzling pendant. "You don't want to get that confiscated."

"Mr. Alder wouldn't dare," replied Bella feistily as she

turned to run.

"I love you, Bella," said ⎯

But Bella was already gone⎯

Today, as always, Bella was in a ⎯

"Hang on, Prakash," she cal⎯ alongside her old adversary. Since ⎯ Eugene Briggs' gang, Bella had found s⎯ She sat next to him in Numeracy and ⎯ ⎯ad the welcome knack of helping her with her w⎯ ⎯hout making her feel stupid.

"Are you running in the cross-country today?" Bella panted.

"Yeah," he replied with a big grin. "But why'd you make such a fuss about the girls starting the race at the same time as the boys?"

Bella hadn't given Mr. Alder any peace over the matter. He had come to dread his playground duties on Tuesday and Friday mornings.

"If you start the girls five minutes before the boys like you always do, we'll never get a chance to prove we can beat them," she would complain as she trailed around after him. "They'll always have an excuse. It's not fair!"

Fairness was Bella's passion. She knew that she could outrun Eugene Briggs over meadows and through woodland. After all, she'd had enough practice when he'd hounded her in the past. But these days, verbal abuse and hollow teases were as much bullying as Eugene could muster. Following his father's arrest last Christmas for archaeological fraud, Eugene had been keeping a low profile. He was still mean and prided

...e cruellest thing he could think of to upset ...e had also nurtured a new subversive code of ...n. Eugene kept himself to himself so successfully that ...ctually came across as a model pupil to some teachers. This in itself was highly suspicious.

As Bella and Prakash continued their walk to school, they passed the medieval tower where the Quetzal had first come to Bella's rescue last December.

"Does this place give you the spooks or what?" Prakash asked with mock trepidation.

Now it was summer, many children were using the shortcut through Oxleas Wood that took them past the derelict tower. Bella looked up at the wonky guttering in the vain hope of seeing the Quetzal. She'd seen nothing of the colourful bird since his brief visit at Easter when he had stopped by to tell her he was off to India to visit a Bengal tiger in Mumbai who was in desperate need of his help.

"I hope you're going to keep an ear to the ground for any news of my father while you're on your travels," she'd told the Quetzal.

"The man is as dead as a Dodo," he'd squawked, a little too sharply, considering the delicacy of the subject. This didn't faze Bella at all. She was used to everyone assuming that her father was dead.

"Still, I want you to try," Bella told him firmly, convinced he was still alive and, even now, fighting against incredible odds to find her.

The wheezing sound of someone running up the hill behind them caused Bella and Prakash to turn.

"Hey, Charlie!" Bella beamed at her friend as she took her

place alongside them. Charlie was Bella's best friend. Her distinctive auburn hair and brown freckles made her easily the prettiest girl in the class, in Bella's opinion.

"Our last day at Hawksmore Primary," Charlie gasped, running her hand through her freshly trimmed bob. "Do you feel sad?" Charlie's blue, twinkling eyes and cheeky grin looked anything but gloomy.

"No," replied Bella sharply. "I've had enough. I'm more sad about having to get up in the middle of the night and fly to India tomorrow."

Bella and Charlie had had a number of conversations about this unwelcome change of plan over the last two weeks. Annie, unaware of Bella's Guatemalan adventure last year, had booked a flight to take Bella to Guatemala this summer. They had planned to visit Bella's birthplace in Quezaltenango and make enquires after her father. Unfortunately, this didn't fit into Bruce's schedule.

"Bruce and I have been talking," was how Bella's mum had broken the news. Her stomach had been all churned up even before she saw the disappointment on Bella's face. "Rather than go to Guatemala for two weeks this year, we'll go to India and help Bruce with his charity work in Delhi." She went on hopefully: "I'll do some voluntary work at the clinic attached to the children's centre, and you can use the cameras to work on your exhibition idea with the street-children."

"But you promised we'd go to Guatemala!" Bella objected.

Annie had felt awful, but Bruce had been very persuasive. Since his return from India last month, his relationship with Bella had taken a serious nosedive, as he presented more and more reasons why they should all accompany him to Delhi.

"I know, darling," replied Annie, attempting to calm her irate daughter, "but . . . " As soon as she started trying to explain things, the whole India idea sounded like a big mistake. But then, what could she do? She was stuck between promises, caught between two people who she loved beyond measure and who were increasingly at each other's throats.

"This is impossible!" thought Annie, flopping her arms against her sides in resignation, as Bella's eyes filled with angry tears.

For Bella, her casual dislike of Bruce was rocketing to the dizzy heights of absolute hatred. Even the pendant, previously as ambivalent as she had been towards her mum's boyfriend, was showing tendencies to form icicles whenever he brought up the subject of India.

"I bet he told you it would be a great chance for me to take photos with the street kids," Bella had shouted. "Some sweet-talking argument about putting together an exhibition to help with his fundraising." Bella's mum went bright red. "But that's exactly what I suggested we should do this summer in Guatemala!" Bella had pleaded, with tears rolling down her face. "For *Guatemalan* street-children!"

It was eight-forty when the children got to school, just in time to see Mr. Alder unlock the main doors. With a familiar downtrodden look, Mr. Alder stepped out in his khaki slacks and white open-neck shirt and, before a sea of blue-and-white uniforms, screaming toddlers and battle-weary carers, raised the school bell. One chime, and they were off! Unusually for Bella, who could push and shove her way into the cloakrooms with the best of them, she ignored the familiar ruckus and stood back to admire the daunting, red-brick façade of her primary school for the last time as one of its pupils. Next term, most of the children in Bella's class would be moving on to Crown Woods Secondary School at Avery Hill. Bella was excited. She'd had enough of primary school and was up for the challenge of life in a bigger institution with more opportunities.

"Come on," Charlie urged, grabbing Bella's arm and dragging her back into the moment. "Let's get our presents in first." And into the crowd they pushed.

The noise from Mr. Alder's classroom was bedlam. When Bella and Charlie walked in, there wasn't a single pupil in their seat. Instead, Mr. Alder was under siege, trying to get to grips with the sheer quantity of shabbily wrapped chocolate oranges and cheap wallets piling up on his desk.

"Thank you, Melanie, thank you, Rahina . . . you're all going to get me very fat, you know . . . " Mr. Alder was doing his best to sound grateful, but things were getting out of control. "Will you please sit down?" he beseeched them finally, when every last drop of congeniality had been drained from him by the relentless pushing and shoving. His plea made no impact whatsoever on the ruckus around him. "Don't make me have to shout!" he yelled, standing up to survey the anarchy of his crumbling domain. "We may have survived leavers' assembly yesterday without too many hiccups, but we've still got Sports Day to get through." The children slowly started to retreat. "Let's keep our fingers crossed for the weather," he concluded in a gentler tone. Bella thought he made it sound more like an exam than a day of celebration, but looking out of the window she saw that there were ominous black clouds in the distance. She grabbed the bottle of wine from her bag, plonked it on the desk, and earned herself the biggest smile Mr. Alder had given out all term.

"Thanks, Bella," he chuckled. "Excellent choice."

Bella felt a warm glow inside. Mr. Alder was far and away the nicest teacher in the school. She guessed that it must have been a tough two terms for him, having to take over as acting headteacher from the fearsome Mrs. Sticklan and still teach his Year Six class Literacy and Numeracy every morning. In the afternoons, 6TA had been assigned a regular supply teacher called Miss Swinburn, whose confidence and enthusiasm for the job had all but been obliterated by a war of calculated attrition by the children. She'd be lucky to get a bar of chocolate.

The rest of the morning was a bit of a blur to Bella. She later remembered Mr. Alder strumming his guitar and everyone having to sing a medley of 1960s pop songs in assembly, playing a half-hearted game of *Simpsons* chess with Winston Geoffrey and helping Mr. Alder get all the staples out of the wall, but that was about it. Apart from desecrating each other's uniform with markers as they signed their names and goodbye wishes, everyone was waiting for an early lunch and the start of Sports Day events. Luckily, the rain was keeping off.

For Sports Day, each pupil had been allowed to put themselves down for three races. Bella had ignored all the silly themed events like "Midsummer Madness", where pupils would have to dress up as pirates and work as a crew to get two large gym mats (pirate ships to the uninitiated) across twenty metres of manky grass (supposedly the Caribbean Sea) without falling in. Instead, she'd picked the hurdles, the 100 metres and the blue-ribbon event: the cross-country. This was the one everyone wanted to win because the local sports shop on Eltham High Street was giving away a pair of designer trainers to the first girl and the first boy home. The actual winner also got to have their name engraved onto a large trophy that was displayed inside a cabinet by the school office for everyone to see. Bella knew the instant Winston Geoffrey, the fastest runner in school, had suspiciously failed to put his name forward for the race, that Eugene was out to win. In over a century of Sports Days, no girl had ever won the trophy without the instigation of various handicap and advantage gimmicks to help them. Bella had had her heart set on winning it fair and square since Year One.

"If you think I'm going to cheat and use the pendant to help me, you're wrong!" Bella told the portrait in the attic that morning.

"But you're still going to wear it," replied the voice sarcastically.

"So?" was Bella's obstinate reply.

As the children started to carry the grey plastic chairs from the hall out to the playing fields for the parents and visitors to sit on, not only were the dark clouds starting to gather, but other, more sinister, forces were busy preparing themselves for the afternoon's events.

A magical pendant might just come in handy.

CHAPTER TWO

SPORTS DAY

Bella sat at a table with Rahina Iqbal, Melanie Roberts, Imogen Meeks and Charlie Stevens. They were eating their packed lunches in the classroom at half-eleven – much earlier than usual.

"As soon as you're finished, I'd like you girls to help me get all the PE equipment out and organize the bunting," Mr. Alder whispered, crouching down. "Just don't tell anyone else." Too many helpers tended to escalate the chances of bad behaviour.

The girls found it quite chilly outside in their summer dresses. With the easterly wind picking up, the bunting was flapping with such ferocity it gave Rahina quite a lashing when she passed by carrying a box of beanbags. By twelve-thirty they'd just about finished setting up, as parents and carers, many of them with preschool children in tow, started to arrive.

"Thanks, girls," said Mr. Alder, blowing into his hands and rubbing them together. "You'd better head back to the classroom and get changed. We need to be out here again by one o'clock if we want to be finished by half-two."

"Great," thought Bella dejectedly. Bruce wasn't even picking her mum up from work at the hospital until one. "My final chance to win something, and he's going to deliberately make sure my mum misses it," she muttered. "I hate that man!"

The boys had to change in the corridor while the girls used the classroom. It wasn't fair, but it was never an issue Bella took up with Mr. Alder on the boys' behalf.

"Alright, pig-face?" sneered Eugene Briggs, as he pushed Bella's chair on his way out. Bella had once stuck up her nose and flared her nostrils at him – hence the nickname. But Bella had come a long way since her pre-Christmas adventure with the Quetzal. Her habitual impulse to retaliate when riled by Eugene's provocations had been replaced by a dignified silence. Eugene, however, was in no mood to let Bella block him out – not today. He pulled her chair around and stamped on her right foot with all his might.

"Ow!" cried Bella, grimacing in pain.

"I hear your mum's got a new boyfriend," Eugene sneered, twisting his foot to maximize Bella's discomfort. "Maybe having a stepdad will sort you out." That was it. Bella thrust out her fist when Mr. Alder stepped in.

"Briggs – out!" he demanded. Eugene pulled himself up and glared into Mr. Alder's eyes. For a moment, it looked as if he might defy him, but then, with a sly grin and a dismissive toss of his shaggy blond hair, he turned and sloped off towards the door. Mr. Alder turned to Bella: "Don't be an idiot," he whispered into her ear. "He's not worth it. Just win the race. That will show him."

"Where's Connor Mitchell?" Rahina asked Bella when all

19

the boys were finally out and they were able to slam the classroom door. "He hasn't come back in from play."

"I haven't seen Ratty either," Imogen added.

Roland "The Rat" Richardson and Connor Mitchell were the two members of Eugene's gang who'd stuck by him. No one had seen either of them since lunch.

Mr. Alder didn't even bother with the afternoon register. When everyone was changed, he took the battery-operated megaphone from his cupboard and marched his long, straggly line of Year Sixes out into the dismal summer's afternoon for the final hurdle of the academic year. Despite the miserable weather, there was quite a big turnout of spectators, with all the seats alongside the track already taken. Once all the classes were sitting down, shivering on the damp grass opposite the expectant crowd, the teachers wandered up to take refuge around Mr. Alder by the starting line. Bella had a quick look around for her mum. She could see Charlie's mum, Mrs. Stevens, talking with Mr. and Mrs. Iqbal and Winston Geoffrey's parents. In fact, she could see almost everyone's parent but her own.

"Where's your mum?" Charlie asked.

"She's waiting for Bruce," Bella mumbled with disgust.

"Why's he coming?" exclaimed Charlie.

Bella shrugged her shoulders.

Mr. Alder greeted the parents with a meandering speech that thankfully few could hear through the distortion of the megaphone. The expressions on most of the other teachers' faces were as bleak as the weather. Mrs. Gudgeon and Miss Swinburn, in particular, looked like they were freezing in their floral dresses and flip-flops.

"I'm never going to be a teacher when I grow up," sniggered Imogen Meeks through chattering teeth. "They all look knackered and fed up." Finally, Mr. Alder's speech ran out of steam.

"Let the games begin," he announced in a triumphant tone that implied some great, gladiatorial event was imminent. There was a long pause, while Mrs. Otter organized six cold, wind-blown and clearly bored Year One children into a starting line-up for the first of at least eight consecutive egg and spoon races.

Event after event passed with the usual raucous interventions and applause from children and parents. Occasionally, someone would fall over, which always got a laugh, and of course there were the endless disappointments and tears of defeated children, requiring hugs and stickers for being brave. Bella was aware that she felt detached in a way she never had before. In truth, she wasn't the only one. Many of the Year Sixes felt as if they had seen one too many Sports Days at Hawksmore Primary. The time for moving on had definitely come.

Like everyone else, Bella got a "well done" sticker for taking part in the hurdles and 100 metres, even though they only ran mixed heats with no overall winner. Along with a good number of upper-juniors, she ended up pulling her stickers off her top and reapplying them to the sole of her trainers.

"They treat us like we're kids," Bella moaned. "Who, over the age of six, wants a sticker for anything?"

The only race all day where there would be an obvious champion and a decent prize was the cross-country. As the black clouds finally blocked out the sun, and the first spots of drizzle began to dampen everyone's spirits still further, Mr. Alder called all the contestants for the final event of the day to the starting line.

"Got your heart set on a new pair of trainers, have you?" Eugene goaded as the contestants wandered up to the starting line. Bella turned away, choosing instead to search the crowd for any sign of her mum rather than waste her energies on negative banter. "Love, learn, forgive and move on," she reminded herself. These were the words that Bella had first heard spoken in ancient K'iche' from the portrait of Itzamna in the attic. Later, those very words had opened up the entrance to the Great Temple of Tikal. She knew the advice to be good. Only it was hard not to hold onto old grudges sometimes, especially when there were bullies like Eugene Briggs around.

Just when Bella was about to give up any hope that her mum was going to make it, she caught sight of her face, bobbing up and down at the back of the crowd. To Bella's absolute joy, Bruce was nowhere to be seen. But her happiness was short-lived.

"Go, Bell, go," came the nauseating call from the sidelines.

Only one person in the world called Bella "Bell". It irked her beyond measure. She turned around to see Bruce, looking stupid in the blue suit, white T-shirt and trainers he wore to work at that trendy charitable trust in Lambeth. But that wasn't the worst of it. To Bella's absolute horror, standing alongside him was a man in a shabby khaki suit and white safari hat. She recognized him at once.

Ted Briggs relished the moment. It had been seven long months since he'd last set eyes on Bella Balistica, and to turn up now alongside her mum's boyfriend was bound to cause offence. The second their eyes met, he saw the shock on Bella's face and gave her a wily smile. The calculated gesture revealed his yellowy teeth, while his brown, shady eyes glared with familiar menace. Bella's pendant went cold just at the sight of him.

"Hey, Fiona!" Bella heard Miss Swinburn exclaim to Mrs. Gudgeon as the Year Sixes took their place on the starting line. "That man over there," she said, gesturing with her head. "The one with the tatty grey beard and hunched-up shoulders – isn't that Eugene Briggs' dad?"

Bella watched what little colour there was in Mrs. Gudgeon's face drain away and was aware that quite a number of children and parents were looking at this most unwelcome visitor with an air of disdain.

"He looks like a demented wolf," she heard Miss Swinburn comment.

"And what's that on the end of his arm?" whispered Mrs. Gudgeon under her breath.

Bella was too scared to look at the lifeless artificial hand attached to Briggs' left arm. She felt sick when she recalled how the three-headed jaguar had torn his hand from him as he tried to re-enter the Temple of Tikal in an attempt to steal the Itzamna Emerald. Bella had initially felt distressed about Briggs' injuries and a little guilty too, when, as a result of her revelations, the police had raided his London house. Later, however, when no stolen artefacts, no illegally acquired skins of endangered species were found – in fact, nothing to incriminate him at all – her suspicions began to erode her sympathies.

"He must have tipped off his wife," Bella told Charlie, upon hearing the news of Briggs' release from police custody a few days after Christmas. "I've seen the tablets of hieroglyphics on his landing and a tiger-skin rug on his living-room floor with my own eyes."

Following the accusations, Briggs had lost his place on the school's Board of Governors, but he was appealing against the action and threatening to sue the school for unlawful dismissal.

"Even your lucky pendant can't help you today," hissed Eugene, sidling up to Bella's ear. Bella quickly covered her pendant with both hands. Twice now, Eugene had managed to guess when she was wearing it and had tried to snatch it from her. "My dad's going to really enjoy this," Eugene grinned. Bella looked up and stared into Eugene's gaunt, pale-skinned face. "You're so dead," he sneered, his narrow, slitty eyes full of nasty pleasure.

"Everyone to their starting positions!" shouted Mr. Alder, raising his starting pistol.

"Good luck, son," Ted Briggs howled.

BANG! And they were off.

The route around the playing fields, back through the playground and out onto the streets via the main gate meant that the runners could be seen by everyone. After that, they raced to the end of the street, where a friendly policeman was holding off what little traffic passed that way, before the runners headed into the woods. The contestants were to stay on the main path, which took them up and round the old watchtower. Here, a member of the PTA would tick off their names before they headed across the fields and meadows to Rochester Way, where they could pick up the path back to school. It was impossible to take a shortcut and to turn back before reaching the tower without being caught. A fair race. Or so everyone thought.

By the time Bella had circled the playing fields and passed the cheering crowd she was already fifty metres clear of Eugene Briggs and the chasing pack. This gap, when converted into time, had been extended to about thirty seconds as Bella found herself running up Oxleas Mount towards the old watchtower. Her strategy had been to open up as big a lead as she could in order to stave off the danger of Eugene's superior sprint finish. Unfortunately for Bella, this idea dovetailed perfectly with Eugene's plan.

Connor Mitchell and Roland Richardson had bunked off after lunch and were now lurking in the bushes halfway up the steep incline to the tower. The spot was perfect for an ambush because it was unseen from the path and was at a point where anybody running up would be too exhausted to scream.

"Here she comes, Ratty." Connor hissed as loudly as he dared, the second Bella's wildly flying hair came into view. The two boys were crouched on opposite sides of the track holding a long skipping rope they'd stolen from the PE cupboard. It was extended across the path, covered with dust and soil.

Bella was quickly approaching, literally only strides away.

"Now!" Ratty hollered.

The two boys yanked the rope. In a cloud of dust, Bella came crashing down. Her hands and knees smacked the ground hard. As she slid, Bella felt her skin grate and tear against the grit. Too dazed to move, she listened to the stampeding thud of approaching footsteps.

"Ow!" she cried, as someone jumped on her back.

"Alright, pig-face?" came Eugene's familiar taunt. "Catch up with me now." He thrust himself onwards with a spiteful dig of the foot.

Bella pulled herself up, raring to go, but the sudden rush of blood made her feel faint. With the world spinning before her eyes, she fell back to her knees and then flat on her face.

"Bella, are you alright?" Charlie puffed, running up and bending down to check on her friend. "I've just seen Connor and Ratty sprinting off into the woods."

Bella heard the voice as if she were coming out of a dream. She felt herself being dragged onto the grass, as a steady trail of breathless runners passed by.

"Bad luck, Bella," she heard someone wheeze. Charlie and Imogen were now crouching alongside Bella, examining her bloody wounds. Bella fumbled for her pendant but realized a quick fix was out of the question. The force of the pendant was a secret – even from Charlie. Any supernatural powers she might call upon to help now would expose her secret and involve a great deal of explaining.

"Ow!" she groaned, feeling the throbbing pain in her knees. "I should have been prepared." But there was no point in complaining. The race was lost.

Burying her pride, Bella swore to her friends that she felt fine and that they should continue the race for first-placed girl, while she turned around and limped back to school on her own.

"You'll be OK for football later, won't you?" Charlie asked hopefully. "I'll come round straight after tea." Bella nodded, and her two friends rejoined the race. When no one was looking, she focused her powers and used the pendant to heal her wounds so that by the time she reached the school gates they didn't look half as bad as they might have. The last few remaining cross-country runners were staggering home, and she knew that Eugene would already be celebrating victory.

"Bad luck, Bell. At least you tried."

Bella knew he'd call out something like that. Bruce and her mum were standing arm in arm ready to greet her. It was the final insult.

"Bella!" Annie gasped, concerned to see her daughter limping and looking so downhearted. "Did you fall?" Bella gave her mum a kiss and totally ignored Bruce.

"Did Charlie win the girl's race?" Bella asked hopefully.

"Imogen won," Annie replied. Bella nodded.

"That's OK then," she said quietly. "I'll go and get changed." She turned and headed back towards the classroom.

"I don't know what I have to do," she heard Bruce sigh as she walked away. "It's as if I don't exist to her." His voice sounded quivery, as if he was upset. Bella felt sure it was put on.

"I'll talk to her," she heard her mum reply firmly. Annie was worried. If Bella continued to be so obstinate and rude to Bruce, the trip to India was going to be a complete disaster.

Having won the race without any serious challenge, Eugene couldn't resist bounding over to offer his insincere commiserations.

"Oh, Bella, what bad luck. Did you fall?" he teased as he trailed after her for a few strides. "Not waiting for the award ceremony, then?" She didn't answer.

Bella found herself alone in the classroom, surrounded by the chaos of jumbled-up school clothes and scattered shoes. Now that the walls were bare and the work trays empty, it felt depressing. She took off the pendant and rubbed it between her fingers. The familiar rush of its power tingled through her body and brought her comfort. By the time she was dressed, all that was left of her injuries was some grazing on the knee that she decided to leave for effect. Walking across the playground to find her mum, Bella was drawn to the sight of two men who were engrossed in deep conversation some distance away from the crowd. She recognized at once who they were.

"What on earth is Bruce doing talking to Ted Briggs?" she muttered through gritted teeth.

Taking hold of her pendant, she blocked out all her other senses and focused on picking out their voices amidst the general hubbub. What she heard made the hairs on the back of her neck stand on end.

"And make sure it's a Bengal tiger," Briggs growled. "I'm not paying this kind of money if it's not the real McCoy." Bella was reminded of the Bengal tiger that the Quetzal had gone to help in India back in March.

"And why is there a delay on those football shirts?" Briggs went on. "I'm turning customers away in the shop and on the website."

Since the closure of his pet shop and aviary, Briggs had opened a sports shop in Greenwich selling club and international football shirts.

"Apparently, he's got the best deals in town," Charlie had told Bella, sporting her new Real Madrid top.

"Well, I'm not going there," Bella had retorted. "I'd rather die!" The shop also boasted the best range of high quality, hand-stitched footballs in the whole country. Even the

Football Association was buying balls from him. "Bruce must be working for Briggs," Bella reflected bitterly, embarrassed that her mum was hanging around with such an obvious idiot.

"And how's it going with the girl?" asked Briggs snidely.

"Ballistic Bell?" Bruce scorned. "The girl's a brat." Bella's senses were jerked to alarm. Up to now she had only her instincts and a stack of minor annoyances to go on when it came to disliking her mum's boyfriend. Suddenly, everything was becoming clearer and much more sinister.

"Have you managed to get your hands on that Guatemalan necklace of hers?" asked Briggs impatiently. "I have a feeling it's the kind of artefact that might go well with my collection."

"I've been up to the attic and had a look around," replied Bruce, "but couldn't find it."

"I knew it!" thought Bella, feeling vindicated.

"Well, look again," Briggs told him. "Not that I believe in supernatural powers, but that trinket certainly seems to bring her the luck of the devil." Bella winced. Briggs' suspicions were dangerous.

"When I mentioned it to the Diva in Mumbai, she gave me a right old grilling," Bruce went on, fiddling nervously with his earring. "She thinks from what I've told her that the pendant might have mystical qualities."

"You fool!" cried Briggs. "Now she's going to want it."

"Who is this 'Diva' woman?" wondered Bella, feeling exposed.

"The Diva was very keen that I should bring Annie and the girl with me on this trip," Bruce admitted. Briggs shook his head in disgust at Bruce's indiscretion.

"You see?" he snarled, raising his voice so much that a

number of people nearby turned their heads. "Then you better make sure the little brat takes the necklace. She's going to need all the lucky charms she can muster."

Bella couldn't hear what Bruce said next because Mr. Alder was announcing the result of the cross-country through his megaphone and preparing to present Eugene and Imogen with their designer trainers. "And I suggest, since you're there," she heard Briggs say, trying to contain his glee, "you might get Ballistic Bell a job at the circus. They still exhibit freaks there, don't they?"

Bella had to imagine his wry smile because a number of parents were now blocking her view. She held the pendant tightly so as not to miss the end of the conversation. "That, or arrange some tragic disappearance."

The sound of Briggs' howling laughter could be heard even without using her powers.

"Are they having a joke?" thought Bella as she mingled with the crowd, frantically looking for her mum. "Or is Briggs planning some kind of hideous revenge?"

At last, Bella saw her mum talking to Mrs. Stevens. She ran to her as fast as she could and threw herself into Annie's arms.

"I think we need to go home," said Annie firmly, giving Mrs. Stevens a nod as if to say: "See what I mean?" She'd just finished telling her friend how Bella's behaviour had been erratic all day – one minute all argumentative and confrontational; the next, tearful and clingy. The conversation between Annie and Mrs. Stevens had been quite an emotional one – particularly in view of the public setting. If Bella had tuned into that conversation, she would have heard her mum admit to how lonely her life had been before meeting Bruce. Annie bade farewell to her friend and started to pull Bella away.

"You and I have some talking to do," she told Bella, feeling as torn as ever between the two loves in her life. "Now where's Bruce?"

CHAPTER THREE

BELLA'S SCRAPBOOK

It was four-thirty, Friday afternoon. As usual, the southeast London commuter rush was a nightmare. Thankfully, Bruce had the radio on for traffic updates so no one had to talk to him. Annie glanced up to look at her daughter in the rear-view mirror. Bella's arms were folded and clutched tightly to her chest while she stared out the window, her face screwed up with anger and frustration.

"Why does he always do the driving?" Bella grumbled to herself. "It's not even his car!"

"Bad luck about the race, Bell," Bruce called back. Bella saw her mum give him a poke in the leg to shut up.

"It wasn't bad luck," Bella yelled. "He cheated!"

Annie was feeling ravaged with guilt about letting Bruce persuade her that Bella wasn't emotionally ready to visit Guatemala this summer.

"If, as you say, her father really is dead," Bruce suggested upon his return from India, "she's only going to be devastated." Annie loved Bruce and knew that his charity work in India was really important to him.

"It's a project with street-children," Annie had argued to Bella. "One that we might learn so much from, for when we go to Guatemala." All this was going on in Annie's head as she turned down the radio and said: "I didn't see Connor or Roland at Sports Day today." She looked back to face Bella. Bella simply raised her hands. "What's the point?" she thought. Annie let it drop. Bella's run-ins with Eugene Briggs and his gang were never-ending.

"We'll finish our packing while Bruce goes back to his flat to finish his," said Annie, changing the subject. "Bruce is bringing back a computer game for your PlayStation."

"He won't be able to bribe me into being nice to him that easily," Bella moaned to herself. Bruce produced these games almost weekly. At first, Bella had been impressed. But he'd overplayed the gesture. Annie caught the look of utter contempt on Bella's face in the side mirror.

"She's even blaming Bruce for today's disappointments," she thought. "It's not right."

As her battered old Mini rolled up to the kerb to stop outside 14 Birdcage Crescent, Annie leaned intimately towards her boyfriend.

"Don't forget to book the taxi for three in the morning," she reminded him. They kissed. Bella felt her stomach churn.

"You two make me sick!" she shouted, getting out and slamming the door.

Bella stormed up the front path, unlocked the door and threw it open.

"Get out of the way!" she screeched at the mottled grey tabby, who, realizing the danger, squealed and darted up the stairs. Bella and the cat didn't get on. It was a small cat / big bird thing that only someone with inside knowledge of Bella's relationship with a Guatemalan quetzal would understand.

Hearing her mum say her final goodbyes to Bruce, Bella banged the front door behind her and bounded up the stairs after the cat.

"If I hear you've killed anything today – you're dead!" Bella hissed loudly.

"Mercy!" shrieked the cat. "I've been in all day, honest." The two of them were in a standoff on the landing, surrounded by the four doors that led to the bathroom, Bella's bedroom, her mum's bedroom and the tiny spare room her mum used as a darkroom. The cat had nowhere to go but to jump over the banister – which she did.

"Eek!" yelped the cat.

"Bella, I hope you're not teasing poor Prudence again," called Annie wearily as she wiped her feet on the doormat. It was Bella's sincerest wish that Mrs. Stevens would forget to come over and feed her while they were away.

"And don't think you're going to get away with hiding up there all night," her mum warned. She'd just about had enough of Bella's rudeness towards her boyfriend.

While Bella sat at the top of the stairs, contemplating her next move, Annie went to the kitchen to make herself a cup of tea. "Bella's always better when she's had some time and space to calm down," she thought to herself while she filled the kettle. As she rooted around in the cupboards for the peppermint tea, Annie again felt the irksome niggles of guilt. She hadn't yet consulted Bella about her plans to ask Bruce to come and live with them. Annie knew that things were happening far too quickly for all of them, but the practicalities of expensive London rents and her wish to see more of Bruce were things Bella had to understand. And anyway – in the absence of an adoptive father, wouldn't it be nice to have a man around the place? For Annie, who hadn't had a boyfriend for years, the prospect of a little romance and parental support was quite appealing. Taking her tea and flopping into a chair, she reached for the remote control and switched on the TV.

"What's the real reason we're following that man to India and working on his project?" Bella demanded, making such a dramatic entrance at the door that Annie jumped. Bella could see that her mum looked tired and drawn, but she had no intention of standing down.

Annie's heart sank. Even the thought of another showdown with Bella was completely exhausting. Dealing with two strong-willed and opposing personalities such as Bella and Bruce was too much. Mustering all her energies she blurted: "Because I love him, Bella." There – she'd said it. Bella felt as if someone had just kicked her in the stomach. "And I want it to be OK with you," Annie concluded, giving Bella a stern look.

"Well, it's not!" Bella burst out, with daggers in her eyes.

"Then you're just going have to get used to the idea," said Annie firmly.

Bella threw up her arms in despair.

"Never!" she exclaimed and stormed off.

As usual, Bella made her way up to the attic, threw herself into the hammock and gazed up at the skylight. She wished with all her heart Bruce Anders could just be magically made to disappear. She rubbed her fingers over her pendant in the vain hope that its powers stretched that far.

"The power of your will . . . " started a voice inside her head.

"Is a tremendous force – *I know*!" snapped Bella, turning to the portrait of Itzamna. "You've told me a million times!" Bella was always irritated that the portrait's mouth never actually moved. Her words simply resounded around Bella's head, prickling her conscience with infuriating zeal.

"Steer yourself away from anger and direct your energies towards the positive and the practical," instructed the voice in exactly the kind of preachy way Bella hated.

"Tell me something I don't know," cried Bella, banging her fist with frustration into the hammock netting.

"He's getting closer," the voice went on, "gathering his forces . . . " Here the voice stopped suddenly. Bella wasn't sure who or what the voice was talking about. Did it mean Bruce or Ted Briggs? Or did the voice mean someone else?

"Yes," she replied cautiously, "go on . . . "

"You're in great danger," whispered the voice. "Harness your powers, control your anger and follow your instincts."

Sometimes, when the voice said things that were too ambiguous or strange for Bella to understand, she tended to ignore it. This time, something about the directness in its tone made her nervous. She cast her mind back to the disturbing conversation she'd overheard between Bruce and Ted Briggs after the cross-country. To think that her mum's boyfriend could be in cahoots with such a twisted, evil man was deeply worrying. "The portrait must be talking about Ted Briggs," Bella decided. "He's obsessed with revenge."

Bella was still deep in thought when her mum called: "Bella, I've made you chicken nuggets and chips. Are you coming down?" Annie was a great cook and would have much preferred Bella to be eating vegetables, but she chose her battles wisely. Despite all her best efforts, this was still Bella's favourite dinner. Usually, Annie and Bella ate all their meals together, but sometimes, when Bruce was coming over, Annie would hang on so that she could put out candles and eat with him later. Feeling hungry, Bella rolled herself out of the hammock and went down to the kitchen.

"I hope you don't want any salad, because I haven't got any," said Annie bluntly as she scooped up the nuggets from the oven tray onto her spatula. Bella wanted to say that she was sorry, but she couldn't let her feelings about Bruce go. While her mum finish serving up, Bella poured herself a glass of water and waited for her mum to sit down.

"Did you know that Bruce and Ted Briggs were friends?" Bella asked abruptly. She immediately regretted it.

"Bella, if you're going to start . . . "

"It's nothing," Bella interrupted. "What's for dessert?" Bella knew her mum wasn't going to listen to anything she said about Bruce. The problem was, she'd been so stroppy about him from the start – for reasons she wasn't yet ready to acknowledge – that the fact she now had clear grounds for concern wouldn't ring true. "I need proof," Bella told herself.

Bella had nearly finished her dinner when the doorbell rang.

"That's Charlie," said Bella, pushing back her chair. "We've arranged to play football in the meadows."

"Oh no, you're not, Bella Balistica," replied Annie crossly. "We've got all the packing to do."

"But I'll only be twenty minutes," Bella replied innocently, knowing full well she'd be at least two hours, if not more.

"No!" said Annie firmly, popping one of Bella's antimalaria tablets from its packet and handing it to her. "And anyway, it's going to rain." This was hard to deny, given the dark clouds and blustery wind. "Charlie can stay for half an hour, and then I'm going to have to insist that she goes home." While it made her feel bad to play the ogre, Annie really believed it was for the best.

"What if I don't take this?" said Bella defiantly, looking at the white, chalky capsule that she and her mum were taking as part of their holiday preparations.

"Then you'll probably spend the whole trip sick with a fever and a throbbing headache," her mum told her. Bella quickly swallowed the tablet down with a mouthful of water, scowled with disgust and left the table with a calculated lack of grace.

Annie began to clear the table. Bruce had been telling her for weeks she needed to be firmer with Bella. "You're too indulgent with her," he'd told her. "Waiting on her hand and foot and pandering to her every need. No wonder she behaves like a spoiled child," he'd said on more than one occasion.

"I've been too soft on her," Annie told herself as she started to load the dishwasher. "And this is the price."

Charlie looked gutted when Bella told her she couldn't come out to play. "Well, I suppose it might rain," she sighed, trying to console herself. She followed Bella up into the attic.

"I've only got half an hour," said Bella. "But I think we should be able to spin it out to an hour, if we're lucky." Charlie was admiring the beautifully engraved pictures of jaguars and tropical birds on the old Guatemalan chest. Having noticed such a chest inside a creepy tomb on her last adventure, Bella tended to keep a large piece of Guatemalan fabric over it.

"I don't know why you keep this thing covered up," said Charlie, gazing in wonder at the intricate motifs. "It's so beautiful."

"I know," said Bella. "It just gives me the spooks." Unusually, the fabric was lying discarded on the floor. It wasn't a good sign. "Bruce has been up here today," thought Bella. She knew he hadn't found the pendant because of the conversation she'd overheard between Bruce and Ted Briggs.

"Have you finished all your packing?" asked Charlie.

"I haven't even started," said Bella as she clambered into the hammock. Bella knew that Charlie had to pack too. Tomorrow she was going to a Centre Parks holiday resort for a long weekend.

"My dad says he's taking me to Highbury when we get back," said Charlie excitedly, taking a folded football programme from her pocket. "There's some summer school course for overseas coaches or something – I'm not sure. We're going to watch the Under-21 International friendly matches they're playing afterwards." Charlie passed Bella the programme and then sat down on the chest. "Did you know Guatemala is playing?" she asked.

"No," Bella whined, secretly wishing she had a dad who would take her to such things. Her mum took her to see Charlton play at home whenever she could, but Bella knew that she didn't really like football because she had to keep on asking the same old questions about the rules and the players. Bella glanced at the front cover of the programme and felt infuriated with herself for not knowing.

"Apparently, Guatemala has stepped in at the last moment

to take the place of Chile," Charlie told her. "You shouldn't feel bad about not knowing."

But she did. Bella decided to check the list of matches on the official Guatemalan football website as soon as Charlie had gone. Maybe the tournament would still be on when she got back.

"Bella, don't be too freaked out," said Charlie anxiously, standing up and pacing around in what precious little space there was between the rafters, "but while you were in a strop and getting changed back in the classroom, I saw your mum's boyfriend shaking hands with Ted Briggs."

The news came as no surprise to Bella.

"I don't know how I know this," said Bella fiercely, "but I have a strong feeling that beneath that lovey-dovey front Bruce puts on whenever my mum's around, he's bad."

"You just don't want a new dad," Charlie teased, rather unwisely. "No one will ever be good enough for you."

"I don't need a substitute dad!" objected Bella. "I *have* a father!"

Buried inside her mum's Guatemalan chest, Bella kept an album full of articles about the earthquake in which her father was thought to have been killed. Annie had started the album on the advice of the welfare officer assigned to monitor Bella's adoption, but recently Bella had been adding to the book herself.

"Charlie, I want to show you something," said Bella, rolling out of the hammock and going over to the chest to get it. Knowing that her dad was a renowned footballer in his youth, Bella regularly trawled the Internet for news and pictures of Guatemalan players from the mid-1980s. Amongst all the photographs she had assembled, there was an action shot of a striker playing for Quezaltenango that had originally appeared in the sports pages of *La Prensa Libre*, one of Guatemala's leading papers.

"Look at this," said Bella, opening up the book to show off her latest addition. Charlie admired the tall footballer, his long black hair blowing wildly in the wind as he powered home his volley. "The winning goal in Quezaltenango's two–one win against Panajachel," Bella announced proudly, reading from the caption.

"So . . . ?" Charlie queried, a little confused.

"Look at him," Bella demanded. "And look what's around his neck." Charlie peered into the blurred black-and-white printout.

"He's wearing a necklace?" said Charlie, trying to make out if indeed this was so or whether it was a fault in the print. "What does that prove?" she asked, getting more perturbed by the second. Bella pulled out her own pendant and brandished it before Charlie's eyes.

"Don't you remember?" Bella replied, getting snappy with her friend. "My mother and father exchanged pendants as wedding presents. I don't know how I know – but I'm sure this man is my father." Bella hadn't been able to keep her pendant a secret from Charlie, despite her promise to the Quetzal, but she'd stopped short of telling her anything about its powers.

"Wow!" said Charlie, returning her attention to the photo. "What's his name?"

"Eduardo Salvatore," said Bella proudly. "He played for the national team back in the 1980s."

"Have you shown your mum?" gasped Charlie.

"Yes," said Bella impatiently. "She sat me down and calmly told me that I was wasting my time. She thinks she's just trying to protect me by telling me he's dead, but I know it's him, Charlie. And I know he's alive!" Bella's heart was thumping. Charlie gawped at her friend, completely dumbfounded by her revelation. The silence was broken by Bella's mum calling up the stairs: "Charlie, your mum's on the phone. She wants you home right away to finish your packing." The two friends gave each other a resigned look.

"But that wasn't even twenty minutes," Bella complained.

"Bella, I want you to sort out your T-shirts and trainers," Annie went on, ignoring Bella's retort. "We're not dragging your entire wardrobe to India, so you'd better decide which ones you're taking." And then, almost as an afterthought: "Oh, and pack one of your colourful Guatemalan dresses. Bruce says we need to look smart when we go to the children's centre."

Bella persuaded Charlie to stay for a little while longer.

"We can say we're tidying up," Bella told her, as the two of them climbed back up into the hammock.

"Is your mum alright?" asked Charlie. "You two seem to argue all the time these days. And she hasn't baked us a chocolate cake in months!"

"It's because of that stupid boyfriend," Bella lamented. "It's like he's cast some spell over her that makes her grumpy all the time."

"I think your mum's acting funny because you're being so mean about Bruce," Charlie told her flatly. "If you keep on being so horrible to her about him, it's bound to make her cross."

"You don't know what he's like," warned Bella, irritated by Charlie's unwelcome advice. "I do!" A creak on the landing made them jump.

"Coming," Charlie called, rolling out of the hammock. "Send me an email from India," said Charlie as she climbed down the ladder. "And call me as soon as you get back."

CHAPTER FOUR

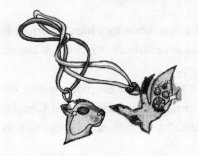

SHIPS THAT PASS

The trouble with having a mum with a medical background was the sheer amount of health aids that needed to be packed on a trip to India: malaria tablets, antibiotics, aspirin, throat lozenges, allergy medication, antiseptic cream, band-aids, insect repellent, sun block – the list was endless. On top of this there was the long checklist of important documents such as passports, health insurance, hotel confirmation letter, and so on. Bella was also surprised at the full array of waterproof clothing they were packing.

"It's the monsoon season," Annie explained to her.

"Great," said Bella. "We could have stayed in England if we wanted a wet and windy summer."

After two hours of solid packing, Bella still hadn't organized the cameras she would need for the trip. Over the past few months she'd managed to collect a range of them from donors interested in her idea to help Guatemalan street-children photograph their lives. It was Bella's ambition to put an exhibition together to show at school and hopefully the local library to help raise public awareness and funds. The more cameras they had, the greater the number of children who could take part and the wider her choice of images. Making such a fuss about diverting this project to India actually made Bella feel guilty when she thought about the children they might help there. According to what she'd read on the Internet, India had the largest population of street-children in the world. Bruce's charity had established one of many children's centres teaching a whole range of skills – how to repair bicycles and scooters, sew clothes, make candles and handicraft knickknacks for tourists – just the kind of project Bella wanted to support in Guatemala.

"I think I'm just going to take the digital cameras," Bella told her mum, heading for the attic to collect them up. "I'll save all the pictures onto your laptop while we're away, then edit and print them here when we get back."

"Fine," said her mum calmly, relieved at last that she and Bella were getting on – at least for the moment. "I'll go downstairs and prepare the stir-fry veg for Bruce and me."

Bella went to her bedroom and logged on to the Internet. She quickly discovered that the Guatemalan team was both arriving in the UK and departing on dates and times that crossed almost to the hour with her own holiday flights.

"I don't believe it!" she cried, banging her fist on the desk in frustration.

Her mum was always going on about fate and how things were meant to happen, but Bella wasn't quite so fatalistic. "It's as if someone has worked it out on purpose so I don't get to see them."

True to form, Bruce Anders arrived late. Annie, too hungry to wait, had already eaten, but the sweet smell of ginger and garlic still filled the house. Bella just happened to be passing the front door when he rang the bell a little after ten. She opened it to find him wearing his blue work suit and white shirt. What annoyed Bella was that he still wore his tinted glasses.

"I suppose you need those to keep out the blinding rays of the full moon," Bella quipped as she reluctantly let him in. Since his return from India, Bella couldn't recall seeing him without them.

"Now now, Bell," he replied, lugging his battered old suitcase into the hall. "You should know sarcasm is the lowest form of wit."

"I'm sorry," replied Bella mockingly. "I was only trying to work out if it's a medical condition or your version of fashion."

"I have to wear tints to help with my dyslexia," he replied rather unconvincingly before pulling yet another computer game from his pocket.

"Bruce, is that you?" came the call from the kitchen. "I'm clearing out the fridge. Come on through."

"There ya go, Bell," Bruce breezed, nonchalantly dropping the strap of his laptop and passing her the game package. "See ya later." Bella knew that this was her cue to get lost. "At least I don't have to sit in the same room as him," she thought as she took the disk and walked away. In principle, she'd already decided that she had no time for the game, despite the fact that it was exactly the kind of counter-terrorism undercover cop one that she and Charlie loved to play.

Because of the early flight, it had been arranged that Bruce would "stay over" at their house, although it was debatable whether "staying late" may have been more appropriate, as it was hardly worth going to bed at all. Nevertheless, Bella had been uncomfortable about it.

"You're going to have to get used to the idea," her mum had told her. "When we get to the hotel, Bruce and I are sharing a bedroom." Bella was devastated. "You're in the adjoining apartment, which will be great, because you'll have your own TV," she went on. "They'll have satellite, you know."

Bella didn't give two hoots about the TV bribe. That man was going to be sharing a room with her mum!

Bella went up to her room, switched on her TV and started to watch a documentary about a French extreme sport she'd never heard of before called *parkour*. It wasn't long before she was hooked. The athletes were called free-runners and used the rooftops and architecture of the city as a daredevil obstacle course through which to sprint and somersault like superheroes.

"I wouldn't mind having a go at that myself," Bruce yawned as he watched the same programme, stretched out on the living-room sofa.

"Well if you do – don't tell me," said Annie, drowsily pushing a cushion behind her head. "And whatever you do – don't do it after you've had a drink. I don't fancy having to peel you off the pavement." Annie and Bella had noticed on more than one occasion that Bruce fancied himself as a bit of an acrobat. He told them once he was so good at gymnastics as a boy that he almost joined the circus.

"Shame you didn't," Bella had said.

She'd been grounded for a week for saying that.

When the documentary was finished, Bella went up into the attic. She pulled her mum's Guatemalan chest across to the skylight and climbed on top.

"What are you doing?" whispered a voice inside her head.

47

Bella gave the portrait a fierce look.

"I'm going out for some fresh air," she snapped. "And stop talking to me like I'm a child."

"He's getting close," whispered the voice. "And he wants his pendant."

"What do you mean, 'he wants his pendant'?" shrieked Bella, giving the portrait of Itzamna a thunderous look.

"Keep your wits about you," warned the voice. Bella felt unnerved, her thoughts returning to Ted Briggs and Bruce. Reaching up, she propped open the skylight, gripped onto the sill and, rolling her leg up onto one of the lower rafters, hauled herself up onto the slate roof.

"Good evening to you, Miss Bella," hooted a passing owl. "An excellent night for chasing field mice. Would you care to join me?"

"No, I wouldn't!" squawked Bella, who'd spent many an hour trying to convert the local owls to scavenging through rubbish bins for food rather than picking on little mice.

Even though it was dark, Bella looked around to make sure that there were no humans watching. Then, checking that her pendant was secure around her neck, she bent her knees, held out her arms and jumped. Especially since the weather had been getting warmer, Bella had taken to a rigorous regime of flying practice after dark. Like the Quetzal, Bella often got hassled about her colourful plumage by the local crows. However, because they could sense her power and knew that she could transform herself into a potentially deadly human, they'd never yet dared to attack her.

Bella glided down and planted herself on the sturdy metal bar jutting out from the wall by the kitchen window. From there she could eavesdrop on the conversation between Annie and Bruce as her mum cooked Bruce's stir-fry. The bar supported a rather spectacular hanging basket. Bella sometimes watered it in the evening to help her mum – when she was in the mood.

"What are you doing there?'" chomped a precocious young snail who was about to tuck into her mum's geraniums. Familiarity with seeing Bella in her animal form had tempted some animals to be quite cocky towards her. Basically, they could say anything, and she still wouldn't eat them.

"If you take one bite out of that leaf, I'm going in for the salt," Bella warned. In truth, she'd have done no such thing, but the comment achieved its desired effect.

"Sorry, Miss Bella," murmured the hapless mollusc, burying his head into his shell.

Peering through the blinds and the boxes of herb plants lined up along the kitchen window, Bella could see Bruce sitting at the kitchen table with a bottle of beer while her mum stirred the veg in the wok.

"Honestly, the way she attends to his every whim," Bella muttered. "It's like I don't exist. And why is he still wearing those wretched sunglasses?" Using the power of the pendant to enhance her hearing, Bella leaned as far forward as she dared.

"Well, I don't think it's right that just because you work for a charity you should have to advance all your own expenses for this trip," Bella's mum was saying as she shook soy sauce into the mix. "It's unprofessional." Steam from the rice cooker was causing condensation to form on the window, and the amplified sizzling from the wok was deafening. Bella squinted to see Bruce unfasten his ponytail and shake out his long, sun-bleached hair. "What a jerk," she tutted.

"Annie," Bruce started furtively, "I'm going to need a favour. Could you lend me two thousand pounds – just to help us through? I can pay you back as soon as we get home."

"Some chance of that!" Bella snorted. "I tried to get her to lend me twenty pounds for a new football shirt. *She hasn't got any money*," she twittered with the joy of insider knowledge. She watched as her mum reached over to turn off the rice cooker.

"I suppose I could draw five hundred in cash on my credit card and another five hundred on my Switch when we get to Heathrow," Annie suggested. "Then perhaps I could write you a cheque from my savings account for the rest."

"What!" chirped Bella, nearly falling off the metal bar. She felt like flying into the kitchen and giving her mum an earful of the "we haven't got any money" line she was always laying on her. Hopping with rage, Bella had to flap her wings wildly to regain her balance and avoid toppling into the hanging basket.

"How do you think it's going with Bella?" she heard her mum ask as she served up.

"She's acting like a spoiled brat," replied Bruce, reaching for the salt before he'd even tasted his dinner. Bella was ready to smash the window with her beak, she was so angry. She watched her mum trying to signal to Bruce to keep his voice down. Bella decided she could bear it no longer and flew back up to the attic.

As it turned out, no one went to bed that night. Bruce and her mum stayed up to watch a late-night film, while Bella hung out in the attic, fretting about the second conversation she'd overheard that day and rereading for the umpteenth time all the articles she'd ever found relating to her father and his apparent death. She wondered what he was like and how different her life would have been if she'd known him. Whether he'd have had time to take her to football on Saturdays like Charlie's dad, or if he'd be too busy at work to do anything – like Rahina's and Imogen's dads. Thinking about her father always left Bella with a horrible, empty feeling – a yearning for someone she missed beyond measure.

"I wish Charlie was sleeping over," she told the portrait. "And where's that pompous old bird when I need him? He never drops in on me these days."

Her only consolation was that she didn't have to spend any time with Bruce.

At ten past three in the morning, they were all standing by the window in the front room. Annie was wearing a blue cotton dress, white mohair cardigan and sandals, while Bella, as usual, had picked out her red Charlton Athletic football shirt, jeans and trainers and was busy tying back her hair with a colourful Guatemalan scrunchie.

"I think I'd better give the cab company a quick reminder," said Annie.

"I see you're still wearing those fancy glasses," Bella goaded Bruce, the second her mum left the room. Bella was still smarting from the "spoiled brat" comment she'd heard him make earlier. Raising his clawed hands in a mock-spooky gesture, he started to prowl towards her. "All the better to see you with," he growled mischievously.

"I'm eleven – not four!" cried Bella, infuriated that he was turning her comment into a joke. "Grow up."

Bruce smiled to himself. He quite enjoyed winding her up.

Reaching out to try and pull Bruce's glasses from his face, Bella was outmanoeuvred as Bruce stuck out his arm and held her shoulder. The action stretched the collar of her shirt.

"I see you're still wearing that lucky charm of yours," he sniggered. "It didn't bring you much joy in yesterday's race, did it?" Bella jerked away and turned her back on him just as her mum returned.

"He's broken down," Annie told them. "But there's another one on its way." She sensed the frostiness between Bella and Bruce but was too tired and stressed to deal with it. The taxi finally turned up at twenty to four.

The atmosphere in the cab was awful, despite the fact the driver made good time crossing London and got them to the terminal drop-off point with ten minutes to spare before their final check-in time. Bella was angry with the austere man in a grey uniform who systematically emptied her backpack in the security zone. Her guide to Delhi, Gore-Tex jacket, a full range of Guatemalan hair scrunchies, Discman, half a packet of chocolate biscuits, an apple and a carton of juice – all of it, spread out on the table for everyone to see, while both her mum and Bruce slipped right through with their shoulder bags and laptops.

"Aren't you going to help me put it all back?" she asked the dour-faced security guard as he gave her the all-clear and turned away.

"Shh, Bella," Annie hushed, hurrying over to Bella's aid. "This is not the place to pick a fight."

Once in the departure lounge, their flight to Delhi was already being called for boarding.

"I need to pick up some more sun block," said Annie in a

flap, about to head for the shops.

"And don't forget, Annie," Bruce interjected as surreptitiously as he could. "The cash – remember? And leave the cheque blank. I'll fill in the details later." Bella saw the worried look on her mum's face and felt her own body stiffen with rage.

"I'll pick up a bottle of whisky," Bruce added, nipping into the duty-free shop.

"Bella, wait here," ordered her mum, pointing to a row of three empty chairs by the Bureau de Change. She'd decided to sort the money first. Bella threw herself down, too tired and fed up even to sulk, while her mum got out her credit card and chequebook.

The departure lounge was far busier than Bella imagined it might be, given the hour. The seats around her were taken up with people of all ages, shapes and sizes, stretched out in various positions of discomfort, as they tried to steal a little rest before their flight. Strewn all around them was a disarray of shopping bags and fast-food packaging, making the whole area quite treacherous to navigate. Despite the fact that most shops still had their metal security windows down, there was the sense of the day beginning. Groups of shop assistants were already gathering outside a number of outlets, while bleary-eyed managers clutching huge bunches of keys went through the laborious process of opening up and turning off the alarms. Inside and around the shops that were open, there was quite a lot of activity.

"Right," said Annie, when she'd finished her transaction. "I'll just be two minutes."

As Annie hurriedly made her way towards the pharmacy,

Bella's eyes were drawn to a far distant corner of the lounge where, to her surprise, she saw Bruce. With his duty-free bag in one hand, he had found a quiet, secluded spot to use his mobile. Bella reached for her pendant and gathered her powers. "Who could he possibly be speaking to at this hour?" she thought, straining with all her might to hear.

"Miss Devaki? Bruce here," she heard him say. Bruce had cupped his hands around the receiver, making it difficult to hear, even for Bella. "I'm at Heathrow . . . "

"I've heard that name before," thought Bella, suddenly wide-awake. She looked around for her mum. "She needs to hear this."

"Have you got the merchandise?" Bruce went on. Bella couldn't see her mum anywhere. "Excellent," Bruce was saying. "The money? No problem, I have it. And how are the new children working out? Good. Yes, I should be able to gather the rest by the end of the week. Yep, see you at the hotel."

He hung up.

Bella quickly tucked away her pendant and stared at the floor, trying to look as bored and fed up as she could – a skill she was almost flawless at. "What is he up to?" she thought anxiously.

Overlooking the departure lounge was a glass-fronted corridor used by arriving passengers making their way towards customs. As Bella sat contemplating Bruce's phone call, a tall, handsome man in a blue-and-white tracksuit casually glanced down. His abrupt double take and sudden stop so startled the flight attendant behind him that she almost crashed right into him. If Bella hadn't been so consumed with her own thoughts, she might have noticed the striking aura of his reddened complexion and long black hair as he moved closer to the window to peer down at her. To have witnessed the man as he reached for the silver-and-gold jaguar hanging around his neck might have helped Bella understand why her pendant suddenly twitched, drawn as it was towards the old, familiar force of its former master.

Yanked to her senses by the abrupt swish of her pendant slipping from her neck, Bella shot both hands out to grab it, but was too late. She glared in horror as her precious pendant swept across the shiny floor, apparently all by itself. "My pendant!" she cried, thrusting herself forward and darting after it at full pelt. Bella's heart was in her mouth. The glistening chain was sliding towards a heating grate. She threw herself into a desperate dive and skidded into the path of a bleary-eyed security guard whose heel, quite by chance, caught the chain.

"Bella, what are you doing?" her mum shrieked, pushing the sun cream into her hand luggage as she ran. Bella snatched the pendant just as the man lifted his shoe, but even in her fist, it was still trying to get away. Clenching it tightly, she pulled herself up as her mum arrived on the scene.

"I'm terribly sorry," Annie apologized frantically to the bewildered security guard. Then, taking Bella by the arm, she pulled her away. "Come on, Bella, I don't know what you're playing at, but we're late. Now where's Bruce?"

It didn't take long for Bruce to make an appearance. Whisky in one hand, shoulder bag and laptop draped over each shoulder, he was completely unaware of Bella's eavesdropping and her pendant crisis. Even more irritating to Bella, he was in a jolly mood.

"Alright there, girls?" he asked, taking the wad of cash and the cheque from Bella's mum. Bella could feel her anger starting to rise.

"Would passengers Balistica and Anders please make their way to Gate Twenty-Three immediately," came the announcement. "Your plane is ready to depart."

Bruce stuffed the cash and the cheque into his money belt and grasped Bella's arm before she could pull it away. "Come on, we've got a plane to catch," he announced in a jovial voice. With her mum clutching Bella's hand, Bella was dragged to the nearest walkway as the three of them hurriedly made their way to the departure gate.

Back up in the glass corridor, the thirty-three-year old man in the blue-and-white tracksuit tucked away his pendant and moved on towards passport control. The sweat and exhilaration on his face told its own story. Sensing his connection to the wild-looking girl he'd just encountered had been revealing. The power and passion he'd felt when the two pendants engaged had been awesome – far greater than even his most extravagant hopes. His girl was more in touch with her spirit and her past than he ever imagined. "She's learning to follow her instincts," he mused with paternal pride. "I wonder who's been teaching her?" Failing to draw his long-lost daughter to him had been an opportunity missed. But he was on to her.

"Our paths will cross again soon enough," he smiled in gleeful anticipation.

It was their destiny.

CHAPTER FIVE

DELHI

Needless to say, Bella, Annie and Bruce were the last three passengers to board the plane, which started taxiing away as soon as they were strapped in. Bella made sure she got the window seat and forced her mum to sit between her and Bruce, who, with his long lanky legs was only too happy to take the aisle seat. She was feeling so stressed out by the erratic pulls of the pendant and her suspicions about Bruce, she just clenched the pendant tightly in her fist and focused all her attention on the safety demonstration performed by the cabin crew. Closing her eyes and tensing her body as the engines revved and opened up, she felt her mum take her hand as they were thrust back into their seats for take-off.

Some minutes later, as the Air India airliner started to level out from its steep ascent, the pendant gradually calmed down, but still Bella refused to release her grip. She tried with all her might to conjure up the colourful image of her friend, the Quetzal. Maybe if she focused all her energies on him he might hear her cries for help and fly to her assistance. "Quetzal, where are you?" she called, using her inner voice. "I need you."

All around her, passengers were reclining their seats and flicking through the choices of programmes and films on offer for their ten-hour flight. When the captain finally switched off the red "fasten seatbelt" sign, Bruce, along with several other passengers, made a mad dash for the toilet. While all this was going on, Bella continued her chant. "Quetzal, where are you? I need you . . . " She carried on even after Bruce returned with the three cans of Diet Coke and two small bottles of whisky he'd charmed the flight attendants into giving him. Ignoring her drink, Bella became so tranquillized by her repetative chant, she fell asleep.

"Bella, it's time to eat, wake up!" urged her mum, shaking Bella's arm. "You're having a nightmare. The whole plane can hear you groaning." She woke up startled and for a second had no idea where she was.

"What was I saying?" asked Bella nervously. Although she had been asleep, Bella realized that her hand was still firmly gripped around her pendant.

"I don't know what language you were mumbling away in, but it certainly wasn't English," replied her mum sleepily. "It was like Spanish gobbledegook."

"K'iche'," thought Bella. K'iche' was the language of her forefathers, the chosen tongue of Bella's inner voice. She'd realized after her adventure in Guatemala with the Quetzal that it was the very language she used when communicating with the portrait of Itzamna in the attic.

She got up and went to the toilet to check on the damage caused to the pendant's chain by its journey across the airport floor. She'd assumed that the clasp was damaged, but to her surprise she found that it was fine. "It's like someone actually unclipped it without me knowing," she thought, still baffled by the whole event. Deciding that her neck was still the safest place for it, Bella put the pendant back on and tucked it away beneath her shirt. Still feeling tired she threw cold water over her face and tried to wake herself up before returning to her seat.

Breakfast turned out to be scrambled eggs, bacon and tomato served up in a tiny plastic container with a multitude of sachets and a small cup of orange juice.

"Better savour and enjoy," said Bruce, rubbing his hands in eager anticipation. "It's going to be rice, rice, chapattis and rice for the next fortnight."

"No it won't, Bruce," smiled Annie with much more affection than Bella thought his frivolous comment deserved. "We're staying at the Ambassador Hotel. They serve great Indian food. You can even have a full English breakfast if you want." Bella didn't care. She loved Indian food. Her mum used Indian spices and herbs in her cooking all the time.

Bella had been happy to read in her guide book that the hotel had a swimming pool with diving boards and chutes. At least being able to swim everyday would make her feel like she was on holiday. Thinking of her travel guide, Bella reached under her seat for her bag and rooted around until she found it. She flicked straight to the small paragraph about the hotel to reassure herself, before slipping it into the seat pocket containing the in-flight magazines.

Even before the flight attendants had finished clearing away the remains of Bella's breakfast, she was dozing again, dreaming of watching a football match in which her father scored eleven goals and was so pleased to see her after it was over, he gave her the dazzling silver-and-gold necklace he was wearing. When she came round, the lights in the aircraft had been dimmed, and most of the window shutters were closed. Many passengers had reclined their seats and were trying to sleep. Some tried to ignore the incessant snores of neighbours and read, while others had stuck on their headphones and were watching the in-flight film. Annie was resting her head on Bruce's shoulder while they slept.

Bella pressed the button on her armrest to switch on her reading light and returned to her travel book. She read with fascination how the seven cities of Delhi had risen from the ashes of a history fraught with invasions and massacres to merge into one vast metropolis. In spite of her anger at the change of venue for this year's holiday, she was excited. "It's going to be a fantastic experience," she thought. "And I guess there's always the chance that the Quetzal might still be there. After all, he did say that his tiger friend worked in the Mumbai Circus. Maybe he can pop over and visit me."

As she leafed through her guidebook, Bella was blown away by the glossy photos of the national parks, the vibrant city streets and markets and, of course, the mighty temples.

"Can we go to Agra and visit the Taj Mahal?" she asked her mum eagerly, giving her a poke on the arm. "And the Red Fort?" Bella was particularly impressed with the massive, red sandstone façade of the fort and was excited to see that it wasn't that far from the hotel.

"Of course, darling," replied Annie dreamily, opening her eyes for a moment. "It won't be all work, work, work. We can be tourists too, you know."

At two o'clock, the pilot announced that the plane was

starting to make its descent towards Delhi airport and that everyone should turn their watches forward by five and a half hours.

"That's ten past seven in the evening, I make it," Bruce yawned, stretching out his arms and legs in what little space his seat allowed.

"Why are you still wearing your sunglasses?" Bella probed. "Too much glare from your reading light?"

"Come on, Bella," Annie reprimanded, while giving her boyfriend a reassuring squeeze on the arm. "You know they're not sunglasses. Now stop being stroppy and take a look at the fabulous view." Bella looked out of the window to see the intricate and winding network of roads that dissected the sprawling city. Even though the setting sun was casting long red streaks across the sky, it was still possible to pick out the rich greenery of the parks and the gardens surrounding many of the temples and buildings Bella had been reading about.

By eight o'clock the three weary travellers had collected their bags and were making their way through the air-conditioned arrivals building to have their visas checked by the immigration officials. The colourful assortment of official hats, Islamic caps and smart turbans worn by immigration and airport staff presented Bella with her first taste of the vibrancy and variety in the culture that she was about to experience.

With nothing to declare, they walked boldly through customs unchallenged and out into the main terminal building, bustling with wandering travellers and busy shops. The first image that caught Bella's eye was on the large billboard hanging from the ceiling. Bella knew without having to read the English caption that the beautiful Indian woman in the picture was advertising a hair care product. Dressed in a black designer suit with a fine yellow pinstripe and a pointed, upturned collar, she was lying suggestively across a white leather couch, while her long, shiny and richly dark hair flowed gracefully down from her left shoulder. "She's beautiful," thought Bella. "I wish my hair looked like that." Bella gave her wild, knotted locks a quick run-through with her fingers. She admired the assortment of shiny gold bracelets the model wore before turning her attention to her dark, hypnotic eyes as they gazed persuasively down upon the lesser mortals on the concourse below.

"Taxi?" asked an old man with a flamboyant white beard and upturned moustache. "Cheap. Very cheap." The man was dressed in smart trousers and a yellow, open-neck shirt. Before they knew it, they were surrounded by a crowd of taxi drivers touting for business, all of them pretty much wearing the same kind of outfit as the old man. "*Nahin!*" Bruce growled, pushing his way through. "No thank you – *dhanyavaad.*" Bella and her mum followed in his wake, pushing their trolleys. "I want to see at firsthand any taxi I get into," Bella heard him grumble.

Fighting their way through the crowd they exited onto the street via a revolving door.

"Phew!" gasped Annie, struck as they all were by the stifling heat. Bella could feel the sweat forming on her brow within seconds. They made their way down to the taxi rank where a long line of black-and-yellow taxis awaited them beneath a row of flickering lampposts.

"Look!" Bella was pointing to a line of three-wheeled bikes, each of which had a large seat at the back, covered by a canopy. "Rickshaws." Bella had seen a few of the pedal-powered rickshaws in central London. They were great for beating the traffic jams and much better for the environment than regular taxis. "I haven't seen them being pulled by scooters before," Bella commented, admiring some of the larger ones.

"Strictly speaking they're called auto-rickshaws," said Bruce. "The eight-seater ones are *vickrams*. They're considerably more comfortable but cause much more pollution."

"What a shame," sighed Annie. "I guess we'd better stick to the pedal rickshaws, then."

"Mum! You're so boring," Bella protested.

"*Namaste*," said Bruce, greeting the owner of the best looking motor-taxi in the line. "The Ambassador Hotel. But take the scenic route around town for our first-timers," he ordered the driver, gesturing to his travel-weary, yet excited companions.

"Very good, sir," replied the man, clasping his hands together and bowing his head respectfully. Amongst a barrage of complaints from drivers further up towards the front of the queue, the driver collected their bags and loaded them carefully into the boot of his taxi. With Bruce taking his place alongside the driver, they set off.

Last year, Bella's adventure in Guatemala had opened her eyes to the hustle and bustle of urban life in the developing world, but all that seemed pretty calm compared with the outskirts of Delhi. Sitting on the back seat, Bella discovered to her frustration that the handle to roll down her window was broken. Against her mum's express wishes, she clawed it down with her fingers and stuck out her head. Leaning out as far as she dared, she took delight in the relatively cool breeze created by their swift movement through the dusty streets. Even the racket made by the side-street vendors, the crowds of pedestrians, the discordant horns of clapped-out cars and overfull buses, the bells of frenetic cyclists and speeding rickshaws could do nothing to drown out the chatter of a whole host of socializing animals. Not only was the bird life spectacular and raucous, Bella could also hear and see goats, pigs, donkeys, oxen, even the odd monkey, most of them tethered to a lead and in some tug of war hustle with their owners. Even at night, Delhi was a sensory feast.

"What do you think?" asked Bruce gleefully, turning his head to gauge their response.

"It's amazing," cheered Bella, unable to contain her sudden joy, despite her worries. She looked into the eyes of her beaming mum and enjoyed the moment. "Maybe things can work out," Bella tried to reassure herself. "What if I've got the wrong end of the stick about Bruce?" In the excitement of the moment, Bella actually wanted to think so.

They travelled on. Bella became fascinated with the adverts. The familiar signs for Coca Cola shone brightly against the faded posters advertising unfamiliar beers and Bollywood films Bella had never heard of. They passed a well-lit statue of Mahatma Gandhi situated at the edge of a park, beautifully landscaped with flowerbeds full of orange marigolds and fiery red poinsettias.

"I wish my begonias and chrysanthemums looked as good," said Annie wistfully.

There were flowers in many window boxes throughout the city too, their scents lost to the strong spicy aromas wafting out from numerous cooking pots.

"I can smell turmeric," said Bella happily.

"And that's not all you can smell," Bruce butted in. It was true. Mingled in with all these aromatic delights, the putrid smell of kerbside debris and engine pollution made for quite a potent stimulant to the senses.

"Look at that!" squealed Bella, pointing to an enormous bull sitting in the central reservation on the dual carriageway. The bull was stretched out comfortably, casually watching the world go by while giving the occasional disparaging snort to passers-by.

As they stopped for a red traffic light, half a dozen ragged and filthy-looking children suddenly surrounded the taxi.

"Roll up your windows," Bruce ordered, shutting his. But Bella couldn't.

"Street-children," tutted the driver, shaking his head. "The scourge of India."

"Don't give them anything," Bruce shouted through the sound of their pleas. "Whatever it is they're selling – we don't want it." Bella was about to give Bruce a piece of her mind when she was abruptly hit in the face by a hand clutching a packet of tissues.

"Give me money," pleaded the desperate child.

"I could do with a packet of tissues," said Annie, reaching for her purse.

"No," Bruce said firmly, reaching back to stop her from opening it. "We'll be besieged." The light changed, and they skidded away.

Bella felt distraught. What shocked her the most was how scared the incident had made her feel. "They were only children," she told herself. She expected to feel an instinctive camaraderie with street-children – after all, if it hadn't been for her adoptive mum, she would have been one herself. Instead, the brief and chaotic interaction had made her feel instantly like she came from a world so rich in privilege and wealth that they could never have anything in common. She felt wretched.

"I know you want to be their friend," said Annie kindly, taking Bella's hand. "But you have to take it slowly – it's going to take time to gain their trust."

The taxi reached another busy junction where a speeding *vickram* had crashed into a cart full of oranges and spilled its load. On the pavement to their right, Bella saw a charismatic-looking boy wearing grubby green shorts and a black, threadbare T-shirt, juggling knives. He was performing to a small crowd of onlookers. "He doesn't look much older than me," Bella thought, dazzled by the boy's intense concentration and speed.

With incredible skill, the boy came to the end of his act, catching each spinning knife by the handle during a sequence in which any one of them could have sliced his fingers clean off. The crowd around him applauded and threw him coins before quickly disbanding. Bella watched him drop his knives into a bag, turn around and apparently bump accidentally into an old Sikh man wearing a crumpled grey suit and bright orange turban. "No!" gasped Bella in disbelief as the boy somehow managed, within the microsecond of this now clearly deliberate collision, to slip his hand into the man's inside pocket and discreetly lift his wallet. The man had no idea that he'd just been robbed. Bella's exclamation drew the boy's attention, and he was soon bounding across the road to greet them. Bella's head was in turmoil. Following the last incident, she actually wanted the taxi to pull away rather than have to deal with another embarrassing situation.

"A few rupees for a poor orphan," he begged in English, dropping his bag and holding out his upturned hands to Bruce. Bella winced to see his unclipped nails and then stiffened in anticipation as Bruce raised his glasses and turned towards the boy. She followed the meeting of their eyes and was shocked to see the look of revulsion that erupted on the boy's face.

"There you are!" Bruce bellowed as the boy recoiled and turned quickly away. "I'm on to you, you little thief." The boy raised his bag of knives to shield his face and backed away. Bruce lowered his glasses. Bella could tell her mum was tense.

"Now Bruce, I know you're tired," she began, "but he was . . . " But Bella wasn't listening. Her thoughts were centred on the boy as he continued to back away. "Why's he so scared of Bruce?" she wondered. Her mind was in overdrive. "It's like the two of them actually know each other." The incident only encouraged Bella's deepest suspicions about her mum's boyfriend. She was glad her mum was upset with him too.

She watched as the boy retreated into a shop doorway, reached for the blue-and-orange baseball cap in his bag and pulled it over his face as he crouched down. "He's muttering something," Bella thought, using the power of the pendant to pick out his voice amongst all the other sounds in the street.

"Why did I have to choose his car?" she heard the boy grumble in a language she guessed was Hindi. Thanks to her mystical powers, Bella found that she could understand almost any language she ever heard. "Of all people!" the boy went on. She watched him peer up at Bruce one more time. The look of hate and distrust on his face confirmed everything. "There's definitely a connection between Bruce and that boy," she decided.

Suddenly, Bella realized that the boy was now looking directly at her. With the spill of oranges over the road finally cleared, the driver crunched the taxi into gear. Before she knew it, the boy was up on his feet, sprinting towards them. A little taken aback, Bella followed the intensity of his gaze and realized that it was set with deep intent upon her pendant.

"Watch out!" cried Bruce, turning quickly. The engine revved. Bella pulled back her head as the boy thrust out his right arm.

"Aah!" Bella screamed as the taxi jerked away with a sickening screech.

"Is he alright?" gasped Annie, as the boy tumbled backwards onto the street.

"Serves the little beggar right," Bruce snarled as they drove away.

"Scum of the earth," the driver added with an agreeing nod.

"Stop the car!" Annie demanded. "We must see if he's alright."

"He's alright," Bruce shouted over the grind of the engine. "I can see him in the wing mirror. He's already walking away." Bella drew at least some comfort from Bruce's uncaring retort. "That's what he's like, Mum," she thought. "Now you'll have to believe me!"

The taxi driver took a detour, partly because of the traffic problems en route but also because of Bruce's request to show them the sights of the city. In stark contrast to the initial high spirits felt by the weary travellers, the mood in the taxi had become sombre. No one spoke for some time. Bella could sense her mum was upset about Bruce's verbal assault on the beggar boy because she was refusing to join in with any of his chitchat. Bella too was deep in thought. "What did Bruce mean: 'I'm going to track you down'?" she was thinking as she replayed the whole event in her mind. "Why so vicious and personal?" She couldn't get it out of her head, the way the boy had backed away with such terror in his eyes. "The boy recognized him," Bella decided. "I have no doubt about it."

As they drove past a battered old sign that read "Ajmal Khan Park", the city suddenly seemed to disappear into darkness.

"This is a beautiful park to visit during the day, guys," said Bruce, attempting to lighten the mood. Along the road, the travellers could see an explosion of light filtering out into the landscaped gardens. As they approached, Bella was surprised to see a long line of parked lorries and caravans, many of them with their headlights still on. Surrounded by noisy generators and floodlights, the site was a hullabaloo of activity. Annie had plainly decided to let things rest about the incident with the boy, at least for now.

"I guess that's going to be the Big Top," she said, leaning across Bella for a closer look at the massive frame being assembled fifty metres or so back from the road. Bella noticed that many of the lorries were advertising the Mumbai Circus.

"You must go see," announced the driver with great pride. "The greatest circus in the whole of India. They've got the best acrobats, not to mention the tigers, leopards, elephants . . . " Bella screwed up her face. She didn't approve of animals in circuses and zoos.

"Can't see these guys going to the circus," Bruce told the driver. "Too many animal rights issues." Bella hated the way he appeared to be taking the mickey out of them. Secretly though, she loved the idea of seeing the acrobats and clowns perform.

Turning her attention away from the circus, Bella was the first to comment on the loud squawks coming from the colourful array of bird life in the trees.

"What lovely voices," she said admiringly, pulling on her mum's arm.

"What a racket!" growled Bruce. "Let's hope our hotel's got an army of cats in the grounds."

"Look, Mum," said Bella. "Sparrows, crows, kites, hornbills, lapwings, babblers – it's amazing!" She pointed high into the trees. "Even golden orioles."

Since Bella had come to realize her animal twin was a quetzal, she'd become fascinated by ornithology. As the birds busied themselves in the usual scavenging and socializing of park life, Bella thought about her friend. "I'm not surprised the Quetzal likes to visit India," she decided. "I wonder if he knows that I'm here." Thinking about her friend made Bella realize how much she needed to talk with someone who could empathize and perhaps offer some plausible explanation for recent events. "Quetzal, where are you?" she meditated, taking hold of her pendant in the vain hope that he might suddenly appear. "I need you." Her concerns regarding Bruce and this whole trip were growing by the hour.

The taxi driver drove them through the narrow lanes of Old Delhi, blaring his horn at pedestrians and rickshaw taxis, while at the same time driving as if blind to the never-ending trail of obstacles before him. Bella gazed up at the entangled telephone wires draping from crooked posts all around her and wondered how anyone ever got a phone call.

"I remember this part of town from my backpacking days," Annie called from the back. "It's so pulsating with life it simply engulfs your senses." Bella could tell her mum was trying to forget what had happened and lift everyone's spirits. "And smell those delicious sweet spices wafting in from the Sadar Bazaar," she enthused, taking a deep sniff. "Heaven!" Bella had to admit, they certainly freshened the air.

Bella gazed through the window at the wealth of cafés and restaurants, interspersed with extravagant-looking jewellery shops.

"I'll take you here for dinner one night," Bruce announced. It wasn't entirely clear to Bella who this magnanimous invitation included, but she let it go. She could kick up a fuss later if they wanted to go on a date without her.

While the character of each district they passed through varied depending on the distribution of temples and places of architectural interest, one thing always remained a constant: the children. They were everywhere. Children running errands, selling things, sitting by the roadside working small sewing machines, performing all manner of acrobatic skills or simply hanging out; the Delhi streets were full of them. What was really staggering for Bella was the number of children she could see with disabilities trying to compete with the able-bodied performers and beggars. She watched a girl of about her own age with a little stub where her left arm should have been as she performed forward and backward flips for two old men sitting by a wall.

"I hope I'm going to meet some of these street-children," Bella thought.

She'd made great friends with a gang of such children on her Guatemalan adventure. It was thanks to them she had been able to find her way around Quezaltenango and track down Ted Briggs. Surely she could get over the surprising and disconcerting shock of her initial reaction here.

As they headed into the more touristy-looking areas of New Delhi, the streets became lined with yellow-flowered trees.

"Tamarind trees," Annie informed them.

"And what are those?" asked Bella, pointing to a tree with the most magnificent big leaves she'd ever seen.

"Peepul trees," replied her mum. "Aren't they beautiful?"

Bella felt proud that her mum knew so much about foreign places. "It's just such a shame about her taste in men," she concluded.

Annie wiped her dripping brow on her arm. Bella too was sweating. The temperature was rising by the minute.

"I think there's a storm brewing," said Bruce, as a distant rumble of thunder was followed by a fierce bolt of lightning. They watched the sparks fly from the electricity cables as people everywhere ran for cover.

"I'd be surprised if the electricity doesn't go down," said Annie. "It was off more than it was on last time I was here in the monsoon season."

Amidst the chaos, Bella's attention was drawn to the beautiful Indian woman with the dark, hypnotic eyes she'd first seen on a poster at the airport. This time, the stunning model was glaring down at them from another gigantic billboard. "It's like her eyes are everywhere," Bella thought to herself. This time the woman was dressed as a tightrope artist in a tight-fitting, yellow-and-black leotard. She held a long pole and was balancing on what looked like an electricity cable high above a rocky canyon.

"That's Diva Devaki," announced the driver. "The greatest acrobat and illusionist in the whole of India." A roll of thunder rattled the taxi followed by another bolt of lightning that illuminated the heavens. Annie looked quite disconcerted, but Bella was on the edge of her seat.

"They're not going to be interested in her," Bruce told the driver. "Just concentrate on your driving." But Bella was interested. "'Miss Devaki' was the person Bruce was speaking to at the airport," she thought. "She must have been 'the Diva' Ted Briggs was referring to – the one who was so interested in me and my pendant."

"Go on," Bella urged the driver, leaning over and tapping his shoulder.

"Bell! He's driving." Bruce objected, slapping her hand. Again, Bella felt her mum tense. "He's not endearing himself to anyone tonight," Bella mused with some satisfaction.

"The Diva is doing a televised stunt this weekend," the driver continued as the first sheets of rain began to pound against the car. Bruce sighed, visibly irritated by the driver's interjections.

"What's she doing?" Bella asked, trying to stay calm.

"She's walking along an electricity cable stretched across the entire width of a ravine about a hundred kilometres north of Delhi," announced the driver. Annie drew a sharp intake of breath.

"Don't worry, Annie," said Bruce, too patronizingly for

Bella's liking. "The electricity doesn't pass through 'til sunset." Then, turning to Bella, he said mockingly: "If it was – she'd be fried to a crisp!"

"Bruce!" Annie blurted, chastising her boyfriend with a glare. He turned away, but Bella caught his smirk in the wing mirror. "Only joking, Annie. Bell likes a good joke."

They all fell silent as the skies broke and the monsoon rain pummelled the taxi roof. Cold rain was pouring through Bella's window as she tried with all her might to push it up. Another streak of lightning, and the lights went out.

"I told you," said Annie. "Let's hope the Ambassador Hotel has a decent generator."

The lashing rain was so dense that the windscreen wipers were making no difference whatsoever. Bella had experienced tropical rain in the Guatemalan rainforest, but this was unbelievable! All Bella could make out through the front window was the blurred image of oncoming headlights and the occasional flickering of lamplight from the inside of buildings.

"This is Connaught Circus," Bruce announced, as they waited to drive onto a massive roundabout. Bella knew that the word "circus" didn't only mean the theatrics of the Big Top. She watched the unfamiliar image of the traffic policeman in a white uniform standing on a raised and sheltered podium in the middle of the road. Eventually he blew his whistle and beckoned them forward with his torch. "We're nearly there," said Bruce.

A minute later the taxi turned onto the impressive driveway leading up to the Ambassador Hotel.

"Thank goodness," said Annie as she peered through the

windscreen towards the brightly lit foyer. "Electricity."

"It looks like you have celebrities staying," said the driver, nodding to the long black limousine in the car park.

CHAPTER SIX

DIVA DEVAKI

A few moments prior to Bella's arrival, the head barman at the Ambassador Hotel had been distracted from his duties by a glamorous dark-haired woman in a glistening suit. He'd watched as she'd slipped surreptitiously into the bar and taken a seat by the window. Chivvying one of his subordinates to rush to her service, he'd hidden himself away behind one of the large yucca plants next to the grand piano. From there, he'd gawped, mesmerized by the shimmering sequins and tiny mirrors of her extravagantly embroidered black suit as she rolled a silver coin between her fingers, passing it smoothly from hand to hand.

Throughout Delhi – in fact, throughout India – Diva Devaki was the most famous acrobat and illusionist of modern times. Her daredevil feats were legendary. Executed without a safety net, whether she was performing in the marquee of her touring Mumbai Circus, Bollywood films or in TV stunts miles above the jagged boulders of a rocky ravine, her routines were always spellbinding. Her beautiful face with its soft, smooth and bronze complexion, dark sparkling eyes and pouting lips, made her popular amongst advertisers who paid her millions of rupees every year to market their cosmetics. A web of intrigue surrounded her personal and business life, with speculation and gossip filling the society pages of India's glossiest magazines. To be the barman in service to Diva Devaki, otherwise known quite simply as "The Diva", was a rare honour.

The head barman stood transfixed, admiring the Diva's jewel-studded watch and studying the way she slowly fondled the bright golden bangles around her wrist while eying up the new arrivals. He watched her reach for her handbag, pull out a small bottle of perfume and dab the heady fragrance behind her ears. He closed his eyes for an instant to breathe in the sweet aroma. When he opened his eyes, she was gone.

Downstairs, dressed in a long white raincoat, black boots and smart flat cap, the concierge came out to greet the taxi. He was carrying a large colourful umbrella, which he immediately used to give cover to his guests, while two porters wearing smart pinstriped trousers, white shirts and jackets came running down the steps to collect their luggage from the boot. Bruce thrust a wedge of crunched-up rupees into the taxi driver's hand.

"*Dhanyavaad*," he shouted through the storm, giving him a patronizing slap on the back.

"No, thank *you*," corrected the driver, as he stood exposed to the pulverizing rain.

Bella had a closer look at the limousine in the car park. While every other vehicle had mud on its wheels and hubcaps, this one was so highly polished it literally shone – even in the rain. Everything about it implied elegance and class. Sitting in the driver's seat, Bella saw the outline of a head upon which was perched a silver top hat studded with tiny mirrors. Normally, this showy type of hat would have been too impractical to wear while driving because of its height – only this one, as if proving just this point, was squashed down and concertinaed. "Nice car," Bella acknowledged. "Weird hat." Thinking no more about it, she jumped through the puddles towards the hotel's imposing entrance ahead of the porters.

Stepping into the air-conditioned splendour of the lobby with its crystal chandeliers and thick velvety carpet, Bella felt more than a little out of place in her trainers and jeans. The clingy sweat of her T-shirt felt cold against her skin as she slowly became aware of the scrutinizing gaze of the immaculately dressed hoteliers, discreetly stationed around the room waiting to serve her. "How can we afford to stay here?" she asked as she gazed around the five-star extravagance of the lobby. The hotel was so big it housed a number of retail outlets, including a gift shop, bookshop and jewellers.

"Bruce's charity gets a discounted rate here," Annie replied, a little self-conscious.

In truth, both Bella and her mum felt a little awkward about staying in such a luxurious hotel when they would be spending most of their time with children who, in all probability, would be sleeping rough in the streets. Annie had persuaded herself that she needed to break Bella in gently to the reality of how life could be in the developing world. She had no idea that Bella had already spent a night sleeping in a rubbish dump in Guatemala with a gang of street-children and was fully aware of the reality and dangers of street life.

The hotel lobby was so big there was even a small fountain in the middle, surrounded by leather armchairs, where a smartly dressed, middle-aged businessman was reading the *Indian Times* newspaper. To her right, Bella admired the large spiral staircase, lined with impressive photographs of Indian wildlife, the Taj Mahal and the Ganges, as well as a selection of shots taken amongst the narrow lanes of Old Delhi. "This place is amazing!" Bella whispered to herself.

The porters carried their bags over to the well-polished reception desk and rang the quaint silver bell to summon the desk clerk, who humbly asked them to complete the registration forms and hand over their passports.

"I trust they'll be kept in the hotel safe?" said Bruce, brusque to the point of rudeness.

"Yes, sir. Of course, sir. Thank you, sir," answered the painfully obsequious desk clerk. Bruce turned around to peruse the lobby, while Annie peered into the quaintly old-fashioned ledger in which the desk clerk was writing. She quickly identified the error.

"I think there's been a slight misunderstanding," she told the man as courteously as her fatigue would allow. "I specifically requested not to have the family room." She got out her confirmation letter to prove her point. Apparently, a single room attached to a double was an unusual request. To hear her mum reinforce her desire for such an arrangement so that she could share a room with her boyfriend made Bella feel pushed out and alone.

"A thousand pardons, madam," replied the desk clerk,

bowing graciously. "May I suggest you all take a seat in the lobby while we quickly attend to this little problem?" He rang the bell for assistance before leading them to the soft chairs around the fountain.

"Are you alright, Bruce?" Annie asked, laying her hand gently over his.

Bruce seemed edgy, looking around the lobby as if trying to find someone.

"I'm fine," he said uneasily. "Just tired." Unseen by Bella and her mum, Bruce acknowledged the glare of the woman lurking behind the large potted plants under the staircase. Bruce clicked his fingers to summon back the desk clerk.

"I want to see the manager," he demanded.

"Bruce, what is it?" asked Annie.

"We've been travelling for sixteen hours, Annie. They shouldn't leave us hanging around."

The manager arrived dressed in so much black that Bella thought he must be in mourning. In such attire, his beaming smile looked strangely incongruous.

"I booked these rooms two weeks ago," Bruce complained. The manager's expression changed instantly to one of sombre respect. "Show us all the rooms that have an adjoining bedroom right away," Bruce ordered.

"Very good, sir," replied the manager humbly. "If you would be so good as to follow me . . . " Bruce turned to Annie, who looked shocked and embarrassed by his aggressive tone.

"You and Bell go," he suggested. "Choose the biggest and best while I make a quick phone call."

"I'm staying here 'til everything's sorted," snapped Bella, throwing herself down into one of the sofas. "I'm too tired to go traipsing around."

"Just don't go wandering off," Annie huffed as she turned to follow the manager. They were all getting grouchy now.

"I'll keep an eye on her," Bruce mumbled. Bella could tell he was reluctant. As soon as Annie was out of sight, he casually got out his mobile phone and drifted off towards the large potted plants under the staircase. Bella looked around the lobby. The smart businessman reading the paper had left, the manager and desk clerk were suddenly nowhere to be seen, and the porters and waiters, who had once occupied the area in reasonably large numbers, had all mysteriously retreated to other parts of the hotel. The only three people in the lobby she could see were the concierge standing by the door, Bruce and herself. "Where is everyone?" she wondered. She didn't see the tall, shadowy figure engaged in a discreet conversation with Bruce Anders under the stairs as he handed over Annie's cheque and the wad of cash. He hadn't needed his mobile at all.

Attracted to the view of the well-lit hotel gardens, Bella walked up to the glass-fronted exterior by the revolving doors and peered out. Quite by chance, her eyes fell upon the strange-looking figure sitting behind the steering wheel of the limousine. Suddenly, her pendant turned ice-cold.

"Are you trying to warn me of something?" she whispered apprehensively. It was the strangely agreeable aroma of sweet perfume that alerted Bella to the fact that she was not alone. Focusing on the images reflected in the window, Bella saw the outline of a tall, glamorous woman. Her spectacular outfit was so completely dazzling to Bella, she felt almost weak at the knees – as if she were standing before a celebrity.

"I recognize that woman," she thought. "But why?"

"You're not English, I can tell that by your complexion," observed the woman in a sickly sweet voice. Bella turned around.

"My parents are Guatemalan," Bella asserted proudly, quite used to the rude questioning of complete strangers about her foreign looks. No sooner had she looked into the woman's face than she realized who she was.

"You're that model from the advert!" Bella blurted. "Diva Devaki, the TV acrobat!" Devaki's eyes widened, and Bella felt the sharp shock of her displeasure. "Look away from her eyes," warned a voice in Bella's head.

She turned away.

"That's an interesting pendant you're wearing," hissed the Diva, as her hand reached speculatively out to touch the chain. Bella ducked, shooting a suspicious look towards Bruce, lurking at the foot of the stairs to greet her mum's timely return.

"Mum!" Bella shouted, pushing past the Diva and running across the lobby to give her mum a really big hug.

"What's the matter with you?" asked Annie calmly as she looked up to see the blur caused by the revolving doors. But Bella didn't reply. She had no doubt in her mind whatsoever that Bruce and Devaki were involved in some terrible business. The problem now was: how to prove it to her love-struck mum?

Outside, the screech of rubber sent Bella running back to the revolving doors to see the limousine departing at great speed through the main gates. She walked back to the chairs by the little fountain and threw herself down.

"What am I going to say to mum?" she thought, her heart

pounding from the exertion and alarm of the last few seconds.

The hotel manager, a little distracted by the scene and the fact that his entire staff had momentarily disappeared, went to find and reprimand his elusive porters.

"I've seen two good-sized rooms on the first floor that will be fine," Annie told Bella and Bruce. "Let's go and get ready for bed."

Two embarrassed-looking porters soon returned to lead them up to their rooms. For some reason, having caught the Diva's eye a little too intensely, they had both felt a strange compulsion to wander away.

Annie and Bruce took room 101, while Bella took 102. Bella went straight to her room. Closing and locking the door, she went to draw the curtains but was distracted by the view across the street where the Diva's dark, penetrating eyes glared out at her from the billboard in Connaught Circus. It gave Bella the shivers. With all the things that had happened over the last twenty-four hours, Bella was feeling rather restless. Taking hold of her pendant, she closed her eyes and yet again tried to conjure up the image of her estranged friend. "Quetzal, come now. I need your help . . . " she began to chant. But he didn't appear.

Ten minutes later, after a quick shower, Bella briefly rejoined Bruce and her mum in their room for a late supper. Feeling utterly exhausted and far too wary of Bruce to relax, she couldn't face the sandwiches her mum had ordered from room service.

After a few nibbles she said, "I'm going to bed," and left. Her mum followed, bringing her sandwich and a glass of milk.

"Can't you stay in here with me tonight, Mum?" asked

Bella. "I don't want to be on my own tonight." Annie gave her a cuddle.

"You'll be alright," she tried to reassure Bella. "Tomorrow morning, after we've had a lie-in and a late breakfast, we'll take a rickshaw out to the children's centre." She began unpacking Bella's suitcase. Bella wanted to tell her mum everything but she knew there was no point. "I've been so negative about Bruce for so long, she'll never believe me," Bella decided, her mind in utter turmoil about what she should do.

"Tomorrow, I thought I would help out at the clinic," Annie continued as she filled Bella's wardrobe and drawers.

"What am I going to do?" asked Bella as she slipped into her green pyjamas and climbed into bed.

"I thought you might tag along with Bruce," her mum replied cautiously. "Get to know him a bit better." Bella couldn't think of anything worse. Her mum paused for a moment, obviously unsure of how to proceed.

"That incident with the beggar earlier . . . " she began, a little uncomfortably. "I think Bruce was feeling stressed and a bit . . . "

"Tired," Bella interrupted in a tone that was hard for her mum to read. "I know. We're all tired."

"He really is a good man," Annie concluded firmly. Bella was so disgusted she thought she was going to be sick. "He's going to do some work with the street-children on their art and craft skills tomorrow," her mum went on. "Maybe you could help him come up with some ideas on how the children can sell their goods to tourists without coming across as too pushy. At least if you get to know some of the children it will help you gain their trust for your project. Just think what fantastic shots you could get for your exhibition if you had them on board." But Bella's mind wasn't on fundraising. She was trying to adjust to immediate hostilities and the strange events of the last few days. Forces were clearly conspiring against her. She would have to be on her guard.

After giving her daughter a goodnight kiss on the forehead, Annie retreated to the adjoining door and turned out the light. "Sleep tight," she whispered. Bella didn't reply. Instead, she buried her head into her pillow, took hold of her pendant and wished with all her heart Bruce Anders might mysteriously disappear, never to be seen again.

It wasn't the noise of distant traffic or the unfamiliarity of her clinically clean and exuberantly furnished room that kept Bella awake. Instead of shutting her eyes and going to sleep, she used her secret powers to focus on the conversation next door. Bruce must have ordered some wine, because Bella heard the voice of a young man asking if "Sir" would like him to open the bottle and then "Is it to Sir's taste?". After a moment's pause while Bruce must have been considering his response, she heard her mum say, "Excellent wine. And, at last, some quality time alone." Bella grimaced.

"Annie," said Bruce. "I love you." Bella felt the tears welling in her eyes. With all her heart she wanted to shout: "No, no, no! Mum, he's horrible . . . I hate him!"

"I love you too, Bruce," replied her mum, her voice quivering with emotion. "And I think this trip will be a great opportunity for you and Bella to get to know each other properly," Bella could hear her mum saying as she began to punch her pillow with both fists. "When she sees the work you do for orphans and street-children, she's bound to love you too." Bella couldn't listen anymore. She pulled the pillows over her ears and gave way to a few restless hours of tossing and turning.

CHAPTER SEVEN

AT LAST!

A long, ear-piercing squawk jerked Bella to her senses. The digital display on the hotel alarm clock read 2:43. It took her a moment to realize that the incessant tapping that followed was coming from the window. Switching on her sidelight, she dragged herself out of bed and stumbled over to the curtains. She pulled them back. "At last!" she cried, punching the air for joy at what she saw perched on the windowsill. The Quetzal, utterly drenched and bedraggled, gave her a glare of extreme boredom. She quickly pulled up the window and let him in.

"I take it you like monsoons!" he squawked, hopping onto the table and making an instant puddle. His emerald-green feathers were so flattened on his head and chest, Bella could hardly see the finer yellow ones.

"Is it raining?" Bella asked. The Quetzal gave her the kind of look best not followed by words. Instead he opened his wings and gave a big flap, sending a splattering of water everywhere. Bella jumped back. "Well, it's not my fault," she said, feeling the vibe as well as the water.

"You decided to visit Delhi in the rainy season. Of course

it's your fault!" squawked the irate bird.

"Well, it's nice to see you too," Bella retorted. "You didn't have to come."

The Quetzal slapped his left wing to his forehead in a gesture of mock distress.

"Oh, Quetzal, Quetzal, come quickly, I need your help . . . " he scoffed, dripping still more water all over the tabletop. Bella went to the bathroom to get a hand towel and dried the bird off. "I suppose I did go a bit over the top with my constant begging," she thought. "And I do need his help." She knew it would be foolish to let her pride get in the way. But his sarcasm was hard to take when she was feeling so low.

"Quetzal," said Bella quietly as she dried his fiery red body right down to the shimmering blues and greens of his impressively long tail. "So much has happened since I last saw you."

"I hear your mum's got a new boyfriend," the Quetzal interjected.

"How did you know that?" Bella demanded.

"I have my sources," winked her friend knowingly. "What do you think of him?"

"He's a horrible slimy eel," Bella sneered. "Did you know he was friends with Ted Briggs?" The Quetzal nodded ruefully.

"Friends might be stating it a bit strongly but . . . "

"And that's not all," Bella added forcefully. "He's conning my mum out of money and is up to something really terrible with someone called Diva Devaki." The Quetzal's eyes visibly widened.

"Diva Devaki!" he exclaimed with some element of surprise. Bella observed the Quetzal's quizzical expression, as he pondered the full impact of Bella's claim.

"Who is she?" Bella probed. "From what I've seen, she's scary!"

"Bella, are you alright?" Annie called from next door. Bella could hear the gentle swoosh of her mum's feet on the carpet. She picked up the Quetzal and put him in the bin just as her mum opened the door.

"Can't you sleep, my love?" Annie asked sleepily, peering round the door. Bella pretended to yawn.

"I think it was the rain lashing against the window," said Bella hopefully, rubbing her eyes. "I'm alright now." She slipped back into bed.

"Sweet dreams, my love," whispered her mum as she closed the door. The Quetzal, itching with rage, bit his lip and counted to ten.

"Well, I love that!" he snorted finally, his words reverberating around the bin in a fading drone. Bella rolled out of bed and went over. Picking the Quetzal up, she put him carefully down on the carpet and kneeled down beside him.

"Keep your voice down," she whispered. "Do you want to wake up the whole hotel?" The Quetzal gave her a glare.

"Some welcome this is," he chuntered.

"So . . . ?" said Bella, hoping the Quetzal might finally answer her question about the Diva. "Who is she?" The Quetzal looked glum.

"She's the performing impresario who owns and runs the touring Mumbai Circus," he told her. "She's had several run-ins with the police over the years regarding the illegal trading of merchandise made by children, but nothing's ever been proved."

"I'm scared," Bella admitted. "I think she's working with

Bruce, and he can sense that I'm on to them." The Quetzal paused to consider this further.

"Talking about senses," he said, gesturing to Bella's pendant. "What about your own?"

"What do you mean?" replied Bella, reaching for her pendant and giving it a reassuring rub. "Until yesterday, everything was fine. I've been using it whenever I can to practice my flying . . . "

"I don't mean that," interrupted the Quetzal, starting to strut up and down. "I mean – has it been dropping hints? You know . . . trying to warn you about things?"

"Sometimes," she had to admit. "But last night at the airport it jumped off my neck and started to fly away all by itself." This news seemed to hit the Quetzal hard because he suddenly looked very depressed.

"As if someone with immense powers was trying to steal it from you?" he suggested.

"And who might that be, then?" Bella asked wryly. "I don't believe in wizards and witches."

"And quite right too!" the Quetzal affirmed with a little more zest. "But it sounds to me as if someone with a sincere desire to either separate you from that pendant or draw you to them for whatever reason came very close to succeeding." The Quetzal scratched his head with the tip of a wing.

"But who?" asked Bella anxiously. "Could it be anything to do with Bruce and this Diva woman? They both seem interested in the pendant."

"You're supposed to be the intuitive one," the Quetzal niggled. "Weren't you listening to your inner voices?" Bella was getting sick to death of her inner voices. She was in two minds whether to take the portrait of Itzamna down from the attic beam and bury it in her mum's Guatemalan chest as soon as she got home. "Did you see anyone at the airport who looked suspicious?" asked the Quetzal, scrutinizing Bella's face with the ostentatious air of a master inquisitor.

Bella hadn't had a wink of sleep the night they'd gone to the airport. She'd been so tired she could hardly remember anything, apart from how strained relations had been between her and Bruce even before she'd overheard his conversation with the Diva.

"You'd best be on your guard," the Quetzal warned her, lowering his beak and looking rather stern. Bella sat down on the edge of her bed. Pleased as she was to see her good friend, she felt so worn out and would have preferred it if he had just let her sleep. "Oh – and another thing," the Quetzal added. "I should have told you this a long time ago." Bella gave the Quetzal a sleepy, yet sceptical look. "Whatever you do, don't lose your self-control or the pendant when you're in animal form." Bella's eyelids were beginning to droop. "Otherwise you'll get stuck as a bird until you sort it out. And believe me – it could be embarrassing as well as highly inconvenient." He gave his feathers another good shake.

"Why didn't you tell me all this stuff before?" Bella huffed, finding all this new information a little too much to take in. The Quetzal plainly had things on his mind too, because suddenly he was in a rush.

"No time for that now," he announced briskly, as he flew to the windowsill. "I think we need to go and pay this Diva Devaki a visit. Come on."

Bella glanced at the clock and groaned. It was 2:59 a.m.

CHAPTER EIGHT

THE CIRCUS

Bella found her red dressing gown thrown across a chair and sleepily put it on.

"Don't forget your slippers," the Quetzal advised. "They'll keep your toes warm. I find the evenings quite chilly after the rains." Bella opened her window and looked out over the Delhi skyline. Now that the electricity was back on, the twinkling city lights set against the architectural chaos of modern high-rises mixed in with dilapidated old buildings, temples, domes and minarets almost reminded her of London. "I wish Charlie were here," she thought as she hopped onto the windowsill.

She reached for her pendant and was immediately invigorated by the tingles of its mystical force. In the same moment, the ear-splitting buzz of a million flies and mosquitoes became all too audible.

"If any one of you even thinks about biting me, there's going to be trouble," Bella warned the swarm hovering above her head.

"So much for a quick getaway," tutted the Quetzal. Bella

shot the Quetzal a cautionary look.

"How come I'm always in my pyjamas and dressing gown when you want me to fly?" she whined. The Quetzal kept his beak firmly shut. Getting irritated wasn't going to help anybody. He watched as Bella opened her arms and focused all her energies on the task at hand. She jumped, flapping wildly as soon as she was clear of the window.

"Which way?" she called out to the Quetzal, as he flew up to join her.

"Follow me," he chirped. And, with the clammy south-westerly wind blowing in their faces, they set off.

If anything, New Delhi in the middle of the night was even more manic than in the early evening. Bella couldn't believe it. The streets were heaving with pedestrians and animals going about their business with little regard for each other, let alone the mass of swerving bicycles, rickshaws and cars. Not that the skies were much better. Flight paths were dangerously busy.

"Watch where you're going!" screeched an angry sparrow when Bella clipped his wing.

"Duck!" squawked a crazy bird with a huge bill, missing Bella's head by a whisker. The heavy whoosh of its wings pulled her into its jet stream, causing her to spiral downwards quite some way before she was able to regain her balance.

"Hornbills," grunted the Quetzal. "Blind as bats." Bella had little choice but to shake off her tiredness and sharpen up. It was either that or crash.

By the time they landed by the circus in a large peepul tree full of lapwings and babblers, Bella's head was spinning.

"What's that awful noise?" Bella whinged, covering her ears. The Quetzal gestured towards a rather large bird with a huge coloured bill and striking plumage not unlike their own. The peals of its maniacal laughter were annoying everyone.

"That's the Great Indian Hornbill who nearly ran you down," griped the Quetzal. "They hoot like simpletons, crash into everything in sight and can't be trusted to do anything but give you a throbbing headache. Think yourself lucky he's not your nahual." The hornbill was making such a racket it meant that all the other birds had to chirp up just to be heard by the bird right next to them. Bella wasn't surprised to find that she was the major topic of conversation.

"I've heard of such things, but I've never before seen one," twittered a little sparrow perched on the branch below. "A human child who can rise above the confines of her body and mind to become one with all nature – who'd have thought it?"

"Remember," warned the Quetzal. "It's not only the friendly animals who will sense your presence."

"What do you mean?" she asked.

"I mean," said the Quetzal, "that not every animal on the planet is going to be on your side." Bella nodded. It was good to be reminded. She'd experienced how hostile some creatures could be towards her – even in London. "And what's more," the Quetzal went on, "you're not the only human in the world who has the power to call upon their services." This, though, was a new concept. "Follow me," ordered the Quetzal. "Let's have a look around."

With the Big Top still under construction and besieged with the circus crew, the whole site was a buzz of activity. Again, Bella was struck by the sheer number of children around.

"If my mum knew I was out at this time she'd go ballistic," Bella fretted as they circled the site. "She never lets me play outside after six."

"But then, your mum's looking out for you," the Quetzal reprimanded her. "No one's looking out for these children." Bella felt awful. She didn't mean to sound like she was complaining about her mum.

There were tents and lorries spread out over quite a large area. Against the strains of the circus band practice, Bella looked down to see hundreds of circus artists going about their business. Some acts were rehearsing, while others busied themselves with the tasks of setting up their own personal tents and attending to their props. She watched the clowns putting on their garish makeup, the jugglers brandishing their knives and fiery torches, and the acrobats building their human pyramid. She watched with awe the rich array of animals and their tamers, some of whom were going through their acts. Those animals not practising were being brushed down, fed and watered, as if in preparation for an imminent inspection.

A flourish of elephant trumpets drew Bella's attention to the small herd gathered at the back of the camp. Extravagantly gowned in multicoloured saddles and robes, the magnificent beasts stood patiently, as their foreheads and trunks were painted with vibrant icons and patterns. "Wow!" Bella sighed in admiration. "They look beautiful." But she could not help but feel sad that they were, in effect, prisoners of the circus.

Bella and the Quetzal swooped down and flew from tree to tree, taking everything in.

"What are they?" Bella gasped as she gazed down with incredulity at two large, furry creatures incongruously gowned in large orange cloaks.

"Dancing bears," replied the Quetzal, shaking his head in disgust. "It's just so undignified."

A man wearing a gaudy silver suit was baiting the bears with a small piece of meat. The bears danced around on their hind legs making futile swipes for the meat with their blunt claws. Bella was again quickly reminded why she hated the whole idea of zoos and circuses. "The poor things," she thought.

The whole site was lit by huge lights, mounted on scaffolding and powered by noisy generators.

"I was chatting with one of the leopards earlier," the Quetzal told her, pointing across the camp to the large cages parked up on the periphery. "Apparently, they were getting such poor attendances last week in Mumbai, the Diva has demanded that every act has to be more dramatic and original than anything that's gone before. Consequently, everyone's stressed. She's going to have a late dress rehearsal tonight before tomorrow night's opening."

"Mumbai?" Bella queried. "That's where Bruce went last month."

"Probably doing a little business with the Diva, no doubt," concluded the Quetzal. He turned to one of the older-looking babblers nearby.

"We're looking for the Diva," he twittered under his breath. "If you tell the crows, or anyone else, come to that, I'll peck your eyes out!"

"She never goes to the Big Top until everything's ready for her," twittered the trembling bird. "She's in the large square tent at the back of the camp where all the lorries and vans are.

You can't mistake it. There's a shiny black limousine parked right outside and security guards everywhere."

"Did you have to be so mean to that poor babbler?" Bella scolded, as they flew down over a row of cages. "He's hardly bigger than a thrush."

"I'm sending out a clear signal that we're not to be messed with," the Quetzal retorted crossly. "Leave the diplomacy to you, and we'd be locked away in a cage twittering for birdseed before you knew it."

It was quite easy to find the well-guarded tent described by the chirpy little babbler, especially with the limousine outside. They came down to perch by a small tear in the roof.

"It's my guess the place is crawling with snakes loyal to the Diva," warned the Quetzal, lowering his voice. "And whatever you do – don't talk to any crows." He gestured to a nearby tree full of them. Bella didn't have a problem with that – crows were the bane of her life, even in England.

"So the Diva has power over animals?" she queried. Bella had been thinking about the Quetzal's rather ambiguous comment earlier about not thinking of herself as the only human in the world who could call upon their support.

"Yes," replied the Quetzal. "She's studied hard. She knows the ones she can get to through mind games and fear. Generally, she tends to keep to reptiles and black-winged birds. They're always on the dark side of what's going on. My advice is to use quetzal talk and stay in your animal form. If you do try and mingle in as a human, be on your guard, and whatever you, don't look into the Diva's eyes." Bella was shocked by the seriousness of the Quetzal's tone.

"Why not?" she asked. But the Quetzal had already

squeezed through the canvas.

Bella followed the Quetzal into the tent where they sat high on the scaffolding looking down upon the crowded scene below. In the background, Bella could hear the muted, woeful whimpers of a variety of animals but couldn't see any of them. What she could see was about forty children, many of them even younger than herself, who were either bent over machines sewing shirts or sitting cross-legged, stitching together the outer casing of leather footballs. Dressed in ragged old clothes, most of them looked so skinny and exhausted, it shocked her.

"Look at their legs," urged the Quetzal, directing Bella's attention to the manacles and chains around their ankles. Bella felt so distressed, she thought she was going to be sick. "I've seen shackles like that before," sighed the Quetzal. "The chains are so short they have to shuffle. I bet some of these children haven't been able to walk properly for years." This was a new dimension of evil to Bella. Ted Briggs had pushed her down into the dark abyss of an ancient temple and left her for dead, but this woman! Bella dreaded to think what heinous crimes she was capable of.

In the middle of the assembled children was a flamboyantly dressed Indian man in a bright yellow shirt, red sequined jacket, white sparkling trousers and, most eye-catching of all, pointy orange winkle-picker boots! He was sitting on a pile of red-and-white football shirts. Next to him lay a dazzling, gold-plated walking stick and a very theatrical concertinaed top hat.

"The chauffer!" thought Bella. "He was wearing a hat like that." The man's hair was long and had remnants of gel and white powder in it. Bella examined his face closely. He looked quite old because of his hunched-up posture and yet wore the pathetic, sad-looking expression of a child who had just been seriously reprimanded by his teacher. Bella watched as the man peered into a silver box from which he picked out small pinches of dried brown leaves with his hairy-backed hand.

"Tobacco," whispered the Quetzal. "Disgusting habit." The man put the tobacco into his mouth and began to chew. Bella grimaced even before he closed his box, gathered all the phlegm he could muster and spat on the floor. Then, putting on his hat, he reached to his belt and pulled out a large black whip. Without giving it a second thought, Bella glided down to hide herself amongst the piles of shiny off-cut material strewn over the floor.

"What do you think you're doing?" hissed the Quetzal, landing gently beside her.

"I wanted a closer look," Bella whispered. Bella was disturbed by the man's glum face. "He's wearing makeup," she observed, mentally peeling away the foundation that failed to mask the deep, craggy lines of his scaly face. "He's like a lizard."

"And look into his eyes," hushed the Quetzal spookily. "It's like someone has drained all the sparkle out of them." The man's eyeliner had run to form black tears, caked onto his face as if to accentuate his sorrow. His cheeks looked like they'd recently been painted white, while his nose definitely had the hint of red makeup half-heartedly removed. Just looking at him made Bella feel sad.

"If he's the man I think he is, his name's Pramrod," the Quetzal whispered.

"He's a clown." Bella winced. She liked to think of clowns

as funny, happy-go-lucky people. This one looked miserable.

"By night, he performs in the ring," the Quetzal went on. "But in reality, he's nothing more than the Diva's henchman, keeping all these poor children in line."

"In line for what?" thought Bella. Despite the fearful chill that the Quetzal's grim description of Pramrod's role gave her, the pendant didn't go cold.

"I don't understand," she said as she fondled it, "but I think he's good."

"If he were good, he'd go home to his wife and kids in Rajasthan," replied the Quetzal sternly. "Keep away from him! According to my friend the Tiger, he's hardly recognizable as the man he used to be. Apparently, he used to be really kind to all the animals. These days, every animal in the circus is terrified of him."

"What happened?" asked Bella, enthralled by the Quetzal's story.

"From what people have told me," the Quetzal went on grimly, "he and his two elder brothers used to be the top acrobatic act in the circus. 'The Sultans of Swing', they used to call them. Everyone thought Pramrod was the most talented high-flying acrobat India had ever seen. When his brothers retired, Pramrod started to work with a young, ambitious partner. Rumour had it, he'd been so enchanted by her beauty, he'd fallen in love. His career was all set to really take off when he had a terrible fall."

"Wasn't there a net to save him?" Bella gasped in astonishment, trying to imagine the drama of the scene. She turned to look at the Quetzal, who simply shook his head. Bella squirmed at the thought. "But why does he stay here?"

she asked.

"Who knows what hold that woman has over him?" the Quetzal speculated. Just then, Pramrod picked up his walking stick and whip and hopped down. Bella noticed that he had a distinctive waddle when he walked – even with the stick.

"So what's going on?" demanded Bella, feeling more confused than ever.

"Hush!" hissed the Quetzal, waving one of his wings and lowering his head in an attempt to make Bella do the same. "I hear the Diva spends most of her time at the circus in there." He gestured to a black curtain at the end of the room. "They call it her 'den'," he went on. "What kind of spell she weaves over anyone who goes in there is impossible to say, but somehow she always seems to get what she wants." Bella looked with trepidation towards the curtain. She realized now that the sorrowful animal murmurings she'd first heard upon entering the tent came from there.

"Is she some kind of witch?" Bella ventured cautiously. The Quetzal gave her a questioning look.

"What is it with you humans?" he scolded. "Why are you so obsessed with witches and wizards?" Bella felt a little stupid and had half a mind to snap back, but she managed to restrain herself.

"From what I can tell," the Quetzal began, "there are no potions or magic wands. The Diva has made it her life's work to study and meditate around certain mystical and supernatural theories. She has mastered some quite extraordinary disciplines, and this makes her highly dangerous."

"Do you think she had anything to do with my pendant flying away at the airport?" asked Bella nervously.

"Who knows?" replied the Quetzal. "But one thing's for sure: if she ever gets her hands on it . . . " The Quetzal was shaking his head, as if this very thought was too much to contemplate.

"But what are all these children doing here?" asked Bella, peering around the room at the chained and forlorn-looking workers.

"From what I can tell, this is a mobile sweatshop," the Quetzal told her. "It's my guess that these children are working shifts twenty-four–seven, making football shirts and balls to sell abroad."

"I didn't think 'handmade' meant handmade by children!" Bella spat with disgust.

At that moment, one of the children, distracted by Bella's outburst, pricked her finger on a needle and let out a short, sharp cry: "Ow!" To Bella's horror, Pramrod raised his whip and sent it crashing down in the dust by the girl's leg. Bella couldn't help herself. In a mad flap she flew across the room aiming her beak at Pramrod's right hand. But Pramrod was swift. Bella's beak hadn't even touched a single hair on the back of his right hand before his left had her tightly in his clutches. "Aah!" she screamed, as the air rushed from her lungs. "Quetzal – the pendant!" she wheezed, seeing it fall at Pramrod's feet. Before she knew it, Pramrod had scooped it up.

"This must be my lucky day," he croaked. He stuffed the captured bird into the inner lining of his jacket. Giving the pendant an affectionate kiss, he put it on and tucked it away beneath his shirt collar. To Bella, trapped in her animal form, it sounded like the kiss of death.

CHAPTER NINE

THE DIVA'S DEN

As soon as the clown put the pendant on, his old aches and pains instantly disappeared. "I feel twenty years younger," he cheered. Bella felt the vibration of his low gravely voice and marvelled at how she could have been so stupid.

"You idiot," she rebuked herself, spitting fluff from her beak and trying in vain to open her wings. Her heart thundered against her ribcage, as she tried to orient herself to the claustrophobic and musty conditions inside Pramrod's jacket. The Quetzal had warned her not to lose her self-control or the pendant while in her animal form. She had lost both. "Quetzal – help!" she called. But her pathetic chirps were too muffled to be heard by anyone but the Diva's attendant. He simply buttoned up his jacket and continued on his patrol.

What surprised Bella more than anything was how small she felt. While flying as a Quetzal, she'd always felt as big as a fully-grown eleven-year-old girl. This had given her such a feeling of power that she'd thought herself invincible, not only when measured against birds of prey but also against other

103

humans from whom she could always fly. Sensing this inner confidence, most predatory birds gave Bella a wide berth. Against a human, however, she was quite vulnerable at close range. "If only I could turn myself back," she muttered through gritted teeth, finding the rocking motion of her captor's walk quite nauseating.

"Get to work!" shouted the rejuvenated clown. She felt the tightening of his jacket caused by the raising of his whip and then heard another terrific crack. Again Bella cried out, but to no avail. She was powerless.

After the third crack of the whip there was a shrill call. "Pramrod!" The room fell silent. Pramrod stopped, and using his cane to support his injured right leg, swivelled around on his left heel.

"Coming," he called as he began to hobble.

The swishing of a curtain was followed by a voice Bella recognized only too clearly.

"Light the incense," she heard the Diva order. "I need to meditate."

"Yes, mistress," Pramrod replied humbly before limping off on his errand.

It was a jerky ride for Bella, with very little air and no room in which to manoeuvre. She was soon feeling hot and faint. Finally, the Diva's attendant sat down with a thud. Without any warning, Bella's dark, festering world disappeared as Pramrod ripped open his jacket, grabbed her wings tightly down and yanked her out into the gloomily lit room.

"Look what I found," he announced, thrusting Bella out towards his mistress with both hands. Bella's high-pitched squeal attracted the attention of every living thing in the room.

Devaki, still wearing the black sequined outfit Bella had seen her in at the hotel, looked straight into her eyes. Remembering what the Quetzal had told her, Bella quickly turned her head away.

"A strange-looking bird," the Diva calmly considered, giving Bella a cursory examination. Bella shook her head from side to side and tried to wriggle herself free, but Pramrod's grip was too tight. "I suppose it might have some value," she conjectured, "if we get it stuffed." Then, as if she had no more time for the bird: "Stick it in a birdcage and give the taxidermist a call." Pramrod jumped to his feet and went to fetch a box to stand on. He positioned it carefully under an empty cage, stepped up and tossed Bella in.

Through the bars of her prison, Bella peered down to see if she could spot the pendant around Pramrod's neck, but she couldn't. "He's tucked it well away," she thought, relieved at least that he was in no rush to offer it up to his mistress.

While Pramrod finished lighting the candles, Bella turned her attention to the room and perceived that it was filled with cages in which various depressed-looking animals were being held. Normally, using the power of the pendant, Bella could have understood what the animals around her were saying. Today, without it, she realized that the strange murmurings she could hear all around her were completely nonsensical to her. There were monkeys, rats, even a pair of red wolves and four giant panda cubs, as well as a host of multicoloured birds. "She'll probably have us all stuffed," Bella shivered in grim trepidation.

As she examined the room she slowly began to discern the strategically placed mirrors that were giving her the illusion of animal pairings as well as multiple images of the Diva and her henchman. "Where is she?" thought Bella, as she tried to work out which of the many images cast around the room represented their true whereabouts. The reflected candlelight gave the den a strangely church-like ambience, while the decor, which was mainly bamboo with a scattering of large tropical plants, would have been perfect for the panda cub – for Bella was now sure there was only one. But light wasn't the only thing emanating from the candles. The sweet, soporific aroma of incense and the Diva's monotonous murmurings made Bella feel woozy. As her mind began to wander, she found herself staring at the slow, wavy movements in the sawdust below. "There're so many wicker baskets in here," she thought. "I wonder . . . " She felt her body stiffen as a large cobra reared its evil-looking head from the basket at the Diva's feet, its image cast twenty times around the room by the reflectors. It was like being in a hall of mirrors or an electrical shop selling televisions with every set tuned in to the same horror film. Bella watched with foreboding, as snakes all around the room spread their necks to form hoods and uncoiled their long, scaly bodies. The dazzling display of pale yellow cross-bands matched to perfection the pattern on Devaki's dress. Focusing for a moment on what she thought was the real image of the Diva, Bella withered with repulsion, as the Diva took a small mouse from an inside pocket and started to dangle it before the wide-eyed snake. Goading the snake to rise higher and higher until it was level with her gaze, she started to lower the helpless creature into the cobra's wide-open jaws. Bella felt tears forming in her eyes as she watched the mouse frantically kicking its hind legs and letting out an almighty squeal in the moments before its execution. As Devaki released the mouse, Bella turned away only to see twenty snakes thrusting out their vicious jaws to swallow mice in what appeared to be one mass attack. "He's still alive," she squirmed, as the struggling mouse slipped down the snake's throat.

The Diva returned to her cross-legged pose before her henchman and for a short while sat in meditative silence.

"Bruce has given me the money," she announced tranquilly at last. "We should be able to purchase the warehouse sooner than I thought."

"So she's trying to get a permanent sweatshop established here in Delhi," Bella deduced. "And with our money!"

"He says he's seen the boy," the Diva went on.

Bella's mind shot to the knife-juggler.

"He's back to his begging and thieving ways, I'll bet," Pramrod replied gruffly.

"We must see if we can lure him back into our nest," replied the dreamy Diva. "Keep a guard to track his sister at all times – no matter what else is going on."

"Will Mister Bruce have the new children here by the end of the week?" Pramrod asked.

"As many as we need and more besides," said the Diva. "And he's made contact with our British agent in London. Apparently, he's keen to buy the tiger hide."

Bella was so mesmerized by the Diva's soothing voice that she almost keeled over. To snap herself out of her trance she gave herself a good shake out. "I knew Bruce was rotten," she thought. "But this!" The whole scenario was almost too evil to take in. But, in her bird form, Bella was in no position to do anything about it. "Where's the Quetzal?" she wondered, scouring the room but finding no trace of her friend.

Mixed in with the jumble of cages and baskets, Bella realized that there were piles of old books and manuscripts scattered around the room. Many were lying open on the ground, as if a researcher had recently been rampaging through them with no regard to the mess they were making. It didn't take her long to establish how right the Quetzal had been. Apart from the books on cobras, the Diva evidently had a fascination for mysticism and the supernatural, because the collection was completely dominated by such works. Of real concern to Bella was the textbook by the Diva's side entitled *The Secrets of the Maya*. "She knows," thought Bella with dread as a sharp stabbing sensation began to rock her cage. Bella looked up. To her joy, up in the scaffolding, the Quetzal was furiously pecking away at the knot that kept Bella's cage suspended. Animals everywhere were becoming agitated. One jerk – the cage slipped three or four inches – another, then another – they were happening now in rapid succession. Bella looked down and saw the clown scowling up at her. The sound of rapidly unfurling rope banging against the scaffolding and canvas alerted Bella to brace herself as the cage came crashing down.

Everything that followed happened in a blink. Bella saw the Quetzal push away the broken lock and force the cage door open with his beak. She glimpsed the orange winkle-pickers hobbling up towards the cage and looked up to catch Pramrod's determined glare. "The pendant!" she thought. In his rush to bend down, the pendant had popped out from under his shirt and was now swinging from his neck. In the same moment as Pramrod's splayed fingers reached out to grab her, the Quetzal threw himself into his path. Bella jumped, her every thought focused on the pendant. She gripped it tightly in her beak, yanked it off Pramrod's neck and flew with all her might towards the chink of light behind the curtain.

"No!" Pramrod wailed, as his familiar pains came surging back. Bursting through the curtain into the sweatshop, Bella crashed into a pile of deflated balls, quickly regained her balance and ran. She looked down and realized at once that she was still in her slippers with her dressing gown flowing out behind her.

"What if Devaki saw me change?" she panicked, gripping the pendant firmly in her fist. She felt the suspicious gaze of the children and the thud of chasing footsteps behind her.

"This way!" someone called.

She looked across to see a pretty little girl in a bright yellow dress beckoning to her from the far side of the tent. The girl, who looked no older than ten, was sitting at a table, sewing a football. Her sparkling eyes and beaming smile gave Bella the glimmer of hope she needed as she ran with all her might towards her.

"Shilpa, watch out, they're coming," someone whispered.

"Quick," urged the girl.

She pushed Bella beneath the table just in time. From her hiding place, Bella shot a quick look back as the Diva threw back the curtain, her eyes burning with rage.

"Where is she?" she hollered, scouring the room. Bella waited with baited breath for someone to give her away, but no one did. She could see that Shilpa's ankles, like all the other children in the room, were chained to a metal post hammered into the ground. "Come on!" repeated the Diva. "Speak up, or do I have to have you all whipped?" Pramrod was now hobbling up and down the aisles, peering under the tables. Bella watched as Shilpa reached down with her hand to raise a loosely pinned-down stretch of canvas and reveal her escape route.

"Don't get caught," whispered Shilpa.

"I don't intend to," Bella replied softly. "But I'm coming back to help you."

Rolling out onto the wet grass caused a scattering of scraggy cats. Bella made little attempt to avoid kicking them as she bounded off.

"Get out of my way," she screamed. It was a mistake.

"She's outside!" Bella heard the Diva cry from inside the tent. "Alert the guards."

A nearby juggler practising his act was so distracted by Bella's sudden appearance he dropped a flaming torch on his foot. Bella had only a split second in which to decide her next move. She heard a tiger's roar. "Head for the shadows," it was calling.

Away from the floodlights surrounding the Big Top, the rest of the park was set in darkness, lit only by the slithery moon and the night sky. It was no surprise then, she didn't notice the young boy with the blue-and-orange baseball cap hiding in the bushes. Again Bella started to run.

"After her!" she heard Pramrod call as he cracked his whip. Behind her, a number of the Diva's security staff were already in pursuit with Pramrod limping his way after them as fast as he could. There was another roar. Bella worked out that it was coming from a large cage-like wagon she could see on the edge of the circus camp. The wagon was leaning at a slight tilt because there were no horses harnessed to it. Alongside it, lying in a heap on the ground, was the large black cloth that Bella guessed covered the cage in transit, while inside she could vaguely make out the silhouette of a large prowling cat.

"The bolts," the beast growled. "I can't open them with my paws. But be quick!"

Bella was working on instinct. She climbed up the three creaky steps to the cage door, wrenched open the bolts and let herself in. The Tiger pounced up to her side. "Shut the door and lie down," he ordered. Bella pushed the door to and threw herself into the sawdust. The Tiger smothered her, leaving only the tiniest of gaps through which she could catch her breath. Bella was sweating profusely, but still the Tiger felt warm, his heart beating almost as fast as hers. The chasing gang were already by the cage.

"Spread out," Bella heard Pramrod wheeze. "Search everywhere." For a moment it seemed as if they might pass. But then: "Wait!" Pramrod shouted. Bella's heart was in her mouth. "Someone's left the door of the tiger's cage open."

Everyone fell silent.

CHAPTER TEN

SNAKE ATTACK

The creak of three sagging steps was followed by the sound of rusted hinges slowly squeaking open. "They're coming in," Bella trembled. She snuggled even closer into the Tiger's body and through the sound of a hundred flies and mosquitoes, heard the first tentative shuffles of Pramrod's feet through the sawdust.

The Tiger was becoming agitated, his heartbeat more rapid and his panting much more pronounced. Bella popped the pendant into her mouth and peered out through a small gap between the Tiger's neck and shoulder to glimpse Pramrod's orange boots and the tip of his golden cane. She shuddered as the Tiger clenched his powerful claws. There was a sudden crack of a whip. The Tiger gave out such an almighty roar that Bella thought her eardrums would burst. She felt every muscle in the Tiger's powerful body flex, ready to pounce.

"Stay calm, my friend," she purred. "He's wary of you, I can sense it." Bella focused on the pendant and used her powers to amplify the mutterings of her hunters.

"Nah," she heard someone grunt. "There's no way she's in there." Another voice followed: "He might be old, but no one in their right mind would go in there without a whip or a gun." Bella heard Pramrod's limping retreat.

"Right, let's split up," he ordered, slamming and bolting the cage door. "Four of you fetch torches and search the park, the rest check every tent and cage in the circus. Track her down and bring her back to the Diva. Now go!" he yelled.

As the sound of their dispersing footsteps faded into the distance, the old Tiger wearily pulled himself up to allow Bella to roll free. Standing back to admire the Tiger fully for the first time, Bella realized just how magnificent a beast he was, despite the cruel blunting of his teeth and claws.

"Thank you," Bella purred softly, rubbing her hands over the strong vibrant fur of his orange-and-black coat. Then, seeing that the Tiger looked sad, she added: "I don't think you look old. I think you're beautiful and brave."

"Beautiful enough to make a really good rug?" said the Tiger dejectedly. "Because that's what I'm soon to become." Having overheard the conversation between Bruce and the Diva regarding the Tiger's fate, Bella didn't know what to say.

"Bella! Bella!"

Bella could hear the muffled, woeful cries of the Quetzal some distance away.

"My friend!" she gasped, before turning to the Tiger. "He sacrificed himself so that I could escape."

"You mean the Quetzal?" the Tiger enquired grimly.

"Yes," said Bella, amazed. "How did you know?"

"We had a chat earlier in the evening," replied the Tiger. "After your ridiculous attack on the Diva's attendant." Bella bowed her head in shame.

"It was all my fault," she admitted. "I lost my temper and

my head."

"The power of your will is a tremendous force," rumbled the Tiger. Bella had heard these words a hundred times before from her inner voice. "Maybe the spiritual world connects us all," she thought. "Animals and humans throughout the world." She felt an instant connection with the Tiger.

"Are you the Bengal tiger who the Quetzal went to help in Mumbai?" she asked excitedly. The Quetzal had mentioned such a venture way back in March.

"We're old friends," the Tiger reminisced, brushing away the flies with a gentle waft of his claw. "But there's no escape from a place like this."

Bella thought he looked forlorn, like a creature resigned to his fate. "He offered to help me escape, but I refused. How far do you think I'd get before someone put a bullet through my head? I'm safer here. At least while I can still perform."

"Well, the Quetzal came here to help you," Bella reprimanded him. "And now the Diva has him locked up ready to be stuffed. The least you can do is make a little effort to help him." The harsh hiss of a large snake arrested their attention. It was coming from the far side of the cage.

"Get down," ordered the Tiger, hurriedly lowering himself to the ground and crossing his paws. Burying herself into the Tiger's side, Bella peered out into the darkness. Rubbing the pendant and using all her energies to illuminate her view, she began to realize just how perilous their plight was.

"Cobras," she whispered.

"I see them," the Tiger hushed. There must have been a hundred of them, slowly coiling themselves around every bar in the cage.

Looking up to the roof of the cage, Bella could see their yellow underbellies as they weaved their way around the rooftop bars. Some of them were dangling down by their tails and beginning to spit.

"Look to the bushes on the right," panted the Tiger, his heart pounding. "Lurking in the shadows."

Bella looked. At first she saw nothing. Then, by the light of the moon she started to make out a tall, slender figure, its head gently swaying from side to side as if in some sort of trance.

"Devaki," Bella exclaimed, her whole body quivering with fear.

"It's the Diva, all right," growled the Tiger hurriedly. "You'd better fly. It's you they want. My time is coming, but it won't be tonight." He could see his hastily spoken words were doing nothing to quell Bella's concern.

"But who's with her?" asked Bella, peering into the dark. She could just about make out the distinctive outline of the Diva's clown waddling through the bushes. But there was more. He appeared to be dragging someone through the trees by the scruff of their neck. As she used the power of the pendant to magnify her view, she saw the slender figure of a barefooted girl in a yellow dress. "Shilpa!"

"You can't do anything to help your friends now," the Tiger warned her. "You must go. It's far too humid for executions. Unless the taxidermist is around, their bodies soon start to rot – it's disgusting – and the smell!"

"But what about you?" Bella pleaded.

"They plan to kill me tomorrow night," replied the Tiger in a tone of complete resignation. "Somewhere way out of town where they can take my hide and throw my remains to the crocodiles." Bella saw spits of venom firing through the air. The splat of their impact and the tiny crackles of their bubbling poison made her shiver. Time was running out. Snakes were slithering towards them from all angles. "The snakes guard the Diva's den day and night. The best chance of a rescue is under cover of night during the snake act in the second half of the show," the Tiger gabbled. "Now, go!"

Bella quickly wiggled out from her hiding place. "Until tomorrow," she whispered into the Tiger's ear. In pulling the pendant from Pramrod's neck Bella had broken the clasp. She kept it in her mouth and jumped just as the leading cobra thrust itself forward. The cobra, neck spread, tongue flashing wildly in the air, was so close to getting its jaws around Bella's tail, it felt the scratch of her sharp claws on the back of its neck as she flew away.

"Be on your guard," the Tiger roared against a barrage of flying venom as Bella shot a measured course through a small, unguarded gap in the rooftop bars.

Bella fluttered out of the cobras' range, her heart thudding with stress. She looked down to see the face of the Diva burning with rage, her hands stretched out into the night sky in a gesture of hell-defying madness as she wailed abuse at her incompetent army of scaly minions. Bella felt her insides recoil as she watched the Diva swoop up the nearest cobra, grasp it tightly around the neck for so long she thought it was dead, then release it with a kiss.

"She's insane," thought Bella with a chill. "And she senses my power."

It wasn't the first time her secrets had been revealed to an adversary. Ted Briggs had had his suspicions about the power of her pendant, she was sure of that, but this time she was truly exposed.

"She's going to come after me," thought Bella. "She'll definitely want the pendant now!"

With all her thoughts centred on the Quetzal and how he'd sacrificed himself to save her, Bella took her chances with the crows and swooped low over the Diva's tent. With the pendant tightly clasped in her beak, her muffled calls of reassurance were heard by no one but herself. The Diva's crows, not yet briefed to be on their lookout for quetzals, simply watched her fly by. This was a mistake they would later regret when they felt the full extent of the Diva's wrath. Snubbing the help of any bird who offered it, Bella soared as high as her energies would allow until she saw the large roundabout at Connaught Circus.

In the hour before sunrise, Bella found her way back to her bedroom window. No sooner had her slippers touched the carpet than she dropped the pendant into her dressing gown pocket and ran to her mum's room.

"Mum!" she cried, bursting through the door. But Bella simply wasn't thinking straight. What she was hoping to achieve by such a rash manoeuvre?

"What time is it?" Bruce croaked, clearing his throat. Bella didn't notice the small box, lost in the crumpled sheets around them, or the ring on her mum's finger.

"Bella?" Annie groaned, pulling herself up wearily. "Did you have a nightmare?"

"Actually, I did," Bella announced, arms on hips and aiming her remarks directly at Bruce. "I dreamed I was being held prisoner by a snake-like witch who was going to abduct me into the slave labour trade and no one was ever going to see me again." The words tripped out of her mouth too fast for Annie to catch.

"It sounds awful, Bella," her mum yawned, still dazed by Bella's dramatic entrance. "Come here, let me give you a hug." Bella simply threw her arms into the air in disgust, returned to her room and dived onto the bed. If she'd been at home now she would have gone straight to the attic to talk to the portrait. Here, there was no one to comfort her.

After a few moments, Bella heard a gentle knock on the door but didn't answer.

"I'm sorry," her mum apologized, coming over and giving her a warm hug. "Was it a bad nightmare?" She held Bella for a full minute, gently rocking her in her arms. "Now," she whispered, "I don't know what you're doing in your dressing gown and slippers, but let's get you back into bed." Annie lay down with Bella and gently stroked her hair. She wanted to tell Bella her exciting news but decided to wait until the morning. For Bella, worried and distraught about the fate of the Quetzal, sleep did not come easily.

CHAPTER ELEVEN

THE KNIFE-JUGGLER RETURNS

When Annie looked in on Bella at eight o'clock the next morning she decided to let her sleep in. Bella finally woke up around midday, feeling distressed.

"Quetzal!" It was her first thought. She scrambled out of bed to retrieve the pendant from her dressing-gown pocket and was distracted by an old babbler perched on the windowsill.

"Bella, are you there?" twittered the bird. Bella ran to the window to find the very babbler who'd told them how to find the Diva's tent.

"Yes, I'm here," Bella chirped. "What's the matter?"

"It's your friend," twittered the babbler. "I heard him cursing and ranting all through the night."

"Is he alright?" Bella blurted. "I knew he was in trouble, I just didn't know what to do."

"He's worried about you," the babbler went on. "I told him I saw you escape, and he was relieved – but he doesn't want you to do anything rash. He says the Diva knows of your powers and has her heart set on getting her hands on the pendant. Whatever happens, she must never get it!"

"She won't," said Bella clenching the pendant firmly in her fists.

"The Quetzal also wants to warn you that the snakes . . . "

"Will be guarding the Diva's den," Bella interrupted. "I know."

"But there's a window between nine and nine-twenty when the cobras are performing in the Big Top and the clowns will be preparing for their second-half act," the babbler went on. "He says that's when you should come."

"I will," Bella promised.

"Bella, you're up," said Annie cheerily, poking her head around the door. "We'll meet you in the hotel restaurant for a late brunch as soon as you're ready. Wear something nice. Bruce says that Mr. and Mrs. Kamat like all the volunteers to be smartly dressed." Bella turned around to bid the babbler farewell, but he'd already gone.

By the time Bella got to the restaurant, Bruce and her mum were sipping coffee. Bella felt anxious. Her outburst last night would only confirm to Bruce what Diva Devaki had in all probability already told him: that she'd been at the circus last night. "If she's already called him, I'm done for," she shuddered. "What am I going to do?" Rubbing her pendant between her fingers to compose herself, she slipped it into her pocket and sat down.

"Bella, you look wonderful," said Annie. Bella had chosen to wear her favourite Guatemalan dress. Made of traditional fabric, the hand-stitched patterns were a colourful blend of ruby-reds, resplendent blues, brilliant yellow and emerald green, the very same colours displayed by her nahual and the

K'iche' tribe from which she was descended.

"What a handsome threesome we make," Annie concluded. Bella didn't agree. The effect of Bruce's white linen shirt and blue suit was completely ruined by his long, mangy hair and green-tinted shades. She might have told her mum how lovely she looked in her yellow cotton dress had she not felt so nervous about Bruce.

"Did you have a good night's sleep, Bell?" Bruce asked jovially. Bella refused to answer. Instead she screwed up her face and reached for the juice.

"Bella, don't . . . " her mum started, looking flustered.

"How about we all order a good slap-up breakfast and celebrate?" Bruce suggested, trying to move things along.

"Celebrate what?" asked Bella stroppily. She watched her mum glance bashfully over to Bruce.

"Bella," her mum began. "Bruce and I . . . " Annie Balistica was both happy and scared all in the same moment. "Bruce and I have decided that we love each other and that we want to live together." Bella squirmed. Annie's face was suddenly flushed. She reached out and held Bella's hand, revealing a tiny emerald ring, the colour of her eyes. Bella saw it and immediately thought how puny it looked compared with the Itzamna Emerald she'd seen in Guatemala last year.

"What does it mean?" Bella blurted, fearing the worst.

"It's only our way of saying we're together," said Annie calmly. "That perhaps one day . . . not immediately, you understand," she hastened to add, "we might want to get married."

Every muscle in Bella's body tensed, as she tried to suppress the emotional inferno bubbling up inside.

"Bella, you're shaking," Annie fretted. Bella reached into her pocket for her pendant, hoping to find the strength to stem the flow of her tears. "Why?" she wanted to cry. "We were happy, weren't we, just you and me? We had a good time. We did things. We said we loved each other every day. Why did you have to go and fall in love with him?"

Bella was suddenly aware that her mum's hand was trembling even more than her own. "She's terrified," thought Bella. "Not of him, but of me!"

Bella's mum had anticipated that her daughter would make a scene. That she'd throw a tantrum and tell her she hated Bruce – hated her – never wanted anything to do with either of them ever again.

"Congratulations," said Bella quickly. "Could you pass me the toast-rack, please?" Her mum looked befuddled.

"Toast, Annie . . . " Bruce interjected, gesturing towards the rack in front of her. "She said 'congratulations' and now she'd like some toast."

"And some jam," Bella quivered.

"Thank you, Bella," Annie burst out, squeezing Bella's hand. "Thank you."

"Yeah, thanks, Bell," said Bruce sheepishly.

It was excruciating for Bella to have to listen to Bruce's inane thanks. She decided to concentrate on eating.

Neither Bruce nor Annie seemed to know what to say next. To Bella's relief, Bruce mentioned that he needed to recharge his mobile before they left for the children's centre. "Then maybe he hasn't spoken to the Diva," Bella thought, before realizing that it would have been just as easy for the Diva to call the hotel direct. Despite this, her instincts leaned more towards Bruce's ignorance.

Bruce and Annie's food arrived, served on large silver trays with big domed lids. Bella quickly ordered. Feeling ravenous, she and Bruce ate everything the waiters put before them, while Annie sat quietly drinking coffee. Straight after brunch Annie made them all take their malaria tablets.

"But we're not going to get malaria," said Bella, swallowing her chalky tablet down with the dregs of her orange juice.

"Well, I'm not taking any chances," Annie told her sternly.

Before they returned to their rooms to freshen up and prepare for the day, Bella asked her mum to take her to the jewellers to fix the chain on her pendant. To avoid any questions about the pendant itself, she slipped it off and just handed the rather stern-looking jeweller the chain. Meanwhile, Bruce went back to the room, supposedly to charge his phone and gather his things.

"Thanks for being so supportive about our news," Annie whispered, as they waited for the chain to be fixed.

"That's OK," said Bella, trying her best to hide her true feelings. "I was expecting it."

"You were?" asked Annie, surprised. Annie felt strangely unnerved by Bella's quiet acceptance of such monumental news.

When the chain was fixed, Bella put the pendant back on, and they returned to their room. Preoccupied with her concerns about the Quetzal, Bella already felt like the day was dragging.

"Perhaps I should sneak off and go straight to the circus now," she thought.

"No," cautioned a familiar voice inside Bella's head. "Be patient."

"Are you taking the cameras today?" Annie asked, as Bella reached under the bed for her backpack.

"Definitely," replied Bella. "I want to record everything." She tipped the entire contents of her bag out onto the bed and started to sort through the things she wanted to take with her.

"And you'd better get covered up," Annie advised her, getting out the sun cream and passing Bella her Charlton Athletic baseball cap, "I don't want you getting sunburned." She wanted to give Bella a cuddle, but didn't feel confident enough in her reading of Bella's mood. Instead she settled for smoothing in the cream on Bella's face where Bella hadn't rubbed it in properly.

"There," said Annie, finishing the gesture with an affectionate tap on Bella's nose. "You're still my little princess, you know." Bella tried to muster a smile, but she couldn't. The thought of her mum getting married to anyone was horrible. She preferred things to be as they were – before Bruce.

"Don't forget your laptop," Bella told Bruce when he popped his head round to see how they were getting on. "I might need it."

"You could have asked him nicely," Annie reprimanded.

"I did," Bella retorted.

When they were all ready, Bruce retrieved his mobile from the charger and switched it on. Almost immediately it started to bleep with a message alert. Bella watched with unease as Bruce read the text silently.

"Anything important?" asked Bella's mum. Bella felt her stomach turn. She could tell that Bruce was having to think quickly.

"No," he replied casually. "Just a quick 'hello' from the guys at work." They headed down to the lobby, where the concierge offered to call them a taxi.

"No taxi," Annie intervened mischievously. "A rickshaw, please." In the end, they decided to squash up inside an auto-rickshaw.

"It's too far for anyone to cycle," Bruce told them.

It wasn't a comfortable ride for many reasons. Apart from the fact that the back seat was really only designed for two, Bella was finding it impossible to discern Bruce's mood following the text message. "He's toying with me," she thought. "Trying to make out he suspects nothing."

As the rickshaw sped down the road, every bump and pothole was an uncomfortable reminder of why most other vehicles had suspension.

"Isn't this great?" cheered Annie. Bella would have been enjoying the experience much more if she hadn't been worrying about the Quetzal.

"Perhaps I should find a way of sneaking off when we get to the children's centre," she reflected, clenching her fists. "What if the Diva realizes we're together and kills him out of spite?"

"Stay calm and focused," whispered a familiar voice inside her head. "Timing is everything."

"We're entering Delhi Gate," Bruce announced as the rain started to thunder against the canopy of the rickshaw. They all quickly rummaged through their bags for their Gore-Tex waterproofs, but the damage was already done. They were soaked. Bella snuggled up under her mum's arm, but even in the middle there was little protection.

"Isn't this fun?" Annie laughed, pointing to a tear in the roof through which water was pouring all over them. Neither Bruce nor Bella was able to agree.

Trundling into Old Delhi amidst a flurry of pedestrians, bell-ringing cyclists, rickshaws and scooters, Bella considered how, coming from London, she was familiar with the sight of Indian families going about their everyday lives. There were some areas of London, particularly in the east, where Indians made up the largest part of the community. She loved the vibrant colours of the women's saris and the striking turbans worn by many of the men both here and at home. Here the Western-style shirts and trousers worn by the Indian men were much more colourful and patterned than the dreary styles men at home seemed to prefer. What did take Bella's breath away, though, was the architecture.

"What do you make of that, Bell?" shouted Bruce through the hammering rain. He was pointing to a magnificent red-brick fortress capped with spectacular white domed towers. "That's the Red Fort," he announced.

'Wow!" exclaimed Annie, impressed by its symmetry and grandeur. "Look at those two magnificent turrets." Bella glanced up at the domed towers flanking the main entrance but made no comment.

"I once saw the Diva jump off the east tower," Bruce told them with admiration. "She dived headfirst into a large basket full of live spitting cobras."

Annie gasped.

"And . . . ?" urged Bella. Bruce turned back to address them.

"She lived, of course," he replied. "She simply stepped out of the basket to a wild, standing ovation and picked up a cheque for twenty-thousand American dollars." Bella and Annie flopped back into their seats, completely flabbergasted by Bruce's story.

"Take us to Jama Masjid," Bruce ordered the driver.

They turned into a labyrinth of alleys lined with tiny shops. Again, Bella was surprised to see how many children there were out on the streets. Some of them were selling incense and tissues, while others had tea towels, hats, umbrellas, and most impressive of all, beautifully crafted wire sculptures of cars and rickshaws – the range was endless.

"While we really need to encourage these children to be in school, I have to admit that they're very resourceful," Annie observed. "They're out on the streets sewing, boot polishing, cleaning cars, horse grooming, performing acrobatic feats – it's amazing how they can do all this, given their circumstances."

"It's enterprise like this that we try to instil in them at the centre," said Bruce proudly. "After all, they've got to learn to fend for themselves in the end." Bella felt unnerved by Bruce's ability to be so two-faced.

Eventually, they emerged into a vast open area in which stood the biggest, most impressive mosque Bella had ever seen.

"That really is something," Annie remarked with admiration. "Rahina and Charlie would love this," Bella thought sadly. "I wish they were here." Just then a battered old rickshaw with two large speakers on the back swerved into their path.

"Mind where you're going!" bellowed the cheeky driver.

Bruce was distracted, but Bella recognized him at once by his distinctive blue-and-orange baseball cap.

"The knife-juggler," she thought. "The one Bruce was so aggressive towards in the taxi." She wanted to jump out of the rickshaw and run straight after him, but he was already out of sight.

"Wasn't that one of the children's rights radio stations?"

Annie asked, turning to Bruce. "I hear they're recorded on cassettes by street-children to help with raising awareness of their troubles."

"That's right," replied Bruce. "It's one of the projects we actively try to support at the children's centre."

"Then I might yet cross paths with that boy," thought Bella with great excitement.

As the driver of the auto-rickshaw directed his scooter north towards the outskirts of Delhi, the rain started to abate. It wasn't long before the pulsating sun was again dominating the sky, under which a flock of vultures menacingly circled. Staring out across an open expanse of wasteland, Bella noticed that the birds were flying over a small gang of children picking out rubbish from a huge mountain of waste. "It must be the same for street-children all over the world," she thought to herself sadly, as she recalled the life of the street-children she'd met in Guatemala last year. Bruce was shaking his head and pointing to the children on the dump.

"I recognize quite a few of those kids," he tutted. "They come and work with us at the centre when they're hungry and then disappear. It's a crying shame."

"Then I guess we need to find out why that is," said Annie. "Perhaps if the centre could offer them somewhere safe to sleep as well as an education programme they wouldn't wander off." Bella's thoughts again shot straight to the street-children she'd met in Guatemala. They'd been sleeping in a rubbish dump when she'd met them. The youngest, Lucas, had almost died when rain soaked the heap and caused him to sink.

"Perhaps they want to be with their friends," said Bella. "Sometimes friends are more important than anything."

"Particularly if they haven't got a family," Annie added. Bruce seemed to nod thoughtfully but didn't pass comment.

Thinking of her Guatemalan friends made Bella feel sad. She'd wanted so much to see them again this summer. But then, if this trip had taught her anything so far, it was that the whole issue of homeless children was a global one.

"It's not right," she deliberated, feeling more upset by the minute. "Everyone should have a home."

"Bella, are you crying?" asked her mum.

"No, I'm not," snapped Bella, drying her eyes. Just then Bruce's mobile started to ring with yet another text alert. Bruce read the message and looked directly at Bella's neck. "She's asking about the pendant," thought Bella, snuggling up to her mum for comfort. Bruce punched in his reply in silence.

As time went on, the gaps between buildings became wider and wider with more factories and far less traffic on the road. Eventually, even the road ran out. Swerving in the mud, the taxi slid its way towards a ramshackle one-storey building, even more rundown than Bella had imagined. The blue paint on the outer walls was badly faded, and there were gaping holes in the rusty tin roof. Outside the main entrance there was an old Ford Cortina with its tyres off and the chassis held up by rocks. A short distance away Bella could see a large group of children playing football.

"Mum, can I go and play?" she begged, desperate for some time away from both of them. Her mum's eyes brightened.

"Of course," she said, "it will be a great way to dry off. I'll come and watch."

"But we need to greet Mr. and Mrs. Kamat," Bruce protested. "They've probably gone to a lot of trouble to prepare refreshments for us." Annie hesitated. She knew Bruce was right.

"Go on," she told Bella. " I know your dress is wet but try and keep it clean, if you can."

Delighted with her mum's decision, Bella jumped out and ran towards the match. "And keep your hat on. I don't want you getting sunstroke," Annie called.

The sight of a Guatemalan girl, even in southeast London, often turned heads. It wasn't long before every child on the pitch had been distracted by the stunning dress of the girl they'd never seen before. A crowd of children was soon gathering around her. Bella noted how wide the age range was. There were children here as young as five or six, right up to teenagers. Using her pendant, Bella would have loved to show them how fluent she was in Hindi, but her mum was still in earshot.

"Give me money," said a boy in a faded Bart Simpson T-shirt as he held out an upturned hand. The boy spoke as if by rote, giving the impression that he knew perhaps only a few phrases in English. Bella smiled uneasily.

"I haven't got any," she replied, tapping her pockets and raising the palms of her hands in a gesture to prove as much. She felt awkward.

"My name's Bella," she announced.

"You look funny," giggled an older-looking girl in a tattered blue dress.

The girl spoke in Hindi, but Bella understood.

"I'm Guatemalan," Bella announced, without any apparent reason. "But I live with my mum in London." The children mingled around, looking at her elaborate dress with distrust. Bella was becoming increasingly aware of how overdressed she, her mum and Bruce all were. "It's like we're trying to prove a point by showing them just how rich we are," she thought, seething with anger at Bruce's insensitivity.

"You want to play?" piped-up a tall skinny boy with tightly cropped hair, grabbing Bella by the arm and pulling her away. "My name is Rahul."

Seeing as Rahul was holding the ball, Bella guessed he carried some weight amongst the group.

"Come and meet us inside when you're finished," called Annie as Bruce pulled her away to greet the smartly dressed Indian couple walking towards them.

Like the ball the street-children in Guatemala played with, this one was made from blue plastic bags tightly wrapped with lots of elastic bands. The goals were marked out by crushed up Coca-Cola tins squashed into the mud. "I should have brought some footballs from home," Bella scolded herself. "Perhaps we can buy one for tomorrow."

Sensitive to the fact that all the other children were playing in bare feet, Bella kicked off her shoes. She recalled the football match at Hawksmore Primary in December when the Quetzal had encouraged her in her quest to beat Eugene Briggs and his gang of bullies. Taking hold of her pendant she sent out another message to her absent friend. "I'm coming," she chirped. "Be strong."

Just before the match reconvened, Bella gestured to her team to put their hands up so she might quickly try and take in who was on her side.

"This is going to be difficult," she thought, as she quickly tried to memorize their faces.

The match started.

"Over here, Bella!" her team-mates shouted whenever she got the ball or, "Go for goal!" Bella was soon reminded that the things people called to each other while playing football were the same everywhere. Football itself was the language. Bella was soon as mucky as everyone else. After an hour or so, a loud horn brought the match to an abrupt end.

"Time for classes," Rahul told Bella.

"Thanks for the game," Bella puffed, reaching out to shake Rahul's hand. The tall boy looked down at Bella.

"You speak Hindi as well as playing great football?" he queried, noticeably impressed.

"Yes," Bella replied. "But please don't tell Bruce or my mum." Rahul gave her an enquiring look but probed no further.

The children, all of them caked in mud, began to drift back towards the building. Bella had stopped to brush down her dress and put on her shoes when she caught sight of a boy on a rickshaw, hanging around some distance away. It wasn't his torn T-shirt and grubby green shorts that gave him away. It was the blue-and-orange baseball cap.

CHAPTER TWELVE

RANDIR

"Aren't you coming in for classes?" Bella panted in Hindi as she ran up to greet the boy.

"You're not Indian," he replied suspiciously, ignoring Bella's question as he stepped off his bicycle. "Yet you speak like one."

Bella noticed how his eyes were fixed on her pendant, which had popped out from beneath her dress while she was playing football. Remembering how he'd tried to grab it last night she tucked it away.

"I'm good at languages," she replied. The boy looked unconvinced.

"But if you're not coming in, then why are you here?" Bella asked. The boy looked at Bella with deep distrust.

"I came to find you," he answered uneasily. "I was curious. Last night I saw you twice. Once in a taxi with that man with the long hair," the boy spat with disgust onto the ground, "and then being chased from the circus by the Diva's guards." He gave Bella a long, hard glare. Bella observed how drawn and tired he looked.

"But what were you doing at the circus?" she asked him, turning the tables while trying to recall seeing the boy there.

"I was trying to rescue my sister," he told her. "But she was so concerned about making sure you got away, she got herself recaptured. I was lucky to get away myself."

Bella felt a wave of guilt. She had seen the girl who'd helped her escape being dragged through the forest by the clown.

"And how come you and your sister found yourself in such a predicament?" Bella probed, trying to get the boy to tell her more of his intriguing story.

"About two months ago they started this big drive at the children's centre to encourage us to learn circus skills," he told her. "They said it was a way to get work and an education. About three weeks into the training, that man with the long hair you're with turned up, watched us practice and then lured me and my sister, Shilpa, on a train ride to visit the Mumbai Circus. Before we knew it – we'd been sold as slaves to the Diva."

"So that's the Mumbai connection!" thought Bella. She was livid.

"He sold me as a knife artist," the boy continued.

Bella gasped in amazement as the boy pulled a knife from a sheath tucked into his trousers, poised himself theatrically and threw it high into the air. Then, with great aplomb, he performed three back flips – the last one with a twist – landed in the splits and caught the knife. The routine ended with a flamboyant outstretching of his arms. Bella was impressed.

"As long as I performed well, all I had to do was clean and cook," said the boy. "But I didn't." He paused and looked down to the floor. "I was nervous in front of crowds," he went on.

"When the Diva ordered me to start throwing knives to split fruit resting on the heads of other children, I ran away before she could set that clown of hers on me." Bella had seen how mean the Diva's henchman could be. "So that's why I was there," the boy concluded. "Now I'd like to know why you were there."

"I need this boy's help," Bella told herself, thinking quickly. "I have a friend being held captive by the Diva too," she told him. "Perhaps we could work together." The boy didn't look so sure.

"Why were you in a taxi with that man?" the boy asked, pointing towards the children's centre. Bella glanced over her shoulder to see that Bruce was now standing by the old Ford Cortina where a small group of boys were busy changing tyres. He was staring right at them.

"Bell, get away from that boy!"

Bruce started running towards them with some urgency.

"Come and find me at the Ambassador Hotel . . . " Bella started, quickly turning back to the boy. But he was already pedalling away on his rickshaw as fast as he could. She gave a short, sharp cry of frustration and turned back.

"What was Randir saying?" Bruce wheezed the moment he caught up with her. He was sweating profusely.

"Nothing," said Bella innocently, turning her eyes to the floor. "I didn't even know his name."

"That boy's a liar and a thief," Bruce snarled, furrowing his brow. "I don't want you playing with him – is that understood?"

"Perfectly," said Bella, emphasizing each syllable slowly and clearly.

Her ambiguous response confused him.

"Good," said Bruce cautiously as he tried to put his arm around her. "Now let's get inside. I need to introduce you to Mr. and Mrs. Kamat, and then there's work to be done." Bella shrugged herself free and ran on ahead to find her mum.

While Bella made her way back towards the children's centre, Bruce turned to watch Randir pedalling towards the city. Taking out his mobile phone, he quickly typed in the now familiar number.

"He was here," said Bruce coldly. "Driving a rickshaw. Send Pramrod and a small posse out in a van . . . Good . . . I will . . . See you tonight."

He hung up.

As she approached the building, Bella saw a number of children building a human pyramid, like the kind she'd seen street-performers or circus acrobats make. There were other children nearby juggling bottles and rehearsing flips similar to those Randir had just shown her. "I've got to warn these children," thought Bella. "Before it's too late." She noticed a girl with a delicate physique climbing up a ladder to a thick wire that was attached to a hook about three meters up the wall. The wire was stretched some twenty metres or so across to a wooden pole. She watched the girl lean against the building to compose herself, then, taking the plunge, step gingerly onto the wire, stretch out her arms and try to balance. Straight away, she started to wobble, her arms flying everywhere. Then, taking three quick, hopeful steps forward, she somehow managed to keep her balance. Bella was transfixed. She watched as the girl walked almost the entire length of the wire before Bruce passed by and yelled "Boo!"

at the top of his voice. Distracted only for a moment, the girl lost her balance and fell.

"See you inside, Bell," chuckled Bruce. "Don't be long. Mr. and Mrs. Kamat are dying to meet you." He mumbled something else as he turned and walked away, but Bella didn't quite catch it.

Filled with disgust, she screwed up her face and stuck out her tongue. "I wish mum could have seen all that," she thought.

Bella ran to the girl's aid.

"Are you alright?" Bella asked her.

"I'm fine," smiled the girl shyly, taking Bella's hand to help her up.

Undeterred, the girl was brushing away the mud and making her way back to the ladder.

"Would you like to try?" she asked Bella.

Bella was excellent on the beam at after-school gym club and knew that she had good balance.

"OK," she said. "As long as you don't mind helping me."

"Then take off your shoes," suggested the girl. "You'll need to use your toes to help you grip."

The two children introduced themselves.

"Bella's a nice name," smiled the girl.

"And so is Rama," Bella grinned, glad to be making a new friend.

Rama was ten, a little taller and more slender than Bella, with much longer dark hair. She was wearing what at one time must have been quite a nice white cotton dress, which was now torn in several places and in need of a wash. At first, Bella was nervous about walking the tightrope. She kept on forgetting to keep her head up, to grip her toes firmly round the wire and to remain calm and poised as Rama had instructed. She'd flap her arms when all she needed to do was gently lift one up or down ever so slightly. But after only three attempts, amazingly, she was able to walk the entire twenty metres without falling off.

"You're a natural," Rama told her enthusiastically. "You should come and join the circus with us. You could be the next Diva Devaki!" Rama looked so innocent and excited about her own and Bella's future, it broke Bella's heart. "How could I ever convince her?" she thought bitterly. She looked at the children rehearsing circus acts all around her. "These are probably the very children Bruce has already condemned to slavery in the Diva's sweatshop," she thought angrily. "But not for much longer!" She thanked Rama kindly for her help and went to find her mum.

Stepping through the entrance to the centre, Bella was impressed to find a huge open-plan room divided into areas where children were engrossed in an impressively wide range of activities.

"I bet mum thinks this is great," thought Bella in frustration. "Another reason to love Bruce." She began to walk round. There were groups of children working with disassembled bikes and all kinds of electronic equipment such as radios and cassette recorders. Bella thought the elderly Muslim gentleman leading the session looked splendid in his pristine white achkan and white trousers. The way he dressed reminded her of Rahina's granddad, Mr. Iqbal. He came across and shook Bella's hand.

"Hello there, I'm Mr. Omar." He gave Bella a friendly smile that she couldn't help but return.

Alongside Mr. Omar's workshop was a class dedicated to

the kind of wire sculptures Bella had seen being sold in the streets earlier. The teacher here was a younger Indian man in smart trousers and a white shirt. There were also groups of children learning how to use sewing machines as well as others learning carpentry skills to make tables and chairs.

"Bella, over here," called her mum.

Bella found her mum sitting with a very elegant middle-aged couple drinking tea at a small table by the kitchen.

"Oh, Bella," sighed Annie in a tone of familiar dismay. "Your dress . . . " Bella was aware that the three adults were looking her up and down. She stopped to examine the damage herself and was quite shocked to see how filthy she looked.

"I was only playing football," Bella replied, as if it wasn't entirely her fault.

"Well, I think your daughter looks fine," said the kind-looking lady in the beautiful orange-and-red sari. The red in Mrs. Kamat's dress matched perfectly the shade in her husband's tie.

"Bella, this is Mr. and Mrs. Kamat," said Annie. "They're the wonderful couple who take care of all these children."

Mr. Kamat had grey hair and a moustache and was dressed rather conservatively in brown cotton trousers, white shirt and red tie. She could tell right away that they were Hindus, because of Mrs. Kamat's bindi – the spot in the middle of her forehead, believed to bring good luck.

"Welcome," Mr. Kamat greeted Bella, getting up to shake her hand in a way Bella was entirely unaccustomed to. "We're all very excited you're here."

"Me too," said Bella with an embarrassed smile.

Annie could tell that the formality of Mr. Kamat's greeting

was making Bella appear uncharacteristically shy. She thanked the Kamats kindly for their hospitality and then suggested that perhaps it was time for her and Bella to get down to some work.

"I've put all your cameras down over there," Annie told Bella, gesturing to the table in the corner. "I didn't turn on the laptop because I thought we'd better go easy on the battery. Bruce suggested you get the children interested by taking some photographs of what they're doing this afternoon and then do a little presentation with the computer later."

"I thought that was my idea," said Bella indignantly, having suggested the very same thing to Bruce only the other day.

"Whatever," said Annie, getting tetchy. "If you need me, I'm going to be working in the clinic," she gestured to a door at the far end of the room. "It's only a small room, I shouldn't be hard to find."

Bella took one of the digital cameras and made a tour of the centre taking photographs as she'd planned. By the time the centre closed at four o'clock it would be fair to say every child in the project wanted the chance to work with Bella on her exhibition.

"See you tomorrow, Bella," said the children, departing for all corners of the city: to sleep where and do what, no one seemed entirely sure.

"Where are you going?" Bella asked Rama.

"I'm going down to the bus station to help people with their luggage," she replied. "I can make a bit of money, and it's quite a good place to sleep."

"I thought I'd go down to the Red Fort tonight," said the tall skinny boy who had spoken out just before the match. "See if I can clean some shoes for the tourists."

It was decided that Bruce would call Bella and her mum a cab while he stayed a little longer to have a staff meeting and look over the finances with Mr. Kamat.

"Well," said Annie when they got in the cab. "Isn't Bruce amazing? Do you know he's built this whole project up himself from absolutely nothing?"

Annie was playing with her ring as she spoke. She looked so happy it made Bella sick with worry. "If we can get some of the wonderful things they've made into shops in Britain and America, we could raise quite a bit of money towards their education," she went on.

Bella knew her mum was obsessed with getting street-children into schools.

"It looks like the children are getting some good lessons," Bella admitted. "But what's the idea with all the acrobatic stuff?" Bella wanted to know what Bruce had told her mum.

"Bruce says that there are great opportunities for talented performers," she replied. "The circus not only feeds and clothes the children, but it also runs a school."

"So that's how he convinced her," thought Bella. "I'd love to show her how it really is."

"They get to learn while at the same time receiving excellent professional training and a small salary," Annie went on. "It's perfect."

"Then we should go and see," Bella suggested enthusiastically, confident that none of this was taking place at the circus.

"Yes, if there's time," Annie agreed.

Back at the hotel Bella and her mum planned to take an early-evening swim before having a light supper back in their room.

"I'm going to have an early night," Bella warned her mum, conscious that she needed to get back to the circus to rescue the Quetzal. She felt a bit guilty ordering an omelette and fries when there were so many elaborate foods on the menu, but it was exactly what she fancied.

"Feeling homesick?" Annie asked when she heard Bella order.

"I'm just missing my friend," said Bella, thinking of the Quetzal. As soon as she knew he was safe, she could turn her attention to revealing the truth about Bruce and Devaki.

Around seven-thirty, Bella told her mum she was tired and wanted to go to bed. Although it suited her purpose to say it, it was also true.

"That's fine with me," Annie yawned. "I'm bushed too."

Annie came in to say goodnight around eight. "Thank you for being so accepting about Bruce and me," she said. "You know you're always going to be my one and only, don't you, Bella? I'll never let anyone come between us." Bella pretended to yawn. The funny thing was, she didn't have to pretend very hard. "Sleep well, my love," Annie whispered, leaning over to give Bella a goodnight kiss. "See you in the morning." With her eyelids already beginning to droop, Bella persuaded herself that she should lie in bed, just for a minute or so, until she was sure that the coast was clear.

Bella awoke with a start. She sat bolt upright and looked at the clock: 8:22. "Damn!" she thought, "I'm going to be late." She knew she had to be at the circus by nine. A scratching sound coming from the main door arrested her attention. "What's that?" she thought, rolling off the mattress and scrambling under the bed. There was the click of a turning lock. "Diva Devaki," she trembled. The door was ajar.

She was too scared even to scream.

CHAPTER THIRTEEN

EXPOSED

"Don't be scared," whispered a voice.

Bella was holding her breath. From her hiding place beneath the bed, she could see that whoever it was, was walking barefoot. She peered up cautiously. The intruder was wearing a blue-and-orange baseball cap.

"Randir," she exhaled so quickly, she almost fainted with relief. She rolled out and pulled herself up. "How did you know that . . . ?" Bella started, but Randir was in too much of a hurry to be drawn into conversation.

"Listen," he interrupted. "You say that you have a friend at the circus who needs your help." Bella nodded earnestly. "Perhaps we can help each other," he said.

"Great!" Bella cheered, feeling a rush of elation. Then, noticing the cuts and bruises on Randir's legs: "But what happened to you?" For a moment Randir looked a little dazed, as if he hadn't even noticed them.

"Oh, those," he replied. "I had to do quite a bit of fast pedalling earlier. I must have fallen off."

Bella had fallen off her bike a hundred times and could

well sympathize.

"Bruce must have told the Diva where I was because she sent Pramrod and some of her guards to find me, but I got away," Randir continued.

"Are you alright, Bella?" came the call from the bathroom next door.

"Fine, Mum," Bella shouted before whispering to Randir: "Wait for me outside while I get dressed." She made her way towards the wardrobe. "I'm sick of looking like a demented sleepwalker whenever I go out at night."

Within a minute, Bella was wearing her yellow Charlton Athletic away shirt, jeans and trainers. Tucking her pendant safely away, she slipped quietly out into the corridor.

Randir hurriedly led Bella into the service elevator and pressed the button for the ground floor. The doors closed and the lift grinded its way slowly down before jerking to an abrupt halt. Bella had to squint as the doors opened to reveal the stainless-steel design of the hotel's busy and brightly lit kitchen.

"There's that boy again," exclaimed a grouchy-looking chef in a white apron and hat as he looked up from dicing meat. Through a haze of boiling pots and sizzling pans Bella could make out at least a dozen identically dressed chefs, caked in sweat.

"Someone stop him!" demanded the chef cutting meat, flinging down his knife and quickly wiping his hands on his apron. All around them there was the clatter of hastily discarded implements.

"Follow me," Randir urged, bursting quickly through the nearest swing door. Suddenly they were in the storeroom, piled high with boxes and crates. "This way," Randir beckoned, running towards the fire escape. As he pushed down the metal bar the doors parted, and the alarm went off. Dashing down a long, well-lit gravel path, they found themselves in an alley that looped back to the hustle and bustle of Connaught Circus.

"Have you got any money?" Randir wheezed. Bella shook her head. She hadn't a single rupee to her name. "Never mind," Randir panted, glancing back towards the sound of crunching footsteps not far behind. "We'll dodge the fare." Before Bella could ask another question, he grabbed her by the arm and pulled her across the busy road towards a local bus. To the sound of blaring motor horns, bicycle bells and shouts of "Mind where you're going!" Randir jumped onto the rear bumper of the bus and grabbed hold of the window. "Come on!" he urged, as the bus set off.

Bella had to be quick. She reached for her pendant, opened her arms and leaped.

"Wow!" thought Randir, as Bella literally flew through the air before slamming rather gracelessly against the back of the bus. He clasped her firmly by the elbow. "How did you do that?" he asked, completely baffled by Bella's five-metre jump. "I've never seen anything like it." Bella blushed. It was dangerous revealing her powers in public – she knew that – but she was desperate. The Quetzal was in great danger, and she needed to stick with this boy.

"I'm good at gym and athletics," she told him.

"You're telling me!" said Randir, giving her a questioning look.

Five minutes up the road, the two children jumped off the bus at a set of traffic lights and raced several blocks east to find another bus on which to steal a ride. Weaving their way across the city in this way, they eventually found themselves approaching the floodlit park and the hubbub of the Mumbai Circus. The sound of loud applause alerted Bella to the fact that the performance was already well under way.

"Last night, Shilpa was being held in a heavily guarded tent at the edge of the compound," Randir told her. "Where's your friend?"

"He's in a cage inside the Diva's private den," Bella replied, realizing that this might sound a little odd.

"Is she using him as her own personal slave?" Randir asked suspiciously. "I heard she didn't allow anyone but her closest advisers in there."

Suddenly, they were distracted by a mighty roar from inside the Big Top. "The Tiger!" Bella gasped. She stopped and listened. Again the Tiger roared, only this time she realized that it was a cry of pain.

"I want to go in," she told Randir, gesturing to the main arena. "Now!"

"I'm here to rescue my sister," Randir retaliated. "I thought we were working together."

"We are," Bella pleaded. "I just need to take a look inside."

Clearly annoyed, Randir reluctantly led Bella to the back of the huge marquee, where the performers gathered before making their big entrance. He searched around for a poorly fastened section of tarpaulin and lifted it up.

"This way," he gestured. "Quick, before anyone stops us." Bella rolled under.

The atmosphere inside the stadium was electric, full of the

sound of uproarious laughter. By the time Randir was through, Bella was already pulling herself up one of the supporting frames to a position from which she could view the entire arena. Randir, irritated by the distraction from their mission, followed her. Bella watched the scene unfolding in the ring, where half a dozen clowns were hysterically banging drums and blowing horns as they ran around a bemused-looking tiger sitting on a podium.

"Pramrod!" Bella blurted, suddenly aware of the extravagantly dressed clown doffing his silver top hat to the crowd's applause. Even through the din, Bella's outburst attracted attention. The shock of seeing the Diva's clown in full makeup for the first time was a little overwhelming. Gone were the orange winkle-picker boots. As with all the other clowns, Pramrod's red, flat boots stretched out before him like canoes, making it almost impossible for him to walk without falling over. His wizened face was covered with thick foundation, while his cheeks had been painted white to accentuate his bright red nose. Like all the other clowns, whenever he removed his hat, he revealed a head of crazy, gelled-up hair, as if a thousand bolts of electricity had recently shot through his body. His eyes, heavily circled with thick black liner, appeared as big as baseballs. "He looks like a freak!" thought Bella, screwing up her face in revulsion.

"You know him?" Randir asked, surprised by Bella's outburst. But Bella was too upset to answer. "They must have hypnotized the Tiger," Randir giggled. "He looks like he's in some sort of trance."

"It's not funny," Bella retorted, crossly. "He's got feelings, you know." Just then Pramrod stopped and raised his golden walking stick into the air. The crowd hushed.

"And now, ladies and gentlemen," he announced. "I shall, with this stick, produce a ring of flames through which this brave and most fearless tiger will jump." The drums rolled. Bella started to panic as Pramrod waved his stick dramatically in the air. With a quick abracadabra-type flick and a crash of the cymbals, Pramrod's golden walking stick turned into a bunch of drooping marigolds. The audience broke out in laughter. Even Randir, frustrated by this unwelcome distraction, couldn't help but smile. Pramrod's face, all down-turned and theatrically saddened for comic effect, suddenly lit up, as if he'd just remembered what to do. The drum rolls began again. There was the same melodramatic sequence of waves and points, only this time a circle of crackling flames suddenly erupted around the Tiger. Bella watched the Tiger flinch, her heart a flood of pity. The front few rows of spectators, visibly wilting under the intense heat, began to back away.

"The fire's too hot!" cried Bella, shocked at the intensity of the inferno raging around her friend. "It looks out of control." The laughter was already beginning to subside.

"There must be a draft," said Randir with some urgency. "I've never seen the fires so fierce." Bella peered through the heat haze at the panting Tiger. "He's sweating badly," Randir observed, clearly concerned. "The old boy's going to really struggle to jump through this fire tonight."

Bella's heart was in her mouth.

"He's injured!" she hollered so loudly that several people looked up and scowled.

Using the power of the pendant, Bella could see blisters on the Tiger's legs and the blood dripping from his paws. The horn-honking clowns also seemed to be finding the heat too much. What had started out as a farce was now turning into a disaster with Pramrod hobbling around the ring waving his bouquet of marigolds while the Tiger slowly suffocated at the very epicentre of the fire. It was too painful to watch.

"I'm coming to help!" Bella roared in tiger-speak. Randir almost fell off his pole he was so flabbergasted.

"How did you do that?" he cried.

Bella knew that she was exposing herself and her powers, but she was too overcome. Suddenly, a much larger part of the audience was straining their necks to look at her. But it was the piercing glint of a distant eye that caused Bella to falter. A tall, stunningly beautiful woman in a yellow-and-black pinstriped leotard had stepped out from behind the performer's curtain and was glaring right up at her.

"Look away!" the Tiger bellowed, drawing the attention of the crowd once more. Bella turned away and prepared to fly to the Tiger's rescue, just as the mighty beast gave out another ear-splitting howl and raised himself up on his hind legs.

"Douse the fire!" shouted the Diva, stepping into the ring like a paragon of compassion.

"It's the Diva!" exclaimed Randir along with a thousand others. Many of the clowns and circus staff were now running into the ring with buckets of slopping water, but the Tiger's podium was already alight.

"She wants to save his fur," thought Bella bitterly, unimpressed with Devaki's dramatic intervention. The Tiger wobbled precariously. The crowd gasped. Then suddenly, he leaped into the fire. Bella squeezed the bar she was holding with all her might. For a millisecond the deep orange of the

Tiger's coat was lost in the flames. "He's not going to make it," she thought, her knuckles clenched white. But he did. It was unbelievable. The whole crowd shot to its feet with wild, spontaneous applause. But it didn't last. As the Tiger landed awkwardly on all fours, limped three or four strides and then collapsed, a deathly hush descended. Pramrod cracked his whip. There were a few boos from the crowd. He raised his whip again. Bella could hardly contain herself. She was about to dive to the Tiger's aid when the great beast whimpered and pulled himself up just in time to avoid the lash. Hobbling across the dusty ground, the Tiger leaped awkwardly up the steps and into his cage.

"I've got to go to him," Bella blurted.

"Wait for me . . . " Randir implored, looking down so quickly to see Bella's hasty departure that his baseball cap almost fell off.

Leaving Randir behind, Bella ran to the back of the tent and forced herself out through the tiniest of gaps. Scampering through the crowd of meandering artists and circus workers around the outer perimeter, she made her way to the performers' entrance to see the Tiger's cage being wheeled out by a gang of backstage workers. The pained look on the animal's face was agonizing to see. Running into the darkness of the park, she clutched her pendant and took on her Quetzal form as soon as she thought it was safe. From the skies, she watched the pen being pulled to its final resting place in the shadows. When the coast was clear, she swooped down and into the cage. She wanted to tell the Tiger what a great performer he was, how he was the bravest, most fearless tiger she'd ever seen and that she was here to help him. But when she saw his blistered paws and singed coat, she felt utterly miserable. He was lying sprawled out on his side, his head flopped onto the straw so haplessly that Bella felt sure he must be dead.

To retain her animal form Bella knew that she needed to keep in mind the image of herself that she wanted to project to the world. In her distress at seeing the Tiger in so much pain, she let down her guard at the very moment Randir set eyes on her as a quetzal. He watched in wonder as the image of the bird slowly faded away to reveal Bella kneeling down beside the dying animal.

"Don't die," she sobbed as she nestled her head against the Tiger's soft warm underbelly and pushed the pendant against his heart. Everything fell still. Despite the Tiger's warmth, Bella felt as if she were in some cold, dark chamber apart from the real world: a place where only the dead might wander briefly before passing on. She squeezed her eyes tightly shut. An image started to appear. At first she could see nothing but a thick orange mist, but slowly the image of a magnificent tiger slowly prowling towards a distant sunrise began to emerge. She called out to him: "Come back!" The beast turned his head nonchalantly. For a second it felt as if he was going to turn and walk away. Then, with a wise and gentle nod of the head, he began to slowly walk back towards her.

The Tiger's body jerked. He took a deep breath and suddenly started to wheeze. She kissed her pendant. "Thank you," she whispered, sobbing with relief.

Turning her attention to the Tiger's blisters, Bella laid the pendant against his wounds and lightly rubbed it over them. She watched the blisters deflate and dissolve while the bleeding cuts on his paws also began to heal.

"In helping me, you have revealed yourself to evil eyes, my dear girl," grumbled the sleepy Tiger. "Why?"

"Because you are my friend," Bella replied. "And you saved my life." The Tiger sighed and for a moment a look of contentment almost smoothed the creases from his furrowed brow. But it was only a moment.

"I heard the Diva's orders as they pulled my cage from the ring," he told her. "I'm to be executed tonight. Soon I'll be nothing more than an ornamental rug." Bella rubbed her face playfully into his chin.

"I won't let that happen," she tried to reassure him. "We'll soon be far away from this place."

"And what about the Quetzal?" he growled, trying to lift his drowsy head. Bella pulled herself up. Looking around for food, she saw that a slab of meat had been cast into the cage. She went to fetch it.

"Here," she said gently, laying it down before the Tiger. "Eat this. Stay here and rest, and I'll be back as soon as I can." She went to leave. But it was hard. The Tiger was quietly weeping as he chewed.

"I fear your heart is too big, Bella," he slurped. "You take the evils of the world too much on your own shoulders and trust too easily."

"I'll be alright," replied Bella kindly.

No sooner had Bella stepped out of the cage than Randir was there in front of her.

"Are you some kind of witch?" he demanded fiercely. "I saw you transform yourself from a bird and then use your necklace like some kind of magic wand on the Tiger." For the first time Bella considered the fiery, spirited look in the eyes of her friend. "If Randir had an animal twin, it would be a panther," she thought with satisfaction.

"I'm no witch," she replied bluntly. Bella trusted Randir. "You must promise me that you will keep this a secret," she added. Randir nodded cautiously. In truth, he was becoming less trusting of Bella by the minute. Bella lifted up her precious pendant.

"This pendant gives me special powers," she told him. "Without it, I'm lost." No sooner had she said it than she felt guilty.

"I should have told Charlie about this a long time ago," she thought. Thinking of her friend made Bella feel homesick.

"You're taking me for a fool," Randir told her flatly. He was feeling both scared and bewildered by Bella's outrageous admissions. He'd borne witness to the Diva's strange powers over the snakes and knew her to be evil. How was he to know if Bella was any better?

"I'm off to find Shilpa," he told her. "You make your own way." He darted off into the darkness, but Bella was hot on his heels. She found him hiding in a bush outside the Diva's tent.

"Keep away from me," said Randir.

"But I want to help," Bella insisted.

"Shhh!" replied Randir, crossing his lips with a finger and gesturing at the two guards making their rounds. Bella looked up into the trees before lowering her eyes to scour the undergrowth around them. "The animals sense my presence," she thought, searching for any sign of crows and snakes.

Waiting until the guards had passed, Randir crawled across the ground and rolled under the tarpaulin into the sweatshop.

Bella was right behind him. As expected, the room was full of children chained to their machines or to metal posts in the ground, but surprisingly there was little activity. With the absence of the Diva's henchman, even the guards inside were snoozing.

"Shilpa!" Randir whispered as he scurried around the room.

"She's not here," said a small boy, leaning against his machine. "You'll find her chained up in the elephant stable. She's been sent there to mop it out."

That's all Randir needed to hear.

"Help us," some of the children were beginning to call out.

"Shhh," hushed Bella as loudly as she dared. "We're here to help all of you." But Randir was already gone. Bella yanked hard at some of the chains, but it was hopeless.

"You need the keys," whispered the boy. "Pramrod and the guards have them."

Bella made her way over to the black curtain dividing the sweatshop from the Diva's den. She was hoping that Pramrod and the Diva might still be in the Big Top and that they might have left the keys. Unfortunately, as she slipped quietly under the curtain and shuffled along the floor to hide behind a long, bamboo sofa, she recognized the intoxicating smell of the Diva's incense and the grating voice of her mum's treacherous boyfriend. "So much for staying on at work to go over the books," she thought.

Peering around the end of the sofa, Bella saw the Diva, still dressed in her black-and-yellow leotard, staring down into the eyes of a kneeling and pathetic-looking Bruce. "He's not wearing his glasses," she thought. "That's strange." Amongst all the other animal cages hanging from the roof Bella saw a tiny birdcage, hardly big enough for a sparrow, let alone a quetzal. If this wasn't bad enough, Bella could see that the wings of her dear friend were bound with thick elastic bands. "He looks so forlorn," she lamented as she tried to catch his eye.

"Why didn't you tell me more about this Bella Balistica before?" the Diva was asking Bruce as she wove her hands hypnotically before his eyes.

Bella sensed that Bruce was dazed, as if the incense was making him light-headed. "She's putting him into a trance," thought Bella, considering for the first time the possibility that Bruce might be powerless against the Diva's will. "I saw her using her pendant to change into one of these," the Diva continued, reaching up and taking the bound Quetzal down from his cage.

Bella tried to see Bruce in a new light, but it was difficult. "I've never liked him," she reminded herself.

"Ted Briggs mentioned his suspicions about Bella's pendant when I spoke to him in London," Bruce told the Diva humbly. "But it all sounded too farfetched to believe. I tried several times to get my hands on it but could never find it."

"Well, I want it!" the Diva hissed, her eyes widening with ferocious intent. "With a pendant like that, I could be the greatest performer the world has ever known!" She inhaled deeply and let out a long, pensive sigh. "Which is why I have no intention of letting this little bird out of my sight," she went on. "He will make excellent bait." She smiled contentedly to herself.

"This is going to be even harder than I imagined," thought Bella, making sure her head was tucked safely out of sight.

Her pendant was starting to turn cold. She looked carefully around between all the other caged animals in the room for any sign of a snake, but there was none. Eventually, the Diva returned to more mundane matters.

"I expect to be patron of the children's centre by the end of the week," she announced. "I want access to all the children's personal files and the pick of any of them."

"As you wish," Bruce replied, putting on his tinted glasses. Any passing doubts Bella had about Bruce were quickly fading.

"Ted Briggs will manage all our European and American outlets," the Diva went on. "You're to do exactly as he tells you."

"I understand," Bruce replied flatly. "When will the tiger fur be ready to send?"

"I'm going out to check on the pylon and cables for my act straight after tonight's show," the Diva replied. "It will be an ideal place to finish him off and have him skinned. The fur might be a little ragged and singed, but it should scrub up well enough."

Her heinous grin cut Bella to the quick as she felt the pendant and the braids of its chain turn ice-cold.

"I've ordered the tiger's meat to be poisoned," the Diva went on. "If he wasn't killed by his exertions in the ring this evening he should be dying even as we speak."

"Oh, no!" Bella gasped, clamping a hand to her mouth for fear of giving herself away.

But it was too late.

CHAPTER FOURTEEN

HELPLESS

Pramrod, returning from the performers' dressing room, was just pulling back the curtain as Bella gasped. Before Bella had time to react, the Diva had shot across the room, jumped over the sofa and thrust her heel into Bella's back, pinning her firmly to the floor.

"Get the pendant!" she ordered the dumbstruck clown. Bella didn't have a second to gather her forces before Pramrod had lunged down and unclasped her precious pendant.

"Yes!" Devaki hissed triumphantly the second the pendant was off. "I knew you'd come back for your little friend."

Bella craned around in an attempt to catch Bruce's eye – maybe even now, he might turn out to be on her side, if only for her mum's sake.

"Bruce!" she pleaded, but to no avail. There were shouts and the sound of a mad scramble coming from the other side of the curtain.

"Hey . . . you! Stop them!" One of the Diva's guards burst through the curtain. "It's that runaway boy, Randir," the guard panted. "He's got his sister. They managed to steal the keys and release about a dozen workers."

Even with the Diva's boot heel pushing firmly into her back, Bella felt her heart jump with pleasure.

"Let me go after him," Bruce raged. "I'll get him."

"Go!" the Diva shouted as Bruce shot through the curtain, then to the dithering guard: "Idiot!"

"Well done, Randir," thought Bella with relief.

With Bruce gone, the Diva's attention returned quickly to the pendant.

"What are you doing?" she yelled to Pramrod, as he put the pendant on. The moment of sparkling joy that erupted in his face wasn't to last.

"Without it, I doubt she has any powers at all," said the Diva, snatching it off him and greedily admiring the multi-coloured gems. Bella tried to wriggle free, which only made the Diva dig her heel into her back even harder. Devaki raised the pendant up to examine it alongside the dejected Quetzal.

"I knew there was something shifty about you," she goaded the Quetzal, comparing the pendant with the bird. "If your little friend decides not to help me use this mysterious trinket, I think I'll stuff you myself." She started to cackle as the Quetzal let out a long, mournful screech. What sickened Bella was that none of the Quetzal's sorrowful protests made any sense to her at all.

"The Diva's right," she sobbed to herself. "Without the pendant I'm nothing."

Bending down and grabbing Bella by her long, tangled locks, the Diva yanked her to her feet.

"You're not getting away this time," she sneered, pulling Bella backwards so fast there was no time for her to react.

"You're going to teach me how to use this pendant of yours."

"You'll never understand," Bella protested. "You're not Mayan."

"Oh, you will make me understand," the Diva chided. "That's unless you want to see your friends suffer interminable pain before your very eyes."

The Diva quickly raised the lid of an empty snake basket and seized Bella around the waist. Hauling her up, she pushed her in bottom first with her arms and legs forced upwards.

"Strap down the lid and throw her in with that pathetic old tiger," the Diva ordered the clown. Bella tried to kick at the lid of the basket, but it was impossible. Gravity and posture were against her. She was furious with herself. She'd allowed her mother's precious pendant to fall into evil hands, and she'd failed her friends.

"Someone help!" she cried. But her pleas were so muffled by the basket, no one but the animals caged inside the Diva's den could hear them.

The smell inside the basket was foul. Bella soon began to feel nauseous. Pramrod had picked up quite a bit of speed as he rolled the basket down the gradient that led to the Tiger's cage.

"Let me out and I'll give you three hours to get away before I tell the police about the sweatshop," Bella tried to bargain, her voice fading in and out of earshot with each rotation. The sound of the Diva's uproarious laughter was answer enough.

The tumbling stopped with an abrupt bang. Bella guessed she'd crashed against the steps of the Tiger's cage. She heard Pramrod haul himself up the steps and unlatch the cage door. She listened anxiously for any sign of the Tiger, but there was none. Then, with an almighty grunt, the clown heaved the basket up the steps and rolled her in. Suddenly she was still. All Bella could hear was the slamming of bolts, the turning of locks and the meaningless squawks of the birds outside. Anyone looking into the cage would only have seen the lifeless-looking body of a once formidable Tiger and a battered wicker basket. If they'd listened carefully, however, they might have just about made out the desperate sobs of a very unhappy girl.

Bella found that with some effort, she could make the basket roll around the cage. Eventually, she felt it come up against a soft, cushion-like object.

"Tiger?" she tried to roar hoarsely. But without the pendant, all she could produce was a throaty growl with no hint of tiger language in it. Whether the Tiger could hear her or not, there was no reply other than an occasional groan.

"Someone help me!" Bella hollered, kicking the sides of the basket to vent her anger. For a moment the ear-splitting hoots of the Great Indian Hornbills drowned out the relentless chatter of the lapwings and babblers; but as for the sound of humans, they could only be heard in the distance as they applauded the acrobatic feats of Diva Devaki in the Big Top.

It wasn't long before the sound of hooves and the neighing of horses drew closer. Bella felt the cage jolt and guessed that the long wooden poles were being lifted up and attached to the horses. Then followed the sound of unfurling cloth all around her. Fresh from her triumphs in the Big Top, the Diva returned.

"What news of Bruce and the escapees?" Bella heard her ask the clown. Luckily for Bella, the Diva often preferred to speak in English. She strained to hear Pramrod's reply, but it was obscured by the squawks of the crows. Suddenly, there was a firm snap of the reins, and they were off, bumping along at a brisk canter across the park to join the bustling New Delhi streets.

Amongst all the muffled cacophony Bella could still hear the pitiful shrieks of the Quetzal. "She's got him," thought Bella, relieved at least, that her friend was still within earshot.

"I'm sorry," she called, hoping that her voice might calm him. The only other sound that brought Bella comfort was the deep and monotonous moan of the Tiger. "His body's trying to fight off the poison," she thought, her resolve stiffening. "The Diva hasn't beaten us yet."

The Tiger wasn't the only one being sick. Bella couldn't remember how many times she threw up on the long bumpy ride. She kicked and struggled and tried to turn herself around so that she could use her hands to punch open the lid, but it was no use. After about an hour, she began to notice that the sounds of the city had faded away and that the horses were able to break into a gallop. It was then that she realized how thirsty she was. The bumpy ride became even more unbearable, as the wagon began to slip and slide over dirt tracks. Even though it was difficult to catch every word that passed between Pramrod and the Diva, one thing was clear – they weren't getting along.

"Let me wear the pendant," Bella heard Pramrod beg. "It was like some awesome power shot through my aching body and took away the pain."

"You're pathetic," the Diva sneered. "So you can do what? Return to the dizzy heights of your long lost career?"

"So I can go home, get a job and be with my wife and kids!" he exclaimed angrily. "You know I was the greatest acrobat in India."

"You were a mediocre acrobat, and now you're nothing but a sad old clown," snarled the Diva.

"You owe me compensation!" Pramrod hissed. "And goodness knows, you should be ashamed of the weekly pittance you pay my brother to mop out the cages. What about a pension for all those years of loyalty they gave to this circus? They have families to support too, you know."

"I owe you and your brothers nothing," the Diva retorted. "I'm sick to death of hearing about your precious little family. I'm not a charity. If you decide to up and leave, I'm telling you, they're out of here! Who else would employ a bunch of has-been circus performers?" Bella tried to stop the basket from rolling backwards so she could focus on the conversation at the reins, but it was difficult over such a potholed road.

"Oh, you do owe me," Pramrod corrected her, his voice getting more sinister. "I know that you deliberately dropped me. I saw it in your eyes. You had me in your grasp and you simply let me slip. Go on, admit it and stop this pitiable charade that it was an accident."

"So it was the Diva who dropped him!" thought Bella, recalling the Quetzal's story about the ambitious young acrobat who'd become Pramrod's partner after his brothers had retired.

That was all the conversation Bella heard before the monsoon broke and the rain began to pelt against the wagon, drowning out all other sounds.

The rain soaked through the cover and dripped heavily onto Bella's basket, allowing her to catch small drops of seeping water in her parched mouth. The downside was yet more steering problems for the wagon. Eventually, however, this all gave way to a long period – perhaps five, six, maybe even seven hours, Bella wasn't sure – of relative comfort as they travelled over what she guessed was a tarmac road. Sheer exhaustion meant that from time to time Bella's eyelids closed. In the end, it was impossible to fight off sleep any longer.

A sudden bump that caused the basket to roll over the Tiger's limp body and crash against the rear bars of the cage brought Bella back to her senses. She was feeling physically shattered – hungry, thirsty and desperate for the toilet. Judging by the frequency of Pramrod's lashes and the bumpy ride, it felt like the horses were being pushed hard up a steep, rocky gradient, causing such a strain on the wheels and axles, Bella felt sure they would crack at any moment. Finally, they stopped.

"Let the girl out to stretch her legs," Bella heard the Diva snap. "And get her some water. I don't want her passing out before we've had a chance to . . . " she paused, trying to pick the right words, "have some fun."

"Have some fun?" Bella scoffed, recalling the hideous moment when the Diva fed the live mouse to one of her snakes. "She enjoys seeing people and animals suffer," Bella decided. "She's going to torture the Tiger and the Quetzal to make me teach her the secrets of the pendant and then kill me anyway."

Bella listened carefully to the movements outside. She heard Pramrod jump down from the driver's seat, hobble round to the side and pull away the thick black cloth.

Suddenly the cage was filled with dawn sunshine. Bella followed the creak of the steps as the clown made his way up to the cage door. As she listened to the turning of locks and slamming bolts, she clenched her fists hoping for a chance to punch out at his sad, downtrodden face. But it was a vain wish. Before she knew it, he'd unstrapped the lid, tipped her out and flung a bottle of water into her lap.

"Five minutes to stretch your legs and do whatever you have to do," he grumbled. "And no funny business!" He cracked his whip. Bella was too stiff and dazzled by the morning sunshine to do anything other than what she was told. Through squinted eyes she peered down to see the Tiger flopped out on the deck, his eyes firmly closed, with a small pool of vomit by his sagging mouth.

"He's thirsty," she implored.

"He doesn't need water," replied Pramrod in a deep gritty voice. "Not where he's going." Bella was desperate to go to him, but Pramrod was pushing her forcefully towards the cage door. "We must have been travelling for eight or nine hours," she worked out as she walked stiffly down from the cage to find privacy behind a nearby rock. All around her the sound of scampering lizards made her toes curl. She looked around for the Quetzal's cage but could see neither him nor the Diva. "My mum's going to be worried sick," she sobbed as she went to the toilet behind the rock. "She'll have called the police and the British Embassy – surely they'll be able to trace me."

In truth, Bella knew that this would be hard. Her trail from the hotel to the circus was, at best, sketchy.

Before Pramrod had even finished locking her back inside the Tiger's cage, Bella had undone the water bottle and was forcing it into the Tiger's mouth. "Drink," she urged him. Searching for any sign of life, she was relieved to feel the warmth of his fur and the very faintest of heartbeats. "Hang on, my friend," she whispered into his ear.

Bella tried her best to brush away the vomit from her football shirt. "What a disgusting smell," she squirmed as she looked out through the bars to examine the wilderness to which the Diva had brought them. What really shocked her was just how high into the mountains they had journeyed.

"There's no chance of any help around here," she rationalized, feeling depressed. "It's too barren for anything but lizards and snakes."

If she'd had the pendant Bella might have tried to elicit the support of passing animals, but the sight of three scraggy-looking vultures perched on a nearby rock was a reminder that the Diva too had her allies.

"What kind of powers does this woman already possess?" Bella wondered in trepidation at what was to follow. She had no doubt in her mind that the Diva's nahual was a cobra. The question was: could she use the pendant to become one, in the same way Bella used it to become a quetzal?

Bella gazed up at a huge electricity pylon. From it, a cable of immense length stretched across the deepest canyon she had ever seen. She remembered the poster advertising the Diva's live televised stunt. "What has she got in mind?" thought Bella with a lump in her throat.

The stirring of the Tiger's tongue as the water fell upon it aroused some hope. Bella poured as much of the water as she could into his mouth, gave herself the last two swigs and made her way to the front of the cage. She saw Pramrod chewing tobacco as he sat beneath the shade of a nearby tree. Unfurled before him was a long piece of hide, sheathing at least twenty glistening knives of all shapes and sizes. "He's going to skin the Tiger right before my eyes," she frowned in disgust. Alongside his impressive weaponry was a long, cylindrical case, already marked up "fragile" and "airmail".

Sitting by a small, shaded rock pool, the Diva was admiring the dazzling pendant hanging around her neck. Alongside, the three vultures were now standing guard over the small birdcage containing the bound Quetzal. Bella watched with deep unease as the Diva fondled the pendant and gently hummed some unknown chant that Bella couldn't follow. Suddenly, she jumped up and stretched open her arms as if to fly, only to land, with obvious disappointment and a certain lack of grace, on the muddy terrain.

"Damn and blast!" she cursed. "How does this thing work?" She turned around to the cage where she caught sight of Bella staring at her with so much rage that it made her laugh. "Look at you," she taunted as she started to make her way towards the cage. The Quetzal let out an almighty squawk.

"Whatever you do – don't look into her eyes," Bella remembered the Quetzal had warned her, and immediately she diverted her gaze to the floorboards.

Suddenly, the Diva was standing right before her.

"I saw you transform yourself into a quetzal," the Diva began. "There's some mystical connection between you and that bird, I can sense that – but how does it work?"

"Give it to me, and I'll show you," replied Bella hopefully. The Diva spat onto the ground. Bella blinked, and the Diva was gone. Suddenly, she heard laughter behind. She turned around. Miraculously, the Diva was now on the opposite side of the wagon. Bella again looked away from the Diva and began scouring the cage for mirrors. "What trickery is she using here?" she wondered.

"Stop taking me for a fool!" cried the Diva. "I know that this pendant acts like a gateway between the human and animal world." Bella turned around, shocked by the illusion and the fact that any human could be so certain of something so mystical and mysterious.

"You're very well-read in the supernatural, I know," Bella replied, remembering the books strewn around the Diva's tent. She had an idea that she might flatter the Diva's ego to manipulate the situation to her advantage. "But if I'm to help you, I'm going to need more time."

"How about the two minutes it would take for me to throw this helpless quetzal into the path of three peckish vultures, eh?" the Diva suggested meanly. Bella grimaced at the thought. The Quetzal wouldn't stand a chance.

"It's a complex meditative process," Bella argued. "Let the animals go, and I'll help you." Bella felt a snake-like slither in the sawdust around her. Suddenly the Diva was swinging the pendant before Bella's face.

"Such a beautiful thing," the Diva teased, trying to tempt Bella's gaze. "She wants to hypnotize me now," Bella warned herself, as she staunchly kept her eyes on the ground and tried to reach out for the pendant.

"As I said," Bella emphasized. "Let the animals go, and I'll help you."

The Diva scooped up a big handful of sawdust and threw it in the air. By the time it settled, she was again on the outside of the wagon.

"No!" she replied, slipping the pendant into her jacket pocket. "I've got a much better idea."

CHAPTER FIFTEEN

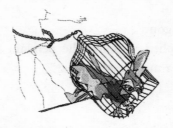

A DEATH-DEFYING STUNT

The Diva left Bella in the cage with the unconscious Tiger for the rest of the morning. With no shade whatsoever, the two prisoners had to lie very still to conserve their wilting strength. When the sun was at its highest point, Pramrod refilled Bella's water bottle and passed a handful of bananas through the bars.

"Here, drink and eat," he said gruffly. "You're going to need your strength."

Bella had the feeling that Pramrod was acting out of pity and was reminded of her first instincts about him. "He's got children of his own," she recalled. "Maybe he's not evil at all. He's just bound to the Diva's service by the hold she has over him through his brothers."

As the sun passed over the ravine and beyond the mountain behind them, the cage at last fell into shade. Half delirious from exhaustion, Bella peered up at the electric cable that stretched out across the ravine and tried to imagine what the Diva's idea might be. "It must be nearly a mile across," she estimated. "Quite a stunt if she can pull it off."

Bella had no idea how long she'd been asleep when the

170

Diva tossed a bucket of cold water on her face.

"Wakey, wakey," she teased. "Time to examine the view, I think." She gestured to the pylon and the cable.

"Do you really think that you can tightrope walk all the way across?" Bella asked doubtfully.

"I can," replied the Diva. "The question is: without the pendant, can you?" Bella felt her whole body go rigid with shock. It took a moment for the full horror of what the Diva had in mind to sink in.

"But if I die, you'll never be able to unlock the secrets of the pendant," Bella told her. "My mum's bound to have called the police. You don't know how stubborn she is. She'll never stop looking for me, and if you do anything to harm me, she'll make sure you go to prison." Tears of laughter were cascading down the Diva's face. Even Pramrod, lurking behind her, was crying, his thick eyeliner trickling down his painted cheeks. Bella thought he looked too dispirited to be crying for joy.

"You've become a liability to my business," said the Diva with a knowing smile. "I'll discover the secret of the pendant with or without your help. But if you change your mind, at least you might be able to save yourself and your friends from a painful death." Then, looking up to the wire, she said: "What makes this death-defying stunt so dramatic is the variety of possible outcomes." Bella had a feeling that she wasn't going to like what was coming next. "At this time of year the electricity cable is live from seven-fifteen in the evening to seven-fifteen in the morning – sunset to sunrise," Devaki went on, stopping to check her jewel-studded watch. Bella glanced across and could see that it was almost 6:45 p.m. "Any creature unfortunate enough to have even the smallest part of their body on an exposed section of the cable during this time . . . " here she paused with gratification, "will be fried!" Bella felt her legs wobble as the Diva started to shake with laughter. "That's if they haven't already crashed into the crocodile-infested ravine below." The Tiger howled in pain, as Bella fell to her knees.

With Bella too dumbfounded to move, Pramrod, following orders, hobbled quietly into the cage and put her into a painful arm lock. Pulling her up, he dragged her from the cage over to the foot of the pylon. "You better start climbing," he sighed, pulling out his whip.

Bella could see that a ladder had been built into the pylon, presumably to help with maintenance. She started to climb the metal ladder as slowly as she could. "Without the pendant, I'm lost," she quietly sobbed. "What am I going to do?" Every two or three steps, the Diva's attendant, who was never far behind, lashed out with his whip – never hitting her, but always giving her a jolt which forced her to take the next step. "Maybe I can do it," she tried to convince herself. She thought of her tightrope walk with Rama, the girl from the children's centre, and how quickly she'd taken to it. "You could be the next Diva Devaki," Rama had told her.

At the top, Bella found that there was a small platform on which she could stand and collect her thoughts. Pramrod, perhaps fearing that Bella might try to pull some stunt, hung nervously back. Bella gazed out at the long, fraying cable before her. In many places the protective insulation had all but worn away.

"The power of your will is a remarkable force," said a familiar voice inside her head – whether it was just whispers in the wind, Bella couldn't tell.

"Itzamna?" Bella thought at once of the portrait in the attic at home. "I'm forgetting who I am." Bella reminded herself for the first time in ages that she was the direct descendent of the Mayan goddess. "But I've lost the pendant," she blubbered. "Surely without it, I'm nothing more than an ordinary eleven-year-old girl."

"Oh – ordinary," whirled the voice. "A Mayan girl who has tamed a three-headed jaguar, spoken in a hundred animal tongues and even flown like the mighty Quetzal himself."

"Then I can do this," Bella tried to convince herself, "if I focus my mind."

She edged nervously towards the cable. "At least it looks thick," she thought as she kicked off her trainers and wrapped the toes of her right foot around it. Opening her arms to take her first tentative step onto the wire, her concentration was suddenly broken by the call from below.

"Wait!" shouted the Diva, scaling the pylon at a breathtaking pace. Bella could see that she was carrying something but couldn't make out what it was until she was standing alongside her. To Bella's surprise, the Diva was holding a length of rope and the cage that imprisoned the terrified Quetzal.

Bending down, the Diva took the rope and ran it around Bella's waist and through the bars of the cage.

"There," she sighed with delight once the cage was firmly attached. "Your fates really are inseperable. You have less than fifteen minutes until the cable becomes live." Bella just had enough time to glance down to her feet before the Diva gave her a big push. "Aah!" Bella cried, taking three quick steps along the cable before managing to fling out her arms and steady herself. Two more steps and she would be directly over the precipice. The cage around her waist was swinging too violently for her to hold her balance with any poise. To make things worse, the Quetzal, who had finally pecked through his bonds, was flapping so wildly he kept head-butting the top of the cage, causing it to swing.

"For goodness sake, keep still!" Bella shouted. Crouching down to lower her centre of gravity, Bella waited until the swaying of the Quetzal's cage finally ran out of momentum. Bored by Bella's slow progress, the Diva started to wobble the cable with her foot. The resulting tremor forced Bella on.

"Ten minutes," the Diva bellowed.

"Don't look down," Bella told herself. But she did.

Hundreds of metres below, the rocky ravine looked to Bella like one of the many three-dimensional scale models Mr. Alder was always getting them to make in Geography. For the first time since her arrival, she could make out the brown murky waters of the slow-moving river below. The thought of her body being chomped to pieces by greedy crocodiles flashed through her mind and for a second threatened to break her concentration. "Keep your head up and your toes tightly curled around the cable," she said out loud. "Take one step at a time. And whatever you do – stay focused."

It was highly distracting to Bella that the Quetzal chose that moment to lean through the bars and peck furiously at her knees.

"Stop it!" Bella barked, getting dangerously niggled. "Or we're going to fall." But still the Quetzal kept on.

"Five minutes," called the Diva, her echo fading into the

ravine along with Bella's hopes.

Bella blocked out everything, even the Quetzal's incessant pecking, and focused all her energies on taking one step at a time across the wire. The tension caused by tightening her leg muscles to keep her balance was causing her great discomfort. Every minute, the Diva's countdown reverberated around the ravine. Bella glanced back to see how far she'd come and saw that the Diva and the clown were now perched on a well-situated boulder. "Probably taking bets on when I might lose my nerve and fall," she muttered. With one minute to go, Bella knew she was doomed. The sun was already sinking behind the rocky outcrops to the west.

"What are we going to do?" Bella wailed into the wind. The strain on her tensed muscles was excruciating, not to mention the bruising caused by the Quetzal's unremitting pecks at her knees. Bella shot a quick look past the cable down into the ravine. Feeling dizzy, her arms flapped wildly as she tried to shift her body weight from side to side to hold her balance. She'd just regained her stability when a sudden shot of pins and needles went up her leg.

"Ow!" she yelped, as the Quetzal chose the moment to peck through her jeans in a desperate attempt to get her attention. For the first time in the entire stunt, Bella glanced down to her friend. "Quetzal!" she gasped.

With time almost out, Bella reached out to try and release her friend. But the move was ill advised. She felt the transference of her weight push the cable out to the right. In trying to straighten herself up, she overcompensated with her arms and swung too far the other way. As she started to fall, Bella managed to twist her body just enough to grab hold of the cable with both hands. "Get ready to fry!" hollered the Diva with glee, as Bella swung from the wire. Her words and subsequent laughter echoed through the ravine, stripping away any hope Bella had. Bella could see the sparks bolting across the cable towards her. The Quetzal, swinging helplessly in the cage, was screeching at the top of his little lungs.

"Let go!" cried a voice in Bella's head.

But then she was already falling.

CHAPTER SIXTEEN

CROCODILES!

Bella plummeted from the electricity cable at the very moment it became live.

"Ahhhhh!" she screamed, the rushing air howling in her ears. She bashed her elbow on the cage as she shot past it and just managed to grab the rope. As she tumbled in freefall she kept glimpsing the Quetzal's head, sticking out through the bars.

"What's he holding?" she thought.

Whatever it was glistened even in the fading light.

"The pendant!" Bella burst out.

They were going to crash into the ravine at any moment. She yanked the rope in a desperate attempt to draw the Quetzal in, but the jerk caused him to lose his grip of the chain. Bella let go of the rope and made a desperate lunge to catch the pendant. The cage shot up like a parachute until the rope reached its limit and snapped with a violent jolt, breaking away from her waist.

"How could I miss?" she thought, casting a desperate look down at her clenched fist as the cage flew away. But then, the tingle of the cold braids on the palm of Bella's hand swiftly filled her with a sense of power. Bella couldn't believe it. She hadn't missed at all. Within a second, the pendant was on and Bella was soaring away from danger.

"Quetzal!" she screamed. But there was nothing she could do. She watched the cage plunge into the murky waters. Swooping down to skim over the surface, her heart hammering against her chest, Bella saw a cluster of black, beady eyes pop to the surface in the shallow waters near the bank.

"Crocodiles!" she squealed. Bella plunged down into the river and grabbed the rope tied to the cage just as the jaws of an enormous crocodile opened up behind her. "No!" she wanted to cry, but her beak was full. Yanking with all her might, she turned to the skies as the full force of the crocodile's jaws came snapping down. The water beneath his belly-flop sprayed into the air, covering her in cold droplets. But he'd missed.

It was all Bella could do to carry the cage back to the bank. But the crocodiles weren't done yet. Returning to her human form, Bella quickly released the spluttering and half-drowned Quetzal.

"Quick!" she panted, seeing the crocodiles scurrying frantically from the river on their stumpy little legs, their mouths drooling with expectation. But the Quetzal was too soaked and shell-shocked to fly. He simply slumped to the ground and began blowing bubbles of frothy water into the air.

"What am I going to do?" Bella panicked. And then it hit her. "Remember who you are," she told herself sternly. Turning towards the crocodiles and raising the palm of her right hand she shrieked: "How dare you! Can't you see we need help?" The crocodiles flopped into the mud, some of them skidding several metres on their bellies before coming to rest at Bella's feet.

"Say that again," one of them snapped suspiciously, completely taken aback by Bella's outburst.

"I don't believe it," snarled another.

"Let's eat them, anyway," croaked another, rising from the mire with an evil grin. He was quickly slapped on the head by the tail of one of the others, but his suggestion quickly aroused a ferocious debate. Bella had no time for it.

"How do you expect to nurture a positive relationship with humans if you go around ripping them limb from limb?" she demanded. "It creates a bad image." The crocodiles looked baffled, although Bella had rather been hoping for a few signs of remorse. She had absolutely no idea where her rant was going to take her so she brought it to an abrupt end.

"So back off!"

Slowly, and with many provocative snaps of their great jaws, the crocodiles started to retreat.

"There was a time when no one would dare speak to us in such a way," Bella heard one of them whinge. "Now it's – don't do this, do that . . . I mean . . . we're crocodiles, for goodness sake!"

The Quetzal was lying flat on his back gazing into the slowly fading blue of the sky. Before the crocodiles had a chance to change their minds, Bella bent down to pick him up, put him over her shoulder and started to wind him. He coughed and wheezed, drew a deep breath, then let out an almighty belch. Bella gave him another pat on the back. With one final wheeze, the drenched bird choked up water for the last time and gave himself such a shake that Bella had to turn away.

"What the hell were you playing at?" he spluttered at the

top of his lungs, water flying everywhere.

"What do you mean?" Bella protested, putting him down on the ground.

"Turning up at the circus in your human form," said the Quetzal, preening himself irritably. "All you needed to do was drop in from the roof."

"I came with a friend," Bella retorted.

"I came with a friend," the Quetzal mimicked, screwing up his face. "And you lost the pendant to the one person in the whole of India who could have used it for evil ends," he added, throwing up his wings in exasperation.

Bella felt awful.

"At least you had the sense to gather your wits on that tightrope, I'll give you that," he grudgingly conceded. "Remember who you are, will you? And stop all this 'Without it I'm lost' malarkey. It's . . . so . . . so . . . " the Quetzal was trying to think of a fitting insult. "So human," he concluded in the most disparaging tone he could muster.

Bella wanted to be cross, but she was just so happy to have him back she couldn't help but bend down and give his head feathers an affectionate ruffle.

"But how did you get the pendant?" Bella asked.

"I leaned over and picked her pocket as she tied the cage to your waist," he told her, flicking up his tail with great aplomb and using his wings to brush up his head feathers. Bella gave him a big fat kiss on the cheek.

"Yuck!" spat the Quetzal. "And you can cut that out!"

Meanwhile, back on the steep mountain incline, two Indian children riding circus horses had just appeared on the scene. Slipping off their weary mount, they found refuge behind the boulders and watched as the Diva and her henchman stood on the precipice and peered down into canyon.

"Where's Bella?" whispered the girl.

"I fear we may be too late to save her," replied the boy with tears in his eyes. "But the Tiger's still alive." They looked on with relief to see the dazed beast slowly prowling around his cage.

"Then we must free him," replied his sister. "Come."

Back at the bottom of the ravine, the Quetzal was still complaining about Bella's failings at the circus when he was interrupted by an earth-shaking roar. Suddenly, small boulders and stones were skipping and scattering down the slopes all around them. They shot each other a wide-eyed look.

"The Tiger!" they gasped in unison.

The two friends flew at great speed towards the pylon that towered over the ravine. As they wound their way up and over the cliff top they saw the Diva, whip in hand, trying to keep the Tiger at bay, while Pramrod scampered away towards the wagon as fast as he could. Bella could see that the doors of the Tiger's cage were wide open and the horses, who had been drinking from a small puddle nearby, were now rearing up and shaking their manes in distress.

"How did that happen?" asked Bella, puzzled by the dramatic turn of events.

"Look at the boulders by the trees," replied the Quetzal. "I can see two children with horses." Bella looked and knew at once who they were.

"That's Randir and Shilpa!" she cried. "They must have followed us here and released the Tiger."

Suddenly, there was a colossal roar from the Tiger. Undeterred by the Diva's whip, he pounced. Bella winced and turned away as the Diva screamed. She thought the Diva was done for. Peeping out from under her flapping wings, Bella could see that the Diva had managed to dive away just far enough to stop one of the Tiger's claws tearing into her leg. But the Tiger wasn't to be outmanoeuvred. He turned and swiped viciously, this time catching the Diva's left leg. Bella grimaced as the Diva dragged herself away just in time to evade a third strike from the ferocious and aggravated beast.

"I fear the Tiger's claws have been clipped too short," sighed the Quetzal as he and Bella landed in a nearby tree. "He's going to have to get his teeth stuck in to her to do any real damage." The thought made Bella's stomach churn. Hating the Diva as she did, the thought of her meeting such a gruesome end filled her with pity.

"We should stop him," gasped Bella, feeling a little squeamish.

"And have her live to kill us all?" the Quetzal rebuffed. But the Diva had already limped her way up onto the wagon and was reaching out for the reins.

"Go for the kill!" the Quetzal yelled to the Tiger. But for some reason the Tiger was holding back. He took a few unsteady paces in pursuit but was clearly in so much pain he had to lie down. This was exactly what the Diva needed. In no time at all, Pramrod and the Diva were driving the horses at a hurtling pace back down the mountain track.

Diving down to the Tiger's aid, Bella returned to her human form and kneeled yet again to nestle her pendant into his sick stomach.

"He's eaten poisoned meat," Bella told the Quetzal.

"I know," replied the Quetzal. "From what I heard, you gave it to him." The Quetzal's words sounded more cutting than he meant them to. Bella was speechless, wounded by the Quetzal's curt retort.

"But it wasn't your fault," he added quickly in a more measured tone. "You were trying to help, I know."

"Bella?" queried a third voice, the owner of which had been seriously befuddled by Bella's apparently inane chirps as he approached with his sister.

"Randir!" Bella cheered, greeting her surprise ally with a beaming smile. "I thought I'd lost your trust."

"When Shilpa told me how much the Diva hated you it changed everything," replied Randir.

"Are you really having a conversation with that bird?" asked Shilpa, looking sceptically at the chirpy Quetzal.

"A conversation might imply he occasionally listened to what I had to say," Bella replied, giving the Quetzal a sharp look.

While Shilpa went to retrieve their horse, Bella and Randir took care of the Tiger and had a chance to catch up with the day's extraordinary events.

"We managed to free about twenty children and at least half the animals in the compound," Randir told her. "It was wild! The animals stampeded. They brought down tents and stands all over the place."

"What happened to Bruce?" Bella exclaimed.

"It was funny," Randir giggled. "We both mounted horses, but the only thing he could find was an ostrich." Bella and Randir were laughing.

"He chased us for about half a mile through the streets

until the ostrich got fed up and dumped him in a cart full of manure."

"But how did you know where we were going?" Bella chortled.

"To be honest, we didn't," replied Randir, calming down a little. "The horses led the way. It wasn't until we got to the top of the mountain path that we knew for sure they really were following your trail."

While Bella and Randir were talking, Diva Devaki and her henchman, less than a mile down the mountain track, had come across a small gang of renegade animal poachers. Pulling up the wagon the Diva called out: "You wouldn't be interested in the bounty I'm offering to track down a few stray circus animals by any chance?"

The deal she struck up with the hunters – spellbound by her beauty and mysteriously persuasive bargaining powers – was so evil that it begged belief.

CHAPTER SEVENTEEN

THE SEED OF REVENGE

About an hour or so later, as the coolness of the night began to set in, the Tiger was beginning to feel much better. Randir had rummaged through the Diva's hastily discarded bag and found some vegetable samosas and chapattis, which the Quetzal and Tiger graciously declined so that the children could eat them.

"I don't need to eat every day," said the Tiger politely. "And anyway, I need to give my stomach a rest."

After building a small fire and taking water from a spring, the three children relaxed together beneath the twinkling wonder of the Milky Way.

"I'm going to be in so much trouble when I get back," said Bella gloomily. "My mum's going to be beside herself – and I don't know what I'm going to say."

"Tell her you saved the life of a Bengal tiger," comforted the old beast.

"And while you're at it," added the Quetzal pompously, "a beautiful and spectacularly resplendent bird, king of the higher canopies, master of the jungle, the most . . . "

"All right, all right," Bella laughed. "But I'm still going to be grounded. And there's also the problem of knowing what to do about Bruce and the Diva. I don't think they're going to let the events of today go without punishment."

Shilpa and her brother, who were sitting opposite and listening to Bella's intermittent growls and chirps, were left in no doubt at all that Bella was talking to the animals. Seeing the befuddled look on Shilpa's face, Bella leaned across and laid her arm gently on her shoulder.

"I'm sorry," she told her friends. "You must think us all very rude." Both Shilpa and Randir shook their heads.

"I think you're the most amazing girl I've ever met," Randir told her.

The Tiger then told them his plan, which Bella translated for Randir and Shilpa.

"I'm going to retire into the wilderness," he told them. "I've had my heart set on it for years. I have children somewhere out there and while there's still a chance I might one day share even a single meal with them, that is all I wish for."

"Poor thing," thought Bella. "He's been a prisoner of the circus for most of his adult life. To think that his children have had to grow up without their father – it's so sad."

"Shilpa and I have a father too somewhere, " Randir mumbled.

"Me too," said Bella quietly. The Tiger turned to the children with a paternal glint in his eye.

"If your fathers are still alive, their every instinct will drive them to find you," he told them kindly. It was all too much for the Quetzal who was now banging his head against a nearby rock in utter frustration.

"Can we stop with all this mush?" he complained. "We're not out of this mess yet!" Just then, they heard a loud bang from the high rocky ground to the west, followed a second later by a splattering of mud close by.

"Poachers!" hissed Randir urgently, throwing dust over the flames as another shot narrowly missed his foot.

"We'd better split up," suggested the Tiger, then to Bella: "The Diva is injured, but you must not be complacent. Strike while she's weakened. There's nothing more dangerous than a humiliated animal – believe me."

He started to bound away. "Get her before she gets you," he growled amongst a volley of gunshots. "Goodbye."

"Goodbye," they called. The three of them watched in awe as the Tiger charged down the dusty track.

"He's out of range already," Randir observed. "That's one amazing tiger." There was a moment's silence. "An amazing tiger, indeed," Bella agreed as she peered through the dust kicked up in the Tiger's wake and considered whether she would ever again have the privilege to meet such a magnificent beast.

Another gunshot. This one ricocheted off a boulder behind Randir's head. They swung around to see where the poachers were firing from.

"We need to split up," Randir exclaimed. "If the Diva's behind this we're all in trouble."

"You and Shilpa take the horse and head back to Delhi," Bella ordered. "Meet us back at the Ambassador Hotel as soon as you can get there."

"What about you?" Shilpa pleaded.

"I've got this," replied Bella, raising her pendant.

"She's right," Randir reassured his sister. "I've seen some

of the things it can do."

Randir and Shilpa mounted their horses and galloped off down the track after the Tiger. Bella looked out to see shadowy figures in the moonlight starting to make their way down towards their smouldering fire.

"Come," ordered the Quetzal. "Let's fly."

As the two quetzals glided into the ravine, Pramrod, hiding with his boss behind rocks close to the poachers, turned to the Diva with his warning: "You've gone too far this time." The Diva gave him a wicked, reproachful look. "And that girl will be your undoing," he concluded with a wry grin. Diva Devaki knocked off his hat, grabbed the back of his head, and pulled him into her hypnotic gaze.

"No," Pramrod implored. "You promised. Not another one of your trances, I beg you!"

He tried to close his eyes, but she was pinning them open with her thumbs.

"There's something you must do," she started, her eyes rolling before Pramrod's dumbfounded gaze. "It concerns our little, bird-loving friend, Bella Balistica . . . "

CHAPTER EIGHTEEN

OFFICER SINGH

It was eleven o'clock at night and there were at least half a dozen police officers knocking on guestroom doors at the Ambassador Hotel, all of them with a photocopied picture of Bella Balistica in one hand and a notebook in the other. "Have you seen this girl?" "I'm sorry to disturb you, then." "You have . . . " "Where?" "At what time?" "Thanks for your assistance." "Yes we will let you know . . . " and so on.

"What are you going to tell your mum?" asked the Quetzal, as they looked down over the shimmering lights and the dots of moving traffic that marked their return to New Delhi. Bella was apprehensive. Her mum was going to be really angry with her and she had no idea what Bruce might do next.

"I'm going to tell her the truth," Bella decided. The Quetzal gave her a quizzical look.

"All except the parts about turning into a fantastical bird, tightrope-walking halfway across a rocky ravine and talking to a Bengal tiger," she conceded.

"What's left to tell?" asked the Quetzal sarcastically. Bella was confused. "It's true," she thought. "No one's ever going to believe me." For a while, neither of them spoke.

"I think it's best if we land somewhere in the garden," the Quetzal suggested, as they finally swooped down into Connaught Circus. "It won't look great if they see you climbing in through a first-floor window."

"Right," Bella agreed.

Just as Bella prepared for her final descent, the Quetzal bid her farewell.

"Until tomorrow," he said. "But don't forget to be on your guard. We've stirred up a cauldron of evil here, and it's not going to die down without a fight. Sweet dreams."

"Thanks for the reassuring thought," replied Bella with a frown. A good night's sleep seemed like a distant hope.

It was one of the hotel chefs looking out through the kitchen window who saw Bella suddenly pop out from the garden bushes.

"Hey, Ajay," he said to his assistant. "Isn't that the girl we saw charging through the kitchens last night? The one everyone's been talking about all day?" No sooner had Bella walked through the revolving doors than heads were turning.

"There she is!" shouted the desk clerk, attracting the attention of the police officer by the fountain.

Bella's eye was drawn to the officer's bright orange turban, which looked quite distinctive against his khaki uniform. The officer, who was busy interviewing guests in the lobby, stood up.

"Excuse me," he called, starting to walk towards her. But Bella didn't wait. She ran up the spiral staircase, barged through the fire doors and onto the first-floor corridor. When she got to room 101, she found the door ajar and her mum sitting on the bed, looking tired and distraught. By the look of her, Bella guessed that she hadn't got dressed properly all day, because she was still wearing her pyjama top underneath her cardigan.

"Hi, Mum," croaked Bella, feeling overcome with emotion as she entered the room. Her mum looked up.

"Bella, thank goodness you're safe!" she exclaimed, opening her arms. "I've been so . . . "

"Mum, I'm fine," Bella interrupted, running into her embrace. "Don't fret." But Annie was fretting. Playing out late in the street at home was one thing, but here, sneaking out of the hotel in a foreign country – that was too much. "She's up to something," Annie thought, "and I have every intention of finding out." They hugged for a full minute.

"Now, Bella," Annie started. "You're going to have to tell me what . . . " It was then that the policeman who'd seen Bella in the lobby finally caught up with her.

"Good evening," he greeted them as he stood in the doorway. Bella noticed for the first time that he had red epaulettes on his uniform. "My name in Gurmeet Singh," he went on. "I'm the senior officer assigned to this case. I have a few questions I'd like to ask the young lady, if I may." Annie gestured to him to enter. It was then that the inquisition started.

"Where have you been?" It was Annie who was the first to start firing the questions. "I was worried sick." "I called the police, the embassy . . . " "Have you any idea how much trouble you've caused?"

"I was being held captive by this woman called Diva Devaki," Bella blurted. Ignoring any doubts that she might have had over Bruce's complicity, she continued: "And your boyfriend is helping her!"

Bella saw at once how the accusation upset her mum and immediately felt guilty about what she'd said.

"Bella's upset because we told her this morning we might be getting married one day," Annie told the patient policeman as he nodded thoughtfully. "That's what started this whole running away thing. Bella's never accepted Bruce."

"And where is Mr. Bruce now?" asked Officer Singh gently. Annie looked embarrassed.

"I haven't seen him all day," she stuttered, openly worried. "When I woke up this morning, he was gone." Bella wasn't surprised. His cover had been blown wide open. "I've called everyone I can think of, but no one's seen him," she continued. "What a terrible day!"

It was almost midnight by the time Officer Singh had finished taking notes.

"I shall be down in the lobby writing up my report for a while," he told them. "If you think of anything else you need to tell me, ring down to reception."

Despite the circumstances, Bella liked Officer Singh. He was a calm, gentle man and a very good listener. What's more, he took her accusations seriously. As soon as he'd gone, Annie called up room service and ordered hot chocolate and sandwiches.

"You don't believe me when I say Bruce is caught up in all this, do you?" Bella accused her mum the second she hung up. Bella was fuming, tormenting herself with conflicting thoughts about Bruce and refusing to acknowledge why she had always been so hard on him. In the back of her mind was the niggling suspicion she was wrong about him.

"Don't think by deflecting all this onto Bruce you're going to get away with this crazy stunt without a telling-off," Annie warned her. "To think that you deliberately sneaked out of the hotel to go on this mad crusade without any regard for your own safety and my feelings really upsets me." She gave her daughter a long hard stare. "And you look filthy!" she exclaimed. Bella couldn't argue with that – she smelled like a dog on a hot summer's day. "I'm going to run you a bath," Annie told her, heading for the bathroom.

Annie was suffering too. Bruce's behaviour of late had been even more erratic than Bella's. She positively dreaded having the two of them back in the same room at the same time ever again. "I don't think I can cope with this for much longer," she thought as she closed the plug and turned on the tap.

Bella's anger about her mum's relationship continued to fester. "That's what love does, I suppose," she said to herself as she stepped into the bath through a cloud of foamy bubbles. Still, the nagging thought that perhaps Bruce wasn't as guilty as he appeared persisted. "Ah," she sighed, wriggling down until the warm water covered every inch of her body.

Bella loved being in the bath with her head underwater. Next to swinging in her hammock, it was the next best thing for blocking out the rest of the world. She loved how weird things sounded when her ears were full of water. It was a totally different way of tuning in to what was going on. Tonight, the light, crispy sound of crackling bubbles contrasted with the deep muted hum of the air-conditioning. But it was hard to relax. "The Diva must have seen me with the Tiger," Bella thought, kicking on the hot tap with her foot and starting a deafening rush of water. "She'll have Bruce and Pramrod working on some kind of counterattack for sure."

Amongst the cacophony of sound and her disparate thoughts, Bella heard a knocking on the door and presumed it was room service with their late-night supper. She thought nothing more about it and continued to try and second-guess the Diva's next move. Soon after turning off the tap, she became aware of voices coming from the bedroom.

"Who's mum talking to?" she thought, pulling herself up sharply and reaching for her pendant. She got out of the bath, threw on a hotel dressing gown and stepped out into the bedroom.

"Randir!" she cried. "Shilpa!"

Randir and Shilpa were sitting on the bed while her mum kneeled to clean their wounds with moist tissues from the first aid kit on the bed.

"Bella, I think these children must be your friends," Annie started. "Randir's been telling me about some of the things you were talking to Officer Singh about," she went on, pulling back to look Bella straight in the eye. "I can't believe Bruce knows anything about this."

Bella was so delighted to see her friends that she ran and gave them both a big hug. Annie called down to the lobby and asked for Officer Singh to return. Because she always spoke in Hindi when she was with them, Bella hadn't really considered that Randir and Shilpa might speak a little English. She was impressed.

With Randir and Shilpa using Hindi and broken English with Officer Singh, the three children made their accusations about the circus. It was grim stuff: the trade in child labour, the murder of animals for their skins. Annie found it devastating to listen to. It must have been four in the morning by the time the hotel staff had put extra beds up for Randir and Shilpa in Bella's room and they all settled down. Randir and Shilpa fell asleep almost immediately, but Bella took a while to drop off. She'd been reconsidering her attitude towards Bruce ever since she'd become aware of the Diva's powers.

"Maybe if the Diva can hypnotize people," she thought, "Bruce is simply under her spell." For the first time, she started to challenge her instinct to be so negative towards him. "Could it be I wanted to distrust him right from the start?" she wondered. She realized with some shame that when she thought of Bruce and focused on the pendant, it always felt warm. If, and for whatever reason, Bella had misjudged him, she felt that she needed to do something to help – but what? She became distracted by the sound of sobbing from her mum's bedroom. "Poor mum," thought Bella sadly. "It's all been a bit too much for her too." Then, although it still pained her to admit it: "I think she really loves Bruce."

Bella felt upset. She hadn't really considered before how lonely her mum might be sometimes. "Charlie's mum has Charlie's dad," she reflected. "And I can be difficult, sometimes." She tried to roll over and get some sleep. "I don't think I would have been nice to any of my mum's boyfriends," she admitted rather reluctantly to herself as she tossed and turned. "I think seeing my mum with Bruce made me feel jealous, like she was taking some of her love for me and sharing it out."

Full of all these emotions and thoughts, it was a miracle she slept at all.

CHAPTER NINETEEN

CARJACK

It was ten-thirty by the time Annie came in to wake them up. "I've got some news," she announced. Bella opened her eyes blearily. "I've had a phone call from the chief of police. He's delighted with all of you," she went on. Shilpa was wide-awake, but Bella and Randir were still coming round. Bella could tell by the bags under her mum's eyes that she too had had a troubled night's sleep. Shilpa stuck out a leg to give Randir a rousing kick. "He said they raided the circus last night after a number of children came to police stations with similar stories," Annie told them. "All the children have been released, and the circus has been closed down."

"But what's happened to Bruce and the Diva?" Bella asked cautiously, pulling herself up. Her mum looked down to the floor.

"There's no news of either," she replied gravely. "The police have a warrant out for their arrest, as well as that horrible man with the whip you were telling us about."

"Are you alright, Mum?" Bella asked softly. "About Bruce and everything?" Her mum pushed her glasses up over her forehead.

"Bella, I'm so, so sorry," she replied, almost under her breath. She came and sat on the edge of Bella's bed. "I guess we've only known Bruce a very short time, and he's obviously been using us. I had a call on my mobile from the credit card company this morning, and he's drawn more money out against my card in addition to all the cash I've given him." She was fighting hard to hold back the tears. "I'm so angry, Bella," she said. "I feel like I've been taken for a ride and I was the only one not to see it." Suddenly her mobile was ringing.

"Mum," Bella whispered. "I'm not sure if I was right about Bruce. I think he needs our help." But Annie didn't hear her.

They all got up and went down for breakfast. Annie told them that the phone call was from Bruce's charity back in London.

"They're sending someone out as soon as they can," she told the children, as they took their seats in the hotel restaurant. "They asked me if I could stick around at the centre until they can get a representative out here early next week."

"And?" asked Bella. All three of the children had their eyes set on Annie.

"I said 'OK'," Annie told them with a smile.

"Good," said Bella, reaching for her orange juice.

A few minutes later they were all wolfing down toast.

"What's this?" asked Randir, picking up a small red pot from the basket on the middle of the table.

"Jam," said Bella. "It's great on toast."

"But what we need to do today is to get things moving with your project," Annie reminded Bella. "Let's get these kids out and about on the streets of Delhi photographing images of their life. Showing the world what it means to be a street kid in India – or anywhere, at that!"

It felt like a relief to Bella and Annie that they could forget about their recent troubles for a while and focus on something constructive. Bella hadn't felt so inspired for days.

After breakfast they returned to their rooms to shower.

"I've called Mr. Kamat to say that we won't be in this morning," Annie told them. "But we really must make an effort to get there for the afternoon session."

"These towels are so soft," Shilpa called from the bathroom.

Randir and Shilpa loved the showers so much that Bella and her mum decided to leave them for a while and go down to the hotel shop. "I want to get them a present to say 'thank you' for helping my daughter," said Annie. She bought green shorts and a smart white T-shirt for Randir, and a beautiful mauve dress with hanging tassels embroidered into the neck and hem for Shilpa. Annie even bought them both some trainers as well as a new football for the children at the centre.

"Wow!" Randir exclaimed, as Annie handed him his present.

"It's beautiful!" cried Shilpa, holding her dress up and giving a twirl of joy.

"*Dhanyavaad*," they said.

"*Koyibathnahi*," Annie told them. Before they left, Bella gathered up all her digital cameras and decided to help herself to Bruce's laptop. "It belongs to the charity anyway," she told herself. Just as they were waiting for a taxi to take them out to the children's centre, two police officers in khaki uniforms arrived. The elder of the two was Gurmeet Singh, the officer who had interviewed them the night before. The other was much younger, fresh-faced and wearing a khaki beret. Randir and Shilpa were looking distinctly uneasy.

"It's fine," Bella reassured them. "They probably want to ask us a few more questions."

"Good morning," Officer Singh greeted them. "This is my colleague, Daruka." He gestured to his young subordinate. The two officers shook hands with all of them in turn.

"Good morning," Annie replied, turning to the worried-looking children.

"We've arranged, at your convenience, for a room swap to the fourth floor. There are no other guests up there at present so we can make it completely secure," Officer Singh continued.

"Now, perhaps I should have told you before," Annie began to tell Bella.

Bella was shocked by the seriousness of her mum's tone. "The chief inspector thinks that, given recent events, we should have two officers looking out for us wherever we go for the duration of our stay. At least until they've apprehended Devaki and her assistant."

Bella felt quite relieved and recalled the departing words of the Tiger. "You must not be complacent," he'd told them. "There's nothing more dangerous than an injured and humiliated animal." Like Bella, the Quetzal had been in little doubt that the Diva would try some sort of counterattack.

"Personally, if I thought we were in any real danger, Bella and I would be going home right now," Annie went on. "Bruce, I know, won't be any trouble, and if I do see him, I'm going to give him a piece of my mind! I've got every faith that the police here can both sort this mess out and keep us all perfectly safe. Now come on, there's work to be done."

"She's throwing herself into things to forget about feeling so let down by Bruce," Bella thought to herself. She decided that she was going to be on her best behaviour all day.

Officer Singh announced that he would be accompanying them to the centre, while Daruka would stay to guard their room. Bella watched as Daruka bowed graciously and wandered off into the hotel. "He's going to have a boring day," she thought.

With everything arranged, Officer Singh sat in the front passenger seat of the taxi and started chatting to the driver as they headed off. Bella and Randir listened avidly. It was about football. From what they could gather, there was an exhibition match tonight at the National Stadium with many of India's finest footballers playing for charity.

"It should be a great match," Randir predicted. "I'll probably watch it outside a TV shop I know. Do you want to come?" Officer Singh, overhearing their conversation, turned around.

"I can get you tickets," he said, addressing Annie and Bella. "But it will cost."

"Tickets for what?" asked Annie, brought back from her daydream.

Officer Singh told her.

"Oh, Mum, can we?" asked Bella imploringly.

"Forty American dollars a ticket," said the policeman. "But it all goes to charity."

"We'll see," said Annie, far too vaguely for Bella's liking. Bella didn't hold out much hope. She knew her mum only pretended to like football because she loved her.

As they approached the children's centre, they couldn't believe their eyes. There must have been two hundred children, some of them playing football, some juggling, others tightrope-walking or simply hanging around: all of them waiting for the centre to open for the afternoon.

"I think I'm going to be busy in the clinic," said Annie, a little overwhelmed. "How many can you take for your project, Bella?"

"I've got twelve digital cameras," Bella replied, mulling over the logistics. "If we share one between three – I could take thirty-six children. We should get some fantastic shots by tomorrow morning."

At the children's centre there was a crowd of happy children recently freed from the Diva's sweatshop waiting to thank them. While Bella tried to make her way through the crowd, Annie pulled Mr. Singh to one side and had a quiet word. She then spent the rest of the morning in the clinic attending to chafed ankles and sore hands. Bella, with Randir and Shilpa acting as her assistants, went through all the camera functions as well as all the key skills involved in taking a good photograph with her first group of eager students. She taught them how to frame shots, review and judge an image once it was taken, how to store it, delete the bad ones and so on. She spoke mainly in Hindi, but every now and then, when she thought her mum might be listening, she reverted to English or made her Hindi more broken.

"You amaze me, Bella," her mum told her when everyone stopped for afternoon tea. "You can make yourself understood anywhere."

After the break, Bella let every child in her group have a

short time to work with the cameras. Finally, she showed them how their shots looked on Bruce's laptop, so by the end of the session everyone had at least some idea of what to do.

Bella and her mum wanted Shilpa and Randir to come back with them to the hotel.

"Thank you," said Shilpa. "But we really want to take some photographs for the exhibition."

"Where will you sleep?" Bella asked, feeling guilty that she would be tucking herself up into a warm and cosy bed tonight.

"We'll be OK," said Randir. "We can always find somewhere safe for the night, even in the monsoon season."

But Bella and Annie were worried. It was difficult for both of them to accept that these children lived such hard lives, while they could always return to the luxury of the hotel. They arranged to meet the children back at the centre the next morning.

"When I think of all the families there are in the world that would love to adopt two such wonderful children," said Annie as she got into the taxi. "And here they are, living out on the streets!" Bella didn't know what to say. "Just because we know that street-kid culture exists throughout the world doesn't mean we should tuck away our concerns and accept it!" Annie concluded.

During the long ride back to the hotel it bucketed down with rain, making such an almighty din, it was impossible to talk without shouting.

"I hope the children are taking some photographs of this," said Annie. "It would be so dramatic."

Bella gazed out through the raindrops exploding onto her window to take in the chaos caused by so many pedestrians running for cover. Gutters were overflowing, and the pavements and roads were already fast-flowing rivers, awash with debris. Suddenly, the driver slammed on his brakes, thrusting them all forward.

"Get out of the way, you idiot!" yelled the driver as the taxi skidded to a halt. There was a loud thud. Bella shot a look at the figure sprawled on the bonnet. "He's staring right at me," she shivered. The man was wearing a long black raincoat draped over his hunched-up shoulders. In his right hand Bella could make out the glint of his gold-plated walking stick. "Pramrod!" she gasped. Seeing the Diva's clown without his makeup was unnerving, but his presence could mean only one thing. "Where's the Diva?" She looked out of the passenger window and saw the tall, dark figure making straight for her. "Lock the door!" urged a voice inside her head. "Quick!" She felt her pendant turn ice-cold and pushed down the lock. The Diva slammed the window with the palm of her hand in frustration and peered through, her eyes wild with rage.

"What's going on?" Annie blurted.

"Lock your doors!" ordered Officer Singh.

Bella threw herself across the backseat to lock her mum's door just as the Diva landed from her spectacular leap over the car.

"Carjack!" shouted the driver, as he thumped down the lock on his own door.

"Let's go!" ordered Officer Singh. The Diva was violently rattling the door handle on Annie's side of the car. Bella watched Pramrod throw her his walking stick. She pulled it back ready to smash through the glass, but the driver was quick. He revved up and skidded away, sending Pramrod crashing into the front windscreen and up over the roof.

"Ahhh!" Pramrod cried as yet again the dull thud of his impact against the taxi was felt by everyone.

Bella quickly turned to the rear window, but her view was blurred by the monsoon. Officer Singh called for backup.

"Nothing to worry about," he told them, turning back to reassure them. He could see that his passengers were extremely anxious. "It doesn't happen very often, but sometimes the carjack gangs can be big and well-organized. It's better not to try and take them on without support."

Annie had been in a number of tight situations in her life, both on her travels and in London. Only last year, someone had opened the passenger door of her car and stolen her handbag at traffic lights in Eltham.

"Are you alright, Bella?" she asked, putting her arm around Bella's shoulder. Bella reached for her pendant and snuggled up tight. She was scared. The incident did not bode well.

By the time they got back to the hotel it was four-thirty. Daruka, the young policeman guarding their room, stepped forward to greet them.

"I'm going to leave you now," Officer Singh told them. "But Daruka here will help you move all your things up to the fourth floor when you're ready and he'll stay right outside your door. I'll be back later this evening."

"Don't worry," Daruka reassured them. "We'll have Devaki and her gang all rounded up by the end of the week. You can be sure."

Bella and her mum were feeling rather frazzled after the incident.

"I've got a headache," said Annie, "Do you mind if I have a bit of a nap before we move our things?"

Bella didn't like siestas. There were so many things she wanted to talk to her mum about that she couldn't rest. As the rain had passed, she decided to go for a swim. Gathering her swimsuit and towel, she stepped quietly into the corridor and was surprised to find that Daruka was slouched out on the floor, fast asleep. "He's obviously bored out of his mind," she thought. "It must be hard having to stand around all day with nothing to do." She made her way down and got changed in one of the poolside locker rooms. For a glorious afternoon, the pool and patio area were unusually quiet.

Bella dropped her towel onto a sun lounger and dived straight in. The chlorine was more potent than she was used to, and when she came up to breathe her eyes were stinging. She tried to focus on the hedge that bordered the gardens and pool area to help her eyes adjust. As she did, she could have sworn she saw a pair of orange boots through the base of the rustling bush. "Pramrod!" she gulped. Bella frantically swam to the side and pulled herself out. She grabbed her towel and ran back to her room. Giving the sleeping Daruka a prod as she passed, she went straight in and locked the door. "Mum!" she shouted.

She darted across to the adjoining door and was distraught to find it locked. "Wake up!" she cried, banging it with her fists.

But there was no answer.

CHAPTER TWENTY

ANNIE'S BIG SURPRISE

Bella must have been bashing on the door for a whole minute before her mum finally opened it.

"Bella, what is it?" she asked sleepily. "I was out for the count."

"Why was the door locked?" Bella shouted, barging through.

"I didn't know that it was," Annie yawned, giving her arms a good stretch. "Perhaps the cleaners did it." Bella flopped down on the edge of the bed, relieved to find that her mum was OK.

"Daruka's sound asleep," said Bella. "Some protection he is!"

"Don't worry, Bella," said Annie kindly, coming to sit alongside her. "The man's been on his feet all day. I'm sure no harm can come to us here."

"Mum," Bella started tentatively. "I think I saw Pramrod in the hotel garden." Annie looked shocked.

"Bella, are you sure?" she replied quickly. "We should let Officer Singh know at once."

Annie rang Officer Singh, who took the matter extremely

seriously and radioed Daruka to search the grounds.

"I refuse to let this horrible business ruin our trip," said Annie, hanging up the phone. Bella was struck with how resolute she was. "Now we've decided that we're staying, I think we need to get on with things," she went on. "Officer Singh assures me that Diva Devaki and that horrible old clown will soon be in police custody. Until then, he's guaranteed our safety and round-the-clock protection." Like her mum, Bella had been shaken by the incident in the taxi but was equally as determined to carry on.

"We can't let our lives be ruled by fear," her mum concluded. Bella had heard her mum say this many times before when she heard people express their reservations about going into London because of their fears about terrorist attacks.

"I've got a big surprise," Annie told Bella, barely able to contain her enthusiasm. "I made arrangements with Officer Singh. After we've moved all our stuff up to our new room on the fourth floor, we're going to that charity football match you were all talking about earlier. He's going to leave the tickets at reception."

Bella felt an overwhelming rush of love for her mum. "Thanks, Mum!" she cried, thrusting herself into Annie's arms.

With the help of Officer Singh and Daruka, it didn't take long to move up to their much larger room on the fourth floor. Bella was delighted that the room had two double beds.

"There," sighed Annie as they entered for the first time. "Sharing a room will be much better."

Bella could not have agreed more.

When they were settled in, Bella switched the TV onto the sports channel to see if she could find any news about the

Under-21 International Tournament in London and was happy to see that Guatemala had beaten Denmark 2–1.

"Is that the tournament Charlie's dad was taking her to?" asked Annie. Bella nodded. She was still gutted she wasn't there, but it was exciting to think she was going to a football match in Delhi tonight with her mum.

After she'd showered and dressed, Bella sat on her mum's bed and waited for her to finish dressing. Making sure that her pendant was tucked safely away beneath her football shirt, she began to explore an idea that had been bugging her for the last few days.

"Mum," she started, tugging at her own football top, "how do we know that this wasn't made by poor, overworked children?" Annie looked concerned.

"I bought you that top from the official club website," she replied. "They wouldn't risk trading anything dodgy. It's at the markets where you have to be careful." Bella wasn't entirely reassured. Ted Briggs' shop in Greenwich wasn't a market stall. To all intents and purposes, it was a legitimate sports shop, and yet Bella knew for sure that he was importing goods made in the Diva's sweatshops. She wondered how long it would take the police in England to make the link between Diva Devaki and Ted Briggs. Annie had heard Bella mention Briggs in her statement to Officer Singh the other evening but until now had not passed comment.

"What will happen to Ted Briggs if he gets into trouble with the police again?" Bella asked tentatively.

"If he gets into trouble," Annie replied scornfully, "that man could worm his way out of hell, given enough time." She left it at that.

They met Daruka in the corridor outside their room and made their way down to reception.

"The concierge has a taxi already waiting, ma'am," said the desk clerk as he handed them their tickets and took their room keys. "Have an enjoyable evening."

The taxi wasn't able to drop them at the National Stadium because the traffic was so bad. Instead, they got out of the car about three blocks away and joined the endless stream of fans making their way towards the match on foot.

"Isn't it festive?" Annie smiled. "It feels like we're in a carnival." Bella agreed. There was such an array of colours in the crowd that it was impossible to determine the strip tonight's teams might be wearing. The spicy smells from the street-side food stalls were so tempting, Bella and Annie stopped to buy a couple of hot veggie samosas, while Daruka, only ever a few metres away, bought himself a glass of juice from a man crushing sugar cane through a mangle.

"I'm glad we're having some time alone together," said Annie, blowing onto her steaming samosa. "We need to remember that this is a holiday, as well."

Bella was happy with the sentiment but couldn't help but feel excited about seeing the photographs the street-children were taking tonight. "I want to make sure our next fundraising exhibition is the best ever," she told her mum. Annie bent down and gave her daughter a kiss on the forehead.

"I do love you, Bella," she told her.

"I know," replied Bella tunefully.

It took ages to queue up at the turnstiles and get in, but eventually they managed to find their seats on the second tier opposite the halfway line.

"What a great view," said Annie, as she fanned herself with her programme and admired the stadium. Daruka, anxious perhaps not to be in the way, decided not to take his seat but to stand with the security guards at the back where he could keep an eye on them. Bella almost forgot about him completely, as she read her programme and began to get into the pre-match warm-up. The team attacking from the right were wearing a yellow-and-white strip, while the others wore blue and black.

"There must be over twenty-five thousand people here," Annie conjectured. "Who are we going to support?"

"I don't care," Bella had to shout to be heard above the mayhem. "I'm just happy to be here."

Being an impartial observer really had its appeal for Bella, who relished each one of the five first-half goals. The pace of the match was frenetic, with all the players performing with the flare inspired by the friendly nature of the occasion. At halftime, a man in a suit came out into the middle of the pitch, surrounded by cameramen and photographers. He gave a short speech in Hindi over the public address system about the wrongs of child labour and the need to get all children into primary schools. Bella stayed for the speech while her mum went to the toilet. While she was gone, Bella found her eyes wandering around the crowd.

"Be on your guard," came the whispered warning in her head. She looked anxiously round for Daruka and found to her relief that he was standing right by her.

"Everything alright?" he asked.

"Everything's OK," she replied cautiously.

Upon her return, Bella's mum handed her a cola.

"I'm enjoying the match," Annie enthused. "What's the score?" Bella gave her mum a bewildered look.

"Three–two," she told her in despair. Her mum never remembered the score.

The second half was pretty much ruined for Bella, who spent as much time scouring the crowd for signs of the Diva and Pramrod as she did watching the match.

"Are you alright, Bella?" asked Annie, aware that Bella's attention was wandering.

"I'm fine," said Bella vaguely. "I was just checking on Daruka."

Daruka was now standing back in his position near the security guards. Occasionally, he would give Bella a reassuring smile and a wave before returning his attention to the excitement on the pitch. Despite Bella's close scrutiny of the crowd, she saw nothing that warranted her anxiety and the frostiness of the pendant. Eventually, her fears started to abate, and she began to get back into the match. "My mind must be playing tricks on me," she decided.

With only a minute of injury time left to play, and the yellow team winning by six goals to four, Daruka suggested that they made a quick getaway to beat the crowds. They were about to stand up and accompany him to the exit when Bella's eyes came to rest on the back of a woman with long, shiny, black hair sitting twenty or so rows below her. The woman was applying makeup while looking into her pocket mirror. Bella was suddenly aware how ice-cold her pendant was.

"It can't be," she shivered.

"What?" asked Daruka, recognizing at once the fear in

211

Bella's eyes.

Bella pointed to the woman in the black raincoat. Her heart started to race.

"What is it, darling?" asked Annie, taking Bella's hand. The final whistle blew, and the people in front immediately stood up and blocked their view.

"We had better make a quick getaway," Daruka suggested, unsure of what Bella had seen.

"You seem a bit nervous, Bella," said Annie as they wove a pathway up through the crowded stairway. "What is it?"

"I'm just feeling tired," replied Bella, trailing in Daruka's wake.

Once outside, it soon became clear they were not going to find a taxi.

"We'd better walk towards the city centre," Daruka advised. "As soon as I can flag down a police car, I'll get us a ride back to the hotel."

"It feels so humid," said Annie, wiping her brow. "I hope it isn't going to rain." But the monsoon was the least of Bella's worries. As her pendant again began to turn ice-cold, she started to scour the crowd for signs of trouble. Twice, she'd thought she caught glimpses of Pramrod's golden walking stick. "As if he'd still be carrying it while the police are looking for him," she told herself. But he was. As Bella was bundled round the corner by the flow of exiting fans, she saw him examining the scene from the roof of a black limousine, stick in hand. A dazzling flash of lightning ripped across the sky, quickly followed by a crack of thunder.

"Slow down!" Bella heard Daruka call some way back in the distance.

"Mum, I'm scared," Bella quivered, reaching for her pendant and turning to take her mum's hand. But whether by the Diva's mystical powers or simply because she was being swept along by the crowd, neither her mum nor Daruka were anywhere to be seen.

CHAPTER TWENTY-ONE

THE CHASE BEGINS

"Mum!" Bella shouted. "Mum, where are you?" It was a mistake.

"There she is!" cried Pramrod, jumping down from the limousine as the heavens opened. There was nothing to do but run.

"Bella, where are you?" Bella could hear her mum's voice through the monsoon but had no idea where it was coming from. Another bolt of lightning tore through the night sky. She jumped into the road and ran full-pelt towards the next junction. "I must take some quick turns," she thought. "Get him off my trail."

Taking a sharp right at the lights, she skidded and fell painfully onto her side. Covered in dirt, with the heavy raindrops pulverizing her body, she pulled herself up and took an immediate left up a street lined with tailors' and boot-makers' shops. She heard the screech of a car and glanced back in terror to see the Diva's limousine swerve into the road. The driver's door opened, and Pramrod jumped out. She looked around for help. There was no one.

Spotting a light inside a nearby shoe shop, Bella ran to the door and opened it. The shop bell rang as light spilled out onto the street. For sure, Pramrod would have seen her.

"Hello," she whispered. "Anyone here?"

She looked at the array of shoes, boots and sandals crammed onto the shelves. In the middle of the room was a bucket in which a rather forlorn-looking mop lay propped up against a stand of black boots. "Someone's cleaning up," Bella thought, realizing at once that it was far too late for customers. At the back of the shop was another door beyond which Bella could see a light and stairs going both up and down.

"Hello?" she called again, cautiously descending the stone steps to the basement.

She was almost at the bottom when the shop bell clanged, the door banged open, and the sound of bucketing rain burst into the shop. "He's found me!" Bella shuddered as her pendant turned ice-cold.

At the bottom of the steps was another open door, this one leading into a large, dimly lit room in which several upturned metal feet were scattered around amongst piles of discarded soles and leather off-cuts. The cold, damp atmosphere and the sense of imminent danger made her shiver. She looked around quickly. In the middle of the room was a large, medieval-looking machine that looked more like an instrument of torture than a device for stitching thick leather.

"What am I going to do?" she flustered.

The uneven thump of Pramrod's footsteps behind her increased her dread. From what she could tell, the only way out was the only way in, and that route was cut off. She reached for her pendant. "Maybe I could fly," she thought with trepidation. Then, remembering just how easily Pramrod's quick hand had caught her last time: "He'll be ready for that."

Desperately looking around for somewhere to hide, Bella's eyes fell upon a pile of large cardboard boxes at the far end of the room behind which she could see the grate of an open fireplace. With no time to come up with a better plan, she scrambled to the fireplace, dived into a pile of cold ash and pulled the heavy metal doors shut. As she peered through the small chink, she watched Pramrod take his final waddling step into the room.

"I know you're in here," he warned her, looking fiercely around the room. "And don't think I'm going to fall for any of your bird tricks." He slammed the door and bolted it shut.

"I could have done that!" Bella groaned, biting her lip in frustration at her own incompetence. She was aware that her teeth were chattering but couldn't stop them. She turned away and closed her eyes, trembling as she heard Pramrod kick a pathway through the off-cuts and boxes towards her.

It was the steady drip of rain that alerted Bella to an unforeseen escape route up the chimney. Before she could reach for her pendant and gather her forces Pramrod had yanked back the doors.

"Give me the pendant!" he yelled. Bella tried to push herself into the corner of the fireplace, but it was too late. He had her by the arm and was dragging her out into the open where he could best hold her down. Unable to get to her feet, Bella looked up into his craggy, joyless face as he tightened his grip on her arm.

"Don't hurt me!" she begged. There was a bang on the door.

"What's going on in there?" demanded an unfamiliar voice. "Open up at once, or I'm calling the police."

"It must be the cleaner," thought Bella, remembering the mop and bucket upstairs. She seized the moment and kicked Pramrod hard in the shins.

"Ow!" he yelled, releasing his grip as he fell. Bella rolled away, pulled herself up and made to run towards the door. But the Diva's henchman was too determined to be so easily rocked. He dived, grabbing Bella's ankles and brought her crashing down onto the floor, giving her right arm a nasty knock.

"Ouch!" The pain was agonizing. Before Bella had time to pull herself up, Pramrod had pinned her arms against her waist and was dragging her across the floor towards the terrifying machine. Bella battled with all her might to break free, but Pramrod soon had her exactly where he wanted. He kicked the on-switch with his foot, clutched the back of her neck with one hand and forced it down towards the pulverizing stabs of the giant needle.

"Open up!" came the muffled shout behind the basement door.

"Help!" called Bella, over the pounding din. "Kick the door in!" She struggled to gather her powers, but Pramrod's hairy-backed hand had too tight a grip on her neck.

"That's right," Pramrod jeered. "Cry for help. Your magic bird isn't going to get you out of this one."

The Quetzal had arranged to meet Bella tomorrow. Where he was now, she'd no idea.

"Let me go!" Bella croaked.

She somehow managed to jerk herself around to face Pramrod's mesmerized, hate-filled glare.

"How about a few stitches across your smug little face, then?" chuckled the clown, thrusting Bella's head ever closer to the pummelling spike.

Pramrod placed one hand on the machine and heaved Bella's head towards the needle. Just as Bella's resistance faltered, and her eyes started to blur, there was an enormous bang. Pramrod looked up. Bella seized the moment and rolled away, knocking his arm as she did.

"Aah!!!" Pramrod's almighty scream seemed to go on forever, as the needle punched into the back of his hand. He kicked wildly at the off-switch with his foot, catching it quite by chance as he grasped his bleeding hand and slumped to his knees. That was all the time Bella needed. Within a second she'd become her animal twin. But flying wasn't easy. Her right wing was so limp it caused her to spiral almost out of control. Through a flustered sequence of short flights, hops and jumps, she crashed into the open fireplace and manically flapped her way up the sooty chimney to freedom. It was a struggle that made her injury even worse. By the time she stumbled out onto the roof to feel the cool night air against her transformed body, she knew that she couldn't fly without first attending to her wounds. "At least it's not raining anymore," she thought as she slumped down with her pendant and held it against her injured arm. But her relief was short-lived. Looking up into the star-studded heavens, Bella saw the ill-omened silhouette made by a large flock of circling birds. "Crows," she shuddered, recognizing their piercing calls. She put the pendant away. Even if she wasn't injured, flying as a quetzal had its own dangers, and the presence of the crows could only mean one thing: the Diva was close by. She used the grip of her trainers to ease herself down to the gutter where she could see the rusty metal grating of an old fire escape. Putting her foot onto the first rung of the ladder she felt a pulsating vibration and peered down. To her horror, an all too familiar figure was scaling the stairs at speed, her long black hair flying wildly in the post-monsoon breeze.

CHAPTER TWENTY-TWO

FREE-RUNNING

Bella's options were distinctly limited. She couldn't fly, and the fire escape was the only way down.

"Quetzal!" she cried. "I need you now!"

"The power of your will is a remarkable force," a voice inside her head reminded her.

"What does that mean?" snapped Bella aloud. To anyone looking up from the street Bella must have looked suicidal.

"Take a running jump," replied the voice.

"You take a running jump!" Bella rebuffed, looking down to see the rapidly approaching figure of Diva Devaki.

"No," replied the voice in a measured tone. "You take a running jump." And then it occurred to Bella. She remembered those amazing urban free-runners she'd seen on TV the other night in London and how they'd run across the city skyline, jumping from building to building. "They didn't have the advantage of a powerful pendant," thought Bella. She shot a look at the rooftop opposite.

"It must be ten metres, at least," Bella estimated with a gulp. The jump she'd made onto the back of the bus with

Randir the other day had been half that, and without the deadly drop. The Diva's hands clutched the top rung of the ladder. Bella caught a frightening snapshot of her fierce hypnotic gaze. "Don't look into her eyes," she reprimanded herself as she bent her knees, put her pendant into her mouth and jumped.

As she stretched out her arms, Bella had the sense of herself gliding like one of those flying monkeys she'd once seen on the Discovery Channel as they leaped from tree to tree through the jungle. Bella crashed onto the gutter across the street and heard the Diva scream with frustration. But before Bella could clamber to safety, the gutter gave way. As she fell, she grasped the top of the wall and heard the crash of the falling debris hitting the pavement. Terrified for her life, she hung off the edge of the building. She tried to swing her foot up but was put off by a barrage of flying stones striking her back. She glanced down. Having pushed the meddling cleaner down to the floor in his escape, the Diva's henchman was now scurrying around the street in the search for ammunition. But the cleaner was not finished yet.

"Behind you!" called the Diva, warning Pramrod of his adversary's heroic return. With Pramrod distracted, Bella hauled herself up onto the roof and looked around for her next jump. "Keep going," she told herself. "And don't look back."

Like an accomplished urban free-runner, Bella ran and jumped from building to building, her confidence growing so rapidly, she was soon crossing tree-lined boulevards. Several mesmerized pedestrians had to blink twice at the sight of the unidentified creature with wildly kicking legs and flapping arms, as it arced high across the street above them.

"I think I've just seen a flying girl," said a young man to

his friend as they stood on the steps of one of Delhi's many mosques.

"Why didn't I ever try this before?" thought Bella, emancipated by the sense of freedom the jumps gave her. She could have run and jumped all night if she'd had the energy and wasn't so worried about finding her mum. Eventually, she came to rest on the final rooftop before a large expanse of land on which stood the impressive Red Fort. "I recognize this," she thought, recalling the pictures in her guidebook and the taxi ride from the airport the night they'd arrived. She paused to look back. The Diva was nowhere to be seen. "I've lost her," Bella sighed with relief.

She considered how deserted the place had become and was reminded just how late it was. "It must be close to midnight," she guessed. "Poor mum. As if she hasn't had enough to worry about already."

She jumped down onto the street and was almost run over by a speeding taxi. The taxi's horn blasted through the stillness. Looking around for someone to ask for directions to Connaught Circus, Bella noticed the figure of a tall man stretched out on a bench outside the old fort. She would have turned and walked away had she not seen his small silver earring and long, blond ponytail, which was now hanging in a puddle. She approached, cautiously.

"Bruce?"

Bella's inquisitive nature had the edge over her fear. As she got closer she saw an empty whisky bottle lying in the gutter beside him. "He's drunk," she thought. "And why isn't he with the Diva?" She gave him a gentle poke in the ribs. The smell of body odour and whisky emanating from his clammy body made her gag. "He hasn't washed or changed since that ostrich dumped him in a cart of manure," she thought, squirming at the sight of his dirty clothes. Although his eyes were closed, Bella was surprised that Bruce wasn't wearing his green-tinted glasses. She bent down as close to his face as she dared and considered trying to raise his eyelids with her thumb. Her nose was almost touching his when his eyes suddenly shot open. Bella jumped back. But Bruce was staring straight through her.

"Bruce?" Bella gasped. "It's me, Bella." His eyes were so devoid of soul, it was scary. He belched, filling the air with the stench of whisky as he rolled off the bench and landed with a splat in a large puddle.

"You're pathetic!" Bella told him, her anger starting to rise. "Do you know how much upset you've caused?" There was a loud squawk from above.

"Bella Balistica!"

She looked into the sky to see her dear friend the Quetzal. Not blessed with mystical powers himself, the tired old bird had been catching up on some well-earned sleep when a little babbler had woken him up with news of Bella's plight.

"*Harak, karadak, lopatos, almanos,*" called the Quetzal, plunging down towards her. These were the ancient Mayan words Bella had first read at the Great Temple of Tikal.

"Love, learn, forgive and move on," she repeated to herself. The Quetzal landed on the back of the bench.

"What are you waiting for?" he shrieked. "Use the pendant." Bella was baffled.

"Use the pendant to do what?" she shouted.

"To break the Diva's trance, of course," retorted the

frustrated bird. "There isn't much time."

"What do I do?" she pleaded with upturned hands.

"Give it here," sighed the Quetzal.

Bella slipped off her pendant and stuck the chain into the Quetzal's beak. The bossy bird hopped down to perch on Bruce's head where he let the pendant swing gently before Bruce's firmly shut eyes. He started to chant rhythmically through his closed beak while giving Bella a look of indignation.

"Oh, you want me to say something . . . " Bella suddenly realized.

"*Harak, karadak, lopatos, almanos,*" she chanted.

"Uuuhhh!" the Quetzal grunted like he was conversing with an idiot. It finally struck Bella that she needed to open Bruce's eyes. Pulling them open with her thumbs, she took hold of the pendant and started again.

"*Harak, karadak, lopatos, almanos,*" she repeated. "Love, learn, forgive and move on . . . "

"Tell him who he is, for goodness sake!" the Quetzal interjected. "That he's Bruce Anders. An Australian. In love with your mum and no longer under the Diva's spell." Bella told him most of these things and more, though the bit about her mum wasn't so easy to say.

"Now tell him that when you clap your hands everything's going to be as it was before," the Quetzal instructed. Then, as an aside to himself he mumbled: "It's like talking to a baby chick."

"I heard that!" Bella reprimanded him.

She did as she was told, clapped her hands and waited. At first Bruce just groaned and muttered a few inaudible words, but as Bella continued to talk to him about who he was and how he'd got here, she couldn't help but search his eyes for any sign of his animal twin. It didn't take long before the ghostly image of a proud, wild stallion, galloping majestically across a barren wilderness began to appear.

"So that's his animal twin!" she realized. "And all this time I thought he was nothing but a slimy eel."

Lost in their endeavours, neither Bella nor the Quetzal was aware of the danger touching down in the exact spot where Bella had landed only a few minutes before. The Diva, not to be outdone by Bella's free-running, had been hot on her trail since the off. Only the wide boulevards had saved Bella and given her the lead that she'd all but used up while stopping to help Bruce. Slipping surreptitiously through the puddles towards her prey, the Diva finally pounced.

"Watch out!" Bruce hollered, sitting bolt upright and pushing Bella away just in time.

Bella and the Quetzal were thrust violently away as the Diva landed on Bruce, forcing him back to the ground.

"So there you are!" she yelled at Bruce.

Bruce tried to push her away, but he was too drunk. The Diva wasn't interested in Bruce, though. She simply hissed venomously into his face and jumped up to confront Bella head-on.

"And as for you!" she spat with disgust.

The atmosphere was electric. Bella sensed that the Diva's revenge would be quick and brutal. The Quetzal tossed Bella her pendant.

"Look away," the Quetzal warned Bella, as he fluttered around her head. Bella's body was racing with adrenaline. She clipped the pendant on, knowing full well that she was too injured to fly.

In one fluid movement, the Diva bent her knees into a full crouch then pounced with terrifying zeal. But Bella was too quick; with her mind focused on the firm belief that she was descended from an invincible Mayan goddess, she jumped several metres into the air.

"Argh!" roared the Diva, turning round sharply to see Bella land behind her. "Give me the pendant now!" She stormed towards Bella, her fists clenched so tightly, her veins visibly swelled. "I'll never leave you in peace until you do."

Bella ran with all her might towards the fort. Jumping onto the rails designed to control the flow of daily visitors, she then propelled herself up onto the newly erected canopy above the main entrance. She used the momentum of this manoeuvre to leap nearly twenty metres, and made a desperate clutch for the battlements. It was an unbelievable stunt. Pulling herself up, she jumped again, this time onto one of the smaller turrets that adorned the impressive façade. To either side were more such turrets, flanked in a symmetrical design by two much taller towers. Bella looked down to see the Diva's spectacular jump onto the rails and then saw her spring up to reach the canopy. Bella knew she had to be quick. Bounding from turret to turret, she made her way to the left tower and began to scale its high, red-brick walls. "Ow!" she grimaced. Her right arm was as good as useless after Pramrod's assault. She was having to let it lie limp at her side while she took huge risks, snatching at tiny crevices in the brickwork with her left hand and using her legs to power herself up.

"Quetzal, where are you?" she called, scouring the night sky.

"No one's going to save you," hissed the Diva, scaling the tower with such agility and prowess she was now only metres away.

The sound of shouting in the streets alerted Bella to the fact that a small crowd of onlookers was already forming. She pulled herself up into the sanctuary of the small tower just in time to avoid the Diva's swiping hand.

"Arghhh!" snarled the Diva, rapidly regaining her composure, ready to strike again.

Bella quickly scanned the tower as the Diva hauled herself in. There was a wooden door in the far corner. She scampered to it – but it was locked. There was simply nowhere else left to run. She turned to face the Diva. They were both panting, their faces tensed and soaked with sweat.

"Give me the pendant," hissed the Diva, trying to catch Bella's eye.

"Never!" Bella yelped.

"Then prepare to die," shouted the Diva. Bella's pendant was so ice-cold that it was burning her skin.

"She's even more powerful than that three-headed, fire-breathing jaguar in the Temple of Tikal," Bella gulped, in no doubt that the Diva was a force more evil than anything she had ever faced before. The Diva pounced. Grabbing Bella by her tangled locks she dragged her to the edge of the tower.

"She's going to snatch the pendant and throw me over," Bella panicked, kicking at the Diva's shins with all her might. But the Diva's final assault was more calculated and brutal than Bella could ever have imagined. Where she pulled it from, Bella had no idea, but before she knew it the head of a spitting cobra was being thrust towards her face. "Don't swallow any venom!" warned a voice inside her head. As she tried to push her attacker away, Bella screwed her eyes tightly shut and hunched up her shoulders in a desperate attempt to protect her face and pendant. She was so obsessed with her defence that she didn't see the tall figure clambering up onto the tower ledge behind her attacker. With one almighty jerk, the Diva was torn away. Bella wiped the poison from her face.

"Bruce!" she gasped, looking up in total astonishment. Bella reached for her pendant – it was still there. She saw that Bruce had pulled the Diva back by her hair, grabbed the cobra and was now forcing it into her face.

"I can't see!" she wailed, as the disorientated cobra spat its deadly poison over her eyelids. The Diva, with one final surge, pulled herself free with immense force but losing her balance, tripped backwards.

"Aaaah!" cried Bella, unable to bring herself to look. Before Bella or Bruce could do anything to save her, she disappeared over the edge of the tower.

CHAPTER TWENTY-THREE

A HASTY RETREAT

The Quetzal came to land on the turret wall as the sound of sirens could be heard in the distance.

"Do you think she's dead?" Bella quivered, deciding whether or not to peer over the edge at the scene below.

"I'm not sure," Bruce panted, clearly still in shock and a little bemused by the appearance of the colourful bird. "She's an acrobat. They know how to fall . . . if you know what I mean." He dropped the exhausted cobra to the floor.

Bella recalled Bruce's story about the Diva diving from one of the turrets here into a basket full of spitting cobras.

"I'll go and see," the Quetzal chirped to Bella. "Get back to the hotel as quickly as you can, and I'll meet you there."

Watching the Quetzal plunge down to assess the Diva's fate, Bella looked into the gathering crowd.

"Are you alright?" she asked, turning to Bruce and for the first time noticing his warm blue eyes. Bruce didn't seem to know how to answer.

"I . . . I don't know what I feel," he stuttered. Bella assumed that he was still totally fazed by everything. "A bit confused, I guess," he acknowledged.

"So how long has the Diva had you cowering under her spell?" Bella asked. A look of realization slowly swept across his dumbfounded face.

"I haven't felt quite the same since my last trip here," Bruce stammered. "She came to visit me at the children's centre we run in Mumbai. She told me she was interested in offering some of the children scholarships to go and work at the circus. I paid her a visit there one day, and . . . " Bruce was really struggling to recall the details, but Bella had heard enough.

"You'd better come back to the hotel with me," she told him, grabbing his arm. "I think my mum needs to hear all this." Here Bella paused, trying to think of the right words.

"I think she loves you." It made her squirm inside to say such mushy stuff to a man. Bruce gave her an edgy smile as he leaned unsteadily against the wall. The sirens were getting louder.

"Come on, Bruce," Bella urged. "We've got to get out of here quickly. This place is going to be swarming with police before you know it."

There was only one door in the tower. Bella thrust her pendant into the lock, closed her eyes and willed the door to open. It did.

"How did you do that?" asked Bruce, astounded.

"Never mind," replied Bella as they ran down the windy stone steps that led out onto the battlements.

"Keep your head down," Bella ordered, leading Bruce round to the back of the fort. There, they unravelled one of the long chains linking a line of seventeenth-century canons and threw it over the wall.

"Are you up to this?" Bella asked Bruce.

"Get onto my back and hang on," he ordered, pulling himself up onto one of the gaps between the turrets.

Bruce's wits were returning to him with such speed he was now unrecognizable as the man Bella had seen sprawled out on the bench like a hapless drunk. Bella did as she was told and climbed onto Bruce's back, and they were soon beginning their descent. As soon as they reached the ground, Bruce led Bella out onto the street where a steady stream of pedestrians was heading towards the dramatic scene unfolding by the main entrance.

"It sounds as if the police and paramedics have arrived," said Bruce.

Bruce hailed a passing rickshaw and they got on board.

"The Ambassador Hotel," he told the driver. "And step on it, please."

As the rickshaw trundled through the narrow, winding streets, Bella flopped out in the back, utterly shattered by the evening's events.

"What about the clown?" she asked Bruce. "Is he bewitched too?" Several times over the last week Bella had replayed the revealing conversation she'd overheard between Pramrod and the Diva.

"I really don't know him," Bruce murmured. "But I guess if she could have put me in trance, then she could do it to anybody."

"Maybe he's a victim in all of this too," thought Bella. "Just like Bruce. At least with him my first impressions were right."

Bella couldn't stop thinking about her mum. Only yesterday she'd broken up with her boyfriend and tonight, yet again, she'd lost her troublesome daughter. "I'm not going to be any more nuisance," Bella tried to convince herself. "I'm going to do everything she asks and not answer back once." And then, as if thinking through the logistics of such a rash ambition: "At least, not for the rest of this holiday."

Bella and Bruce got out of the rickshaw before it pulled into the hotel.

"Find a way into the hotel garden and wait for us by the pool," Bella told Bruce while he paid the driver. "There's sure to be at least one policeman at the hotel on the lookout for you. You're a wanted man."

"OK, Bell," Bruce agreed, lowering his head in shame. "Only it feels so weird. I don't know what I'm going to say to Annie."

"Let's see what she says," replied Bella, beginning to walk away. "I won't be long. Oh . . . and one more thing . . . " she turned to face him. "Please don't call me Bell. I don't like it."

Putting away the childish instincts that had led her to hate Bruce just because he was with her mum, Bella ran towards the hotel. Officer Singh, observing her return quite by chance as he talked with one of his officers in the lobby, came out to greet her.

"You're back!" he exclaimed. "We've had half the police force in Delhi out looking for you."

"Not again," Bella squirmed to herself. "This is getting embarrassing."

"Where's my mum?" she asked him.

"Upstairs," he replied.

The lobby was full of guests and several policemen. It felt like déjà vu to Bella, who ran past all of them, ignoring their calls to stop as she jumped into the waiting lift and took a ride up to the fourth floor. An embarrassed-looking Daruka was standing guard outside her mum's room. "He must feel really bad about losing me on his shift," thought Bella as she passed by without comment.

"Mum," called Bella as she entered the room.

Annie was on the phone but hung up the second Bella walked in. In actual fact, because of the traffic problems around the stadium, Annie and Daruka had only got back an hour ago.

"Bella, where have you . . . " she started. Bella ran into her arms.

Cuddled up on the edge of the bed, it didn't take long for Bella and her mum to tell their stories. Bella of course cut straight to the bit where, making her way back home, she'd come across Bruce. She told her how heroic and brave Bruce had been in protecting her from Diva Devaki. Given her mum's distress, Bella thought it best to adapt the details of their dramatic climb up to the highest reaches of the Red Fort and replaced them with a much more down-to-earth chase around the streets.

"And now Bruce is waiting for you in the hotel garden by the pool," Bella blurted. "You've got to go and hear his side of the story." Annie went quiet for a moment. "Please," said Bella quietly.

Bella wasn't sure if her mum was ever going to answer. She could tell by her furrowed brow and angry eyes that her head was in turmoil.

"Now you're not going off anywhere, are you, Bella?" Annie asked sternly.

"I'm staying right here," replied Bella.

CHAPTER TWENTY-FOUR

THE BEGINNING
OF THE END

Bella wasn't surprised to find the Quetzal waiting for her on her bedroom windowsill. She let him in.

"Well . . . ?" she enquired, anxious for news.

"She's dead," the Quetzal announced as he landed in the fruit bowl. "And good riddance to her, that's what I say." He started to preen his feathers. Bella felt a quick shiver shoot through her body. She'd never known anyone who'd died before.

"No one deserves to die in such a horrible way," she replied reproachfully. The Quetzal stuck the tip of his right wing into his mouth in a gesture that implied Bella's sympathies were making him feel sick.

"Oh, stop it!" said Bella, dismissing his action with a flick of her hand. "I know you're a big softy at heart."

"So, another mission finally accomplished," proclaimed the Quetzal, jumping onto an orange and performing a quick jig. Bella was at last holding the pendant to her injured arm and enjoying its warm, therapeutic tingles.

"Can I relax now?" she sighed, flopping down onto a

chair. "Things always seem to happen when you're around."

"Exciting, isn't it?" chirped the Quetzal, pecking into an orange and giving Bella an eyeful of juice. "Oh, and you should be pleased to know that the Tiger found his mate and children and is thoroughly enjoying his retirement," he told Bella as she squinted through stinging eyes. "He's a grandfather, no less." Bella felt relieved to hear that the Tiger had found his way to freedom.

"He sends his regards," said the Quetzal.

"And what about all those poor animals held in the Diva's den?" asked Bella.

"They've been taken into care," said the Quetzal. "Some will go to zoos, but those that can cope will get released back into the wild."

Bella felt bad for the animals going to zoos but still, it was better than being skinned or stuffed.

"Now you'd better fill me in on what's been going on," said the Quetzal.

Bella told the Quetzal about events prior to their meeting at the Red Fort.

"Well done," he told Bella when she'd finished.

"Well done?" Bella mimicked.

"Well, you can't expect me to hold your hand through every little problem," retorted the bird. "You have powers beyond your wildest imagination. You just don't bother to explore them." Bella picked up the orange, intending to squeeze it all over him, but was distracted by the call from next door: "Bella, I'm back."

"Coming," Bella shouted, tossing the orange onto the bed.

"When will I see you again?" asked Bella, as she made a

move for the adjoining door.

"I'll come and visit you in London soon," the Quetzal promised. "Oh, and by the way, what happened to Pramrod?" Bella shrugged her shoulders. The question put her on edge.

Annie appeared quite calm upon her return from the garden.

"So?" asked Bella, as she sat herself down on the bed next to her. "What happened?"

"We talked about many things," Annie started. "Bruce feels that he should go back to Australia for a while. He needs to think through what's happened and decide where he goes from here."

"But is he still your boyfriend?" asked Bella, desperate for her mum to cut to the chase. "He's really OK when he's not in some weird trance."

Annie laughed. "Bella, you are unpredictable. You've spent the entire time we've been together being horrible about him and telling me how much you hate him."

Bella looked uncomfortable. "I think I was jealous," she blushed. "I don't think I was ready for you to have a boyfriend. It kind of freaked me out a bit." She started fidgeting with her scrunchie.

"I know, darling," said Annie kindly, putting her arm around Bella's shoulder. "He said he wanted us to come to Australia to be with him."

"What did you say?" asked Bella cautiously.

"I told him that you and I were very happy with our life in London." Bella felt a wave of relief sweep over her.

"We are, aren't we, Mum?" she smiled, giving her mum a really big hug. It had gone two in the morning before Bella and her mum fell asleep together on the bed.

The next morning, Bella woke up shivering and went to close the window. Looking out, she was distracted by two men on long ladders tearing down the poster advertising the Diva's TV stunt. It was disconcerting, but amongst all the flapping strips of torn paper, it was still possible to make out the Diva's dark, penetrating eyes that even now gave Bella the shivers.

"What shall we do after breakfast?" Annie yawned, as she looked up from the bed. "We could always pack our bags and go home."

"But we need to see the children's photos!" replied Bella as she closed the window. "We can't go. And anyway, you promised you'd take me sightseeing." Annie smiled.

"I hoped you might say something like that," she said.

With Officer Singh and Daruka as discreet companions, the last eight days of the holiday passed quite peacefully. Mornings and early afternoons were spent working on the photography project at the children's centre, while the late afternoons were usually taken up with sightseeing: visiting markets and temples, exploring the bustling alleys, shopping for trinkets and presents to take home, as well as hanging out around the hotel swimming pool.

Mr. and Mrs. Kamat had been devastated about the whole murky business with the children and the circus.

"We reported Shilpa and Randir missing," Mr. Kamat told them the very next time they saw them after the whole operation was exposed in the papers. "If we'd had any idea what was going on, we'd have gone straight to the police." The Kamats had wanted to resign, but the charity would not hear a word of it.

"You're doing a great job," Annie had reassured them. And they were.

It turned out that Randir and Shilpa and some of the other children were excellent photographers. "If you find the idea satisfactory, this photography project is one we would want to continue," Mr. Kamat told Bella and Annie when they viewed the outstanding work the children were producing.

"The cameras are yours," Bella told him.

"Many thanks. We will use email to keep you updated with some of the best work," Mr. Kamat replied.

Annie and Bella took Randir and Shilpa to Agra to see the Taj Mahal, and there were several sightseeing tours of Delhi with Randir and Shilpa acting as guides. On the final Friday, Annie took Bella and a small group of children from the centre to show some of their photos on a large computer screen at the National Gallery of Modern Art in New Delhi. Encouragingly, the event was well-attended, with professional photographers and journalists showing up along with the public.

"Now if we can get the same level of interest at home, it's sure to boost our publicity and fundraising," said Annie. Bella was determined that she was going to help make the exhibition as thought-provoking as she could.

And so it came: the last day of the holiday. It was Saturday, so the children's centre was closed. Bella and her mum were booked onto the evening flight and so they decided to spend the day relaxing around the pool with Randir and Shilpa. At lunchtime they took their young friends to eat in the bar where they could listen to a man playing the grand piano and gaze in wonder at the fabulous chandeliers.

"We can pretend we're kings and queens," said Bella cheekily, picking up the posh silverware and stabbing the table.

"Bella, stop that!" snapped her mum playfully. "Kings and queens have good table manners." She gave Bella a big smile.

After lunch, as they were walking through the bar, Randir noticed that there was some football on the TV.

"That's Guatemala playing," Bella declared, recognizing the blue-and-white strip. "It must be from the Under-21 International Tournament in London."

Bella, Shilpa and Randir spent the next hours in the bar following Guatemala's 4–0 thrashing of Finland, while Annie went upstairs to pack. After the game, the children were just about to forego the post-match analysis from the studio experts when Bella noticed a tall man with the long black hair, wearing the blue-and-white tracksuit of the Guatemalan coaches. Frustratingly, the sound was on mute, so she couldn't hear what he had to say – but something about him was strikingly familiar.

Just before four, Mr. and Mrs. Kamat came by to wish Bella and her mum a safe journey home. It had been arranged that Randir and Shilpa would take over the photography project and teach there three mornings a week.

Bella found saying goodbye to Randir and Shilpa hard. She wanted to think that they lived up the road like Charlie did.

"Keep sending those photographs through on email," she told them, as she gave them both a farewell embrace. "We're going to arrange for an exhibition in London. That way, so many more people will get to hear about the great things you're doing at the children's centre."

"You can count on it," replied Randir, pulling back with a beaming smile.

"For sure," said Shilpa.

After Mr. and Mrs. Kamat left with the children, Bella and her mum collected their bags. They met Officer Singh and Daruka in the lobby.

"You've done an excellent job of taking care of us," Annie told them.

"It was our pleasure, ma'am," Officer Singh replied, offering her his hand to shake.

"Did you ever find out what happened to the Diva's assistant?" Annie asked. "The one with the limp?"

Bella caught the look that passed between the two policemen.

A cold shiver trickled down her spine.

CHAPTER TWENTY-FIVE

DANGER LURKS

Luckily, Annie's replacement credit card arrived in time to pay the hotel bill.

Officer Singh and Daruka decided that they would accompany them to the airport. "With Pramrod still at large, we're not taking any chances," Officer Singh told them as he helped them into the taxi.

At the airport, Bella looked up at the billboard that only two weeks ago had displayed Diva Devaki's advert. Bella recalled how hypnotically beautiful the Diva had looked, stretched out across a white leather couch. Today's poster was advertising a brand of chutney.

"You look sad," her mum commented as they made their way through the departure lounge. "What are you thinking about?"

"I was only thinking how some people who seem to have everything end up doing such awful things," she replied quietly.

By the time they were in the departure lounge there was less than an hour before their flight was due to depart.

"Can I go and send Charlie an email?" Bella asked when she saw an Internet café. Bella had meant to email before, but somehow she hadn't had the time or the opportunity.

Bella dropped her backpack at the foot of her chair and logged onto her email account. She wanted to know all about the Under-21 tournament Charlie had been to see and wondered if she'd managed to watch any Guatemalan matches. She was delighted to find two emails in her inbox from Charlie. Bella quickly clicked on to the one entitled: "Guatemala is great!"

Reading Charlie's first email, Bella was reminded of the fact that, according to the official website, the Guatemalan team was scheduled to return home tomorrow. She had no idea of the time of the flight or which airport they were departing from, but she couldn't help but hope that she might at least get to see them at Heathrow. When she finally got round to reading Charlie's second email she found the title "You'll Never Believe It" quite apt.

Dear Bella,
You'll never believe it, but Ted Briggs is in BIG TROUBLE! He was even on the TV news. They say that he's mixed up in some scandal involving footballs from India or something . . .

Surprisingly, all Bella felt upon hearing this news was how hard it was going to be for Eugene and his mum. She typed Charlie a quick reply, slipped her backpack over her shoulder and went to join her mum to do some last-minute shopping.

There were yellow cones outside the duty-free shop to show that the floor on that part of the concourse had recently been cleaned. Bella and her mum had to walk around the cones and an abandoned cleaning trolley to get into the shop. If she'd have looked a little more closely, Bella might have noticed the golden cane tucked in the basket underneath with the dustpan and brushes, alerting her to the imminent danger.

Bella hated crowded shops. She'd already bought Charlie a pair of Taj Mahal earrings and really wasn't that bothered about doing any more shopping. As they trawled up and down the aisles, a dour-faced man in green overalls was limping ever closer towards them. What made this man look so unusual was not so much his ill-fitting uniform or the black bin liner he clutched to his chest, but the jaded orange winkle-pickers poking out from underneath. As Annie and Bella stopped to admire a range of sun-hats, Bella rested her bag on the floor. Seizing his chance, the man carefully undid the zip with his bandaged hand and slipped in his wicked surprise.

"I think I'll get one of those," announced Annie, reaching up for a blue-and-white floppy hat. As she did so, the man with the empty bin liner was already hobbling away up the aisle with a dazed grin on his face. Having timed his deadly manoeuvre to perfection, it was as if he were now gliding through some rudderless trance. Failing to notice the yellow cones he'd placed to alert travellers to the slippery floor, he fell and cracked his head. By the time Bella and Annie left the shop, it was impossible to see the man for the crowd of concerned passengers around him. As the man came out of his trance, the first inklings of what he'd done slowly began to dawn.

"I must warn her," he slurred, staggering to his feet. It seemed the Diva's trances were well woven to keep you locked into your task but soon fell away when it was done.

Annie and Bella were about to show their boarding cards and step into the final jetway that led to the plane when they were distracted by a loud commotion in the corridor behind them. It wasn't clear what was going on, but a scrum of security guards appeared to be wrestling an unwelcome intruder onto the ground.

"Wait! I've done a terrible, terrible thing." The man was shouting at the top of his lungs, but his plea was too muffled for Bella to recognize his deep gritty tone.

"Hurry along there," ushered the flight attendant by the door. Bella wondered what this "terrible, terrible thing" the stranger was referring to might be, never for a moment considering that his guilt-ridden admission was aimed directly at her.

The outward journey to India had been difficult because of the puzzling incident with her flyaway pendant and Bruce's cryptic phone call to the Diva, but usually Bella loved flying. She couldn't wait to get on board and start to play around with the radio and TV controls. But by the time they'd taken their seats and Bella had tucked her backpack safely away in the overhead compartment, she was feeing tired. Despite trying her best to fight off her fatigue, she slept right through the evening meal, woke to watch a bit of TV and then dozed off again, blissfully unaware of the danger lurking in her bag.

CHAPTER TWENTY-SIX

BELLA'S REVELATION

Despite flying for ten hours, by the time they landed at Heathrow, the local time was still only a little after midnight on Sunday morning. In a bleary-eyed stupor, Bella and her mum trudged through the tedious sequence of passport control, baggage reclaim and customs before stepping out into the arrivals terminal a little after one.

"Look out for the Guatemalan football team," Bella told her mum excitedly.

"Don't get your hopes up, Bella," replied Annie. As they made their way across the sparsely populated concourse with their luggage, Bella was speculating why her backpack was feeling so uncomfortable and was considering having a look inside. They had just stepped out of the air-conditioned terminal into the humid night air in the hope of finding a taxi when she felt her pendant turn ice-cold.

"Be on your guard!" cautioned a voice inside her head.

Bella was certain something momentous was about to happen. Something she'd been waiting for her whole life. She looked up and saw a bus from which a large number of men in identical grey suits and red ties were disembarking.

"I don't think that's the Guatemalan team," Annie observed. For a second, Bella was deflated. Then, confused by a blue-and-white blur further up the road, she squinted and realized that there was another bus dropping off passengers directly behind it. Her pendant was so cold it hurt.

"What's wrong now, Bella?" asked her mum cautiously. Bella dropped her suitcase and ran. "Bella!" cried Annie. "Where are you going?"

As she barged her way through the small crowd of men in suits she sensed that something in her backpack was moving. If she hadn't been in such a rush, she might have stopped.

When she got to the second bus, all but a handful of the men in blue-and-white tracksuits had made their way through to the departures terminal. The man she was looking for was nowhere to be seen. She ran with all her might, following the signs for check-in, where she found a few stragglers still in line for the flight to Guatemala City. "He's not there either," she realized, as her mum burst into the terminal building. "He's already gone through customs."

"Bella!" exclaimed Annie.

But Bella was so blinkered by her cause she was again running, this time towards the glass doors leading to the departure lounge. As she ran past the man waiting to check passports an alarm went off. Ahead of her she could see the solitary figure of a tall man with long, dark hair, as he passed through the security screening devices leading to the departure lounge.

"Father!" she cried.

Bella had no idea she was going to blurt out such a thing.

The man turned, his face exploding with joy.

"Stop her!" came the voices from behind.

Bella could feel the heavy clomps of boots echoing all around her. She ran towards the man who was now staring directly at her, his eyes scorched with fear. As he pushed past the security guard who tried to stop his return through the electronic scanner, Bella heard one of his colleagues shout from behind.

"Eduardo!"

A voice inside Bella's head cried: "It's him!" She was exuberant.

"Danger!" warned her inner voice. "Look behind you."

For a few seconds everything seemed to pass in slow motion. As the man she believed to be her long-lost father ran towards her, his hair flowing wildly all around him, Bella caught the ferocious look in his dark eyes and was suddenly frozen with terror.

"There's something wrong," she shuddered. He was literally only metres away. Pouncing towards her, his fingers clawed, his mouth wide open, Bella glimpsed the sliver braids of his pendant as the beast within him let out an almighty roar and knocked her to the ground with brutal force.

"Jaguar!" she heard someone cry.

"Snake!" yelled another.

Suddenly, the action was zooming. Skidding across the floor, she glanced over her shoulder and saw a huge, spotted creature, his shiny fur pulsating to the rhythm of his fast-beating heart.

"Jaguar?" she trembled. "But where's my fa– ?"

And then she stopped. The jaguar had its front paws tightly

clutched around the neck of a massive king cobra. The snake was spitting venom into his face, but the jaguar was refusing to let go.

"Check your line of fire," shouted a red-faced policeman to his colleague.

Bella's eyes darted to the two armed police officers taking aim at the wild cat while another two were running towards her. She leaped without fear towards the Jaguar, stopping only metres before it and turning to face the men with rifles.

"Don't shoot!" she begged them.

"Hold your fire!" ordered the red-faced policeman, seeing that Bella was dangerously close to the target, then: "Move away, miss, you're going to get hurt." But Bella would not retreat. Every instinct in her body told her to defend the animal, despite its apparent attack. The alarms set off by her breach of airport security were still ringing, but alongside this was a cacophony of distorted walkie-talkie outbursts from an army of security men, appearing as if out of nowhere to hold back the gathering crowd.

"This is a security announcement," came the amplified voice reverberating around the airport. "Would all passengers kindly leave the terminal building. I repeat, would all passengers . . . " Bella heard the last hiss of the cobra as the Jaguar ripped off its head. It was then that she realized that her backpack was hanging open. Dropping it from her shoulder she saw at a glance, from the black and yellow scales that covered everything inside, that the snake had been in her bag.

"He saved my life!" Bella gasped, looking up at the Jaguar. With a terrifying growl, the Jaguar pounced back over the security barrier and into the departure lounge. Seeing several policemen heading towards her, Bella was about to chase after the Jaguar when she noticed a glistening pendant and chain lying on the concourse. Even at a glance, she had no doubt that the jewelled figure at the centre was that of a magnificent jaguar. She dashed across, scooped it up and chased after the fleeing beast.

"Run, Bella, run," bawled the Jaguar.

"But, Father!" Bella wailed.

"Use your powers to escape," growled the Jaguar, "but whatever you do, don't give yourself away!" He disappeared up the long corridor that led to the boarding gates. "He's trapped," Bella blubbered, remembering how she too had lost her pendant to the Diva's henchman and got stuck in her animal form. Wiping her eyes, she sprinted towards the toilets with her father's pendant grasped firmly between her teeth. Bursting through the door, she instantly turned herself into her animal twin and just managed to squeeze through the air vent in time.

Flying above the main terminal building Bella could see that a crowd was gathering. "It won't be long before the TV crews get here," she thought.

Concerned for her father, she swooped down to a window ledge and looked on helplessly as two armed policemen made ready to fire at the Jaguar curled up in the corner of the room. "No!" went the scream inside her head as she pecked at the window so hard she thought her beak was going to break. It was then that she saw two red-winged darts fly from the barrels of the guns, hitting the Jaguar's side. As Bella watched the Jaguar fall, first to his knees then, with an awkward flop, onto his side, she felt as if her heart was going to crack with pain. So numb she could hardly move, she followed the arrival of two officers in green jackets as they edged slowly towards the sedated beast. She trembled as they tentatively reached for the Jaguar's head and put a muzzle over his jaws. The men then tied his front legs and back legs together before rolling him onto a large stretcher. Minutes later, eight men were lifting the Jaguar up onto their shoulders. All of them looked as if the exertion was going to break their backs. Seeing that they were heading back up the corridor towards the departure lounge, Bella quickly flew around to the front of the building, coming down to land in a sheltered spot by the entrance to the tube station. Here she transformed herself back into her human form, slipped her father's pendant into her jeans and ran back to the terminal.

Outside the main doors she fought her way through the crowd.

"Mum!" she called. "It's me, Bella! Where are you?" There were policemen standing by the automatic doors, keeping people out, but Bella could still see her mum inside talking to an officer. She ran to a phone box, dug around in her pocket for the right change and dialled her mum's mobile number. It rang for so long, Bella feared it was switched off, but her mum picked up just before the call diverted to voice mail.

"Mum, I'm outside."

Before Bella knew it, her mum was sprinting towards her. They ran into each other's arms.

"Bella, you have to stop doing this! I've had it!" said Annie, exasperated.

"It was my father," Bella sobbed. But Annie couldn't make out what she was saying through the din. Just then, the loud incessant horn of a large police van, making its way through the crowd, caused them both to turn.

"Bella, I think they killed the jaguar," said Annie, wiping her eyes. "I know you were trying to save him but . . . " Clutching hold of her mum's hand, Bella dragged her through the crowd to get a closer look. As the doors opened, Bella got a clear look at the Jaguar's face. Throwing back her head she filled her lungs and howled.

"Father!"

All around her people were slamming their hands up over their ears as they turned towards Bella in disbelief. But Bella's eyes were fixed firmly on the Jaguar. His eyes opened only for a fraction of a second – but it was enough.

"He's alive!" cried Bella, tears running down her face as she clutched her precious pendant with joy.

CHAPTER TWENTY-SEVEN

A PROPHETIC DREAM

Bella wanted to get in a taxi and follow the van transporting the Jaguar, but Annie was having none of it.

"We need to go home and get some sleep," she told Bella, putting her foot down. "First thing in the morning, we'll make some phone calls and find out how the poor thing is." Bella screwed up her face in protest but knew that there was no arguing. She had every intention of transforming herself as soon as she could and flying after him with his pendant.

They took a black cab all the way home. It was almost four o'clock in the morning when Annie put the key into the door of 14 Birdcage Crescent. The cat, who had become quite used to Mrs. Stevens popping around twice a day to feed her, squealed with familiar dread at the sight of Bella and darted into the living room. To the moggy's distress, Bella wasn't far behind, not because she wanted to catch her but because she was so desperate to switch on the TV. As she expected, News 24 was covering the story. Bella sat before the TV and avidly watched the whole report, searching without success for her image in the crowd and grimacing at the footage of the sedated Jaguar being stretchered into the van.

"Now can we get some sleep?" Annie begged after Bella had sat through the whole report twice. This time Bella didn't object, as she too was dead beat. While her mum was using the bathroom she quickly climbed up into the attic, lifted up the floorboards and dug out her jewellery box. "Father, I'm coming to help you," she whispered, opening the secret compartment and giving her father's pendant a kiss before putting it safely away with her own. She then went to her room and fell into bed.

As soon as she awoke the next morning, Bella rushed to the TV, hoping for reports on the Jaguar's whereabouts. She didn't have to wait long. The story was headline news.

"In the early hours of this morning, a wild and ferocious jaguar was caught and sedated at Heathrow Airport," the presenter announced. "While no official documentation about the beast has yet been produced by the authorities, early reports suggest that the animal may have been illegally imported from Guatemala by a private collector. The jaguar, who has been nicknamed 'Eduardo', is now being examined at London Zoo."

"Mum!" Bella called up the stairs. "I want to go to the zoo."

"No way!" Annie groaned, rolling over in her bed. "I'm having a lie-in."

By the time Bella had brought her mum a cup of tea in an attempt to chivvy her out of bed, the unthinkable had happened. Turning on her mum's radio alarm clock, they listened in astonishment to the news that somehow, less than an hour ago, Eduardo the Jaguar had escaped from his cage. Bella sat by the TV for the morning while her mum unpacked and started the washing.

"I hope you're not going to sit there all day without getting showered and dressed," she said to Bella. "We've got work to do."

After lunch, Bella finally got into the shower but was never out of earshot of the radio. It frustrated her that no one could find any explanation of how the Jaguar had both escaped his cage and eluded the zoo's tight security. She learned that police helicopters were now combing the city, while the public was being advised to be on a state of high alert. Still, there were no reported sightings of him.

"It's a mystery," said Annie, as she threw a big basket of tumbled-dried clothes onto Bella's bed. Bella was getting dressed and had no doubt where the beast would be heading. "He needs his pendant," she thought, shaking with anticipation. She left folding the clothes to head straight for the attic to check on her father's pendant and found it exactly where she had left it. While Bella was there, Charlie phoned.

"Bella," Annie shouted up the stairs. "I've told Charlie she can come round and see you as soon as you've finished putting away all your holiday clothes." Bella knew that this was a bluff to get her to hurry up and that Charlie would already be on her way round, but nevertheless she hurriedly went to her room and crushed all her clothes into her drawers and wardrobe. As she expected, Charlie was soon knocking on the front door.

Bella found it hard to keep secrets from a good friend like Charlie. She considered why it was so much easier to share her mystical powers with children in other countries. "I guess it's because I'm so far away from home no one's ever going to tease me and make me feel like a freak," she decided. "Or maybe the children there understand those kind of things more." In truth, Bella doubted both these reasons but had promised the Quetzal that she would never purposely reveal her secret powers to anyone. So that was the end of it. At least for now.

Charlie was so fascinated by the story of Bruce stealing all Annie's credit cards that she was hardly interested in anything else, which was just as well, because Bella wanted to hear all about the Under-21 tournament and get the latest gossip on Ted Briggs.

"All I know," said Charlie, "is that he's out on police bail."

Despite not being able to share everything with her best friend, Bella did tell her all about Shilpa and Randir and how they'd all worked together to expose the sweatshops run by Diva Devaki.

"Bella, you're always falling into adventures," Charlie marvelled with admiration. "I wish I could be more like you."

That night, Bella transformed herself into her animal twin and flew all over London carrying her father's pendant and searching for signs of the missing Jaguar. Finding nothing, she returned home completely dispirited. This sequence of events went on right through to the end of August and into early September. During these weeks, Bella and her mum put a great deal of time into preparing photographs for an exhibition funded by the charity Bruce had once worked for. There was no news on the Jaguar, although there had been several reported sightings of him all over the country. "It doesn't make any sense," Bella would complain. "He can't be in the north of Scotland and the south of England on the same day."

Bella guessed that many of the calls to police were from cranks, designed to muster up local interest and amusement.

With the start of secondary school only two days away, all the TV weather reporters were predicting an Indian summer.

"What does that mean, exactly?" Bella asked her mum.

"It means our summer is going to go on and flourish way into September and early October," Annie explained.

A week or so after their return, Bella got an email from Shilpa telling her how well things were going at the children's centre and forwarding many new shots for the exhibition. The same day as Shilpa's email, Bella heard her mum take a phone call. She knew at once it was from Bruce because her mum didn't seem to know what to say. Bella tried to convince herself that she shouldn't listen in – but she did, at least until she became too bored to follow it any further. "I think mum's OK," she thought, reminding herself that next time her mum got a new boyfriend she would make a bit more of an effort.

The first day of the exhibition was a private view for invited guests only, running from eleven in the morning until two in the afternoon. Bella had asked her mum if she could bring Charlie and Rahina up into London on the train with them.

"Bella, this is so amazing," Rahina told her friend, as they arrived at the station. "To think that this exhibition is happening because of the work you and your mum have done this summer."

"It's not our work," Bella corrected her friend modestly. "It was all done by the Indian street-children."

"You know what I mean," Rahina jibed affectionately.

Like the exhibition in Delhi, Bella and her mum hoped to

lure journalists and art critics as well as representatives from charities working with street-children throughout the world. One of the first images any visitor to the gallery would see was of the Diva's empty sweatshop, where a few half-finished footballs and shirts could be seen strewn around amongst all the sewing machines and posts to which the children had been chained.

"That room looks scary," Charlie commented as they arrived shortly before the actual opening. "To think someone would force children to work all hours of the day to make things that we buy because they're cheap."

It took a while for people to arrive, but almost everyone who did came across and shook Bella's hand.

"I think this shot here is the best," the woman from *The Times* newspaper told her, pointing to a picture that Shilpa had taken at the bus station, showing a young girl sleeping on a sloping tin rooftop. "It looks as if she'll roll over and go crashing down to her death at any second," observed the journalist in a tone that implied both horror and awe.

A photograph by Randir of a seven-year-old girl taking care of her six-month-old baby sister while she slept on the steps of the National Bank in New Delhi also drew great attention. There was a whole range of striking images of dishevelled children selling all kinds of things to bargain-hungry tourists on the street.

"They make those wire sculptures at the children's centre," Bella told Charlie and Rahina with pride, directing their attention to the model rickshaws and bicycles. There were also photos of children performing a range of theatrical tricks on the street, as well as disabled children polishing shoes and sitting with sewing machines on the roadside as they tried to pick up a bit of passing trade.

"Can't any of these children go to school?" asked Charlie a little naively.

About an hour into the exhibition, a tall, lanky man in a shabby white safari suit slipped in. He'd told the woman on the door checking the guest list that he was a personal friend of the Balisticas. Bella smelt the tobacco the second her pendant began to turn cold, but she was in the middle of an interview that she and her mum were giving to a representative from the Indian embassy.

"Bella, look," Rahina hissed, pulling at her arm. "Ted Briggs."

Bella quickly excused herself. Briggs was casually strolling around the exhibition, smoking his wooden pipe, despite all the "No Smoking" signs around the room. Bella was in no mood to be tolerant.

"What do you think you're doing here?" she asked him boldly, storming up to his side.

"Interesting photograph," he remarked snidely, gesturing to the one showing a group of children helping to disassemble the Big Top of the Mumbai Circus. Bella wasn't sure what Briggs was getting at until he pointed to a rather resplendent bird perched in the trees. "If I'm not mistaken, that's a Guatemalan quetzal," said Briggs. Riled by Briggs' arrogant attitude, Bella scrutinized the photograph, noticing her friend in the trees for the first time. "Quite a rare sight in India," Briggs continued, his eyes examining Bella's neck for any sign of her precious pendant. "Almost as rare as a jaguar suddenly appearing at an international airport." He began to smirk.

"Bella, where are you?" Annie called. Bella looked around to find her mum.

"Mum, look who's decided to turn up," Bella announced angrily, turning back to find that Briggs was already weaving his way towards the door.

It was difficult for Bella to relax after that.

"What are you looking at?" asked Charlie, spotting Bella standing alone by the door to the ladies' toilet. Bella had been taking a peek at the newspaper article she'd kept tucked away in her pocket for the last fortnight.

"Oh, it's nothing," she replied, quickly folding it up and tucking it into her back jean pocket. "Is it time to go?" The report had been taken from the Guatemalan newspaper *La Prensa Libre* that Bella had downloaded from the Internet. It was about the strange disappearance of the football coach, Eduardo Salvatore.

Late that afternoon upon her return home, Bella went up to the attic to stick the article into her father's album and check on his pendant. The meeting with Ted Briggs had knocked her off tilt. "What's he planning?" she pondered as she opened the album. "If the Diva really was such a great illusionist, perhaps she's not dead at all. Maybe even now she and Briggs are planning their revenge."

That night, a terrible storm raged. Twice Bella woke herself up with her own screams as she had nightmares of violent tussles with venomous snakes, which kept on appearing, as if out of nowhere, from the floor, the skies, her mouth: everywhere! It was awful! She had a vague memory of someone she thought was her mum coming in to see if she was alright, giving her a long cuddle and soothing her brow with gentle kisses.

"I love you, Bella," the voice had whispered. "I want to take you with me now, but I can't. But please, don't feel sad. Everything's going to be alright."

After that, she'd felt much better. At one point in her dozing she had an amazing panoramic image of a vast, barren terrain on which she saw a multitude of animals migrating towards a distant sunrise. There appeared to be every species imaginable, both on the ground and in the skies. But that wasn't all. Mixed in amongst all the animals, she could see humans – thousands of them. Many were dressed in the simple tribal attire of farmers, shepherds and cattle herders. Those that she recognized included the purple and red tunics of the Maasai, the short stature of the Pygmies and elegant Zulu warriors, as well as countless Mayan and Aboriginal men, women and children, all making their way with the animals towards the lightening horizon. It was as if the animals and the indigenous peoples of the world were all being drawn together for something of immense importance. But what? The sense of expectation was thrilling. "Someone with colossal power is making this happen," Bella mumbled as she tried to hold on to the fading image and block out the awakening world.

"Good morning, Bella," said her mum cheerily as she plonked a mug of tea on the bedside table. "That's the best night's sleep I've had for weeks. How was yours?" Bella was waking up with a throbbing headache, her mind awash with confusion.

"But, Mum, didn't I keep you awake all night with my nightmares?" she asked sleepily. Annie considered Bella's comment with concern.

"I'm sorry, darling," she replied, "I would have come and given you a cuddle if I'd known." Bella was puzzled.

"But you did," said Bella. "And you reassured me by saying that everything was going to be alright?" Annie shrugged her shoulders, distracted by the squelch in the carpet.

"You really need to dry down after you've had a shower, Bella," she said. "The carpet is soaking." She left the room. "Oh, and Bella," she called from the top of the stairs. "For goodness sake, close the skylight window when you go up. We don't want the attic getting damp, or worse still, someone getting in the house while we're out." Bella rolled out of bed and examined the floor. "I didn't have a shower last night," she thought, following the soggy trail to the ladder on the landing. Climbing into the attic, she knew at once something had happened. "I don't remember leaving the skylight open," she pondered as she pulled across her mum's Guatemalan chest so that she might stand up and close it.

"It's gone," whispered a voice inside her head. Bella quickly darted around to face the portrait of Itzamna.

"What do you mean?" Bella implored.

Her eyes shot to the far corner to see her jewellery box lying abandoned on the floor, its secret compartment open. She ran to pick it up. None of the lesser trinkets and bracelets she often played with had been touched, but her father's precious pendant was nowhere to be seen. Then, looking up to the skylight, Bella saw, outlined quite clearly in the dirt and grime, what she knew at a glance was the footprint of a large, predatory cat.

"I love you, Bella," echoed the memory of last night's

dream. "I want to take you with me now, but I can't. But please don't feel sad. Everything's going to be alright."

She started to smile.

BELLA BALISTICA AND THE TEMPLE OF TIKAL

In the first novel in the Bella Balistica series, Bella discovers her birth mother's spectacular, jewelled pendant hidden away in the secret compartment of an old, hand-carved jewellery box in the attic. The pendant, which is crafted in the image of her nahual – a resplendent Guatemalan quetzal – connects Bella with her mystical past and powers beyond her wildest imagination.

Out now: *Bella Balistica and the Temple of Tikal*, the first book in the Bella Balistica series.

BELLA BALISTICA AND THE AFRICAN SAFARI

While Bella struggles with her transition into secondary school, supernatural forces are gathering. The spirits of both Bella's parents are calling her to action – but who's the enemy? And what are they fighting for? Find out in Bella Balistica's next gripping adventure set against the mesmerizing, historical wonders of Ethiopia.

Out soon: *Bella Balistica and the African Safari*, the next book in the Bella Balistica series.

ACKNOWLEDGEMENTS

Thanks to my friend Rebecca Evans, who read my first draft and to Gurudas Bailur who advised me over language issues with regard to the Indian setting. Thanks to my agent, Robin Wade, Sedat Turhan, Patricia Billings, Laura Hambleton and Mehtap Durmus at Milet who have all injected energy, enthusiasm and fresh ideas into the book. Rachel Goslin has again stunned us with her creative, vibrant and engaging artwork, and Ken Hollings has done a great job of editing the book. As always, my beautiful wife Charlotte supported me every paragraph of the way while our darling little boy, George, with his spectacular head of red hair and incredible strength, spent so much of his first three months strapped around me in a sling as I wrote this book. The gentle purrs and fierce roars of his nahual were both the joy and pain of many a long winter's night. A.G.

ACKNOWLEDGEMENTS